Molly couldn't stop herself

"Your daughter let you know exactly how she feels about not having a real home. And what did you do? You put her off. Maybe if she had a taste of the life she so desperately wants to lead, it wouldn't live up to her expectations. But she deserves to find that out for herself. She deserves the best you can give her, Eric Norvald, and the life of a boat bum isn't it."

Stunned, Eric stared at her openmouthed throughout this diatribe. When she stopped, she inhaled a deep breath.

"I'm going out."

Molly set off down the dock at a fast clip and refused to look back. It might not have any effect on what he did, but it sure felt good hauling off and giving him a piece of her mind.

Dear Reader,

When I was a kid, I woke up from a nap one day and found my mother emptying the guts of our vacuum cleaner onto a newspaper. I was convinced she'd killed it, and I was inconsolable. Turns out she was only dumping the dirt, but what did I know? I was only three.

I'm sure I was emotionally connected to that upright vacuum cleaner; otherwise, why would I have cared so much? At the time, I was only a child. Our vacuum seemed friendly, with that little bright light on its face, and all-powerful. It had a bag made of shiny blue material, and I thought it was pretty. Everyone else in our house was tall, but it was just my size.

When friends told me of their grandson, who is fascinated with vacuum cleaners, who wants to play with them, and take them apart, and draw them, I recognized something of myself. Thus I created Phoebe.

Love doesn't exist in a vacuum. The bad things that happen to us cannot be swept away. And sometimes the stars don't have all the answers.

But when love comes along, it has the power to change our lives. I hope you enjoy the story of Eric and Molly and Phoebe, who learned that lesson in a very special way.

Love,

Pamela Browning

P.S. Please visit me at my Web site: www.pamelabrowning.com.

THE MOMMY WISH
Pamela Browning

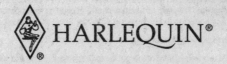

TORONTO • NEW YORK • LONDON
AMSTERDAM • PARIS • SYDNEY • HAMBURG
STOCKHOLM • ATHENS • TOKYO • MILAN • MADRID
PRAGUE • WARSAW • BUDAPEST • AUCKLAND

ISBN 0-373-75074-9

THE MOMMY WISH

Copyright © 2005 by Pamela Browning.

This edition published by arrangement with Harlequin Books S.A.

® and TM are trademarks of the publisher. Trademarks indicated with ® are registered in the United States Patent and Trademark Office, the Canadian Trade Marks Office and in other countries.

www.eHarlequin.com

Printed in U.S.A.

Books by Pamela Browning

HARLEQUIN AMERICAN ROMANCE

With thanks to the real Molly Kate,
for her input into the plot and for Meehan lessons; and
thanks to Ralph and Eileen, whose family vacuum cleaner
stories helped me find Phoebe.

Chapter One

Molly didn't see what caused her to trip and fall. All she knew was that one minute she was walking down B Dock at the Tarheel Marina somewhere in coastal North Carolina, and the next minute she was sprawled across the weathered boards, staring up into the curious face of a bedraggled moppet who appeared to be somewhere over the age of four and under the age of nine.

"You'd better get out of my way or I'll vacuum you up," said the child. She spoke cheerfully and without malice.

Since the fall had knocked the air out of her lungs, Molly was unable to reply at first, although she managed a couple of feeble gasps. It was a few moments before she was able to push a hank of red-gold hair out of her eyes and haul herself up on her hands and knees, all the while glaring balefully at the spike-haired apparition who had witnessed her unnerving tumble.

"And just how are you going to do that?" she asked when she could talk again. Pushing back on her haunches, she inspected her elbows for abrasions and found none. Knees, ditto.

"With my Model 440 Hoovasonic Sweeper. *Varoom, varoom.*" The speaker appeared to be of indeterminate sex and had dark-brown hair that stuck out as if groomed with a glue stick.

Molly leveled a skeptical gaze at the kid, who was about

four feet tall and unaccompanied by a vacuum cleaner as far as she could tell. "All right," she said. "Go ahead and suck me up. I warn you, though, I'm hell on vacuum cleaners."

"Oooh. You said a bad word."

"Not really. I was merely being descriptive."

Round eyes watched as she brushed off her hands and stood. Molly's gaze fell on her Irish harp case, which had landed next to a piling. As she grabbed it, she noticed for the first time that the child wore one pink sock. The other one was a grungy white. The pink sock gave Molly the impression that this was most likely a female child, albeit one that could use some spiffing up.

"Who are you?" the girl said, peering at her through bangs that looked as if they'd been trimmed with a hacksaw.

"I'm Molly Kate McBryde. I could ask you the same question."

"I'm Phoebe Anne Norvald. I'm the only child at the marina. I'm seven and a half years old, and I hate not having someone to play with."

"Okay, okay, I sympathize," Molly said. "Did you trip me on purpose? So I'd play with you?" She poked at a splinter on her left palm, acquired when she fell, and rued the day that she had agreed to a leave of absence from her job as number-two honcho in the corporate accounting department of the family business. Sane people usually did not do such things, even when their grandfathers insisted.

Phoebe shook her head in denial. "Oh, no. It wouldn't be nice to trip someone. There's a loose board on the dock. See?" She demonstrated by stomping on it with one small foot. Sure enough, it wiggled.

"That's dangerous," Molly said. "Someone should fix it."

"My dad's the one. He works around here, but he's been busy lately. You know, people need to be careful around vacuum cleaners because they can trip over the cord. *You* could have tripped over the cord."

"If there *was* a cord," Molly said pointedly.

"Vacuum cleaners don't have to have one. The robotic kinds just wander around your house, whooshing up dirt."

"How lovely," Molly murmured. She wasn't accustomed to children, had rarely been around any. Did they all like to talk about vacuum cleaners?

She picked up her duffel and her harp, and Phoebe skipped along beside her as she limped down the dock. Molly had to admit that this was an appealing child. Or she would be if she'd do something about that awful hair.

"So what is this—you hang out with make-believe vacuum cleaners?" she asked Phoebe. Ahead in the last slip she saw *Fiona,* Grandpa Emmett's fifty-three-foot ketch, its two tall masts towering above all the others.

Phoebe looked very serious. "I can only have make-believe ones until we get a house of our own again. My dad says it's not going to happen soon."

Molly slowed her pace. Her knee really hurt. "Why not?"

"He likes to stay on the move. I'm tired of it. You'll meet him in a few minutes."

"Right now I'm going aboard *Fiona* to put my feet up and have a beer."

"That's where you'll meet my dad. He drinks beer."

"He's on *Fiona?*" All the work that her grandfather had ordered was supposed to have been finished by today.

"We live aboard. Dad didn't want you to come here, but then Mr. Emmett called and made it okay. We like Mr. Emmett a whole lot. I guess Dad'll be glad to see you now. You're going to help deliver the boat to Fort Lauderdale, right?"

"Right," Molly muttered. Grandpa Emmett, when he was arranging for her to supervise the transfer of his boat from the boatyard to his winter home in Florida, hadn't mentioned any live-aboards. Molly couldn't imagine why he'd allow a repairman to stake out residence on *Fiona,* his most prized possession, which at the moment was riding easily on the slight swells, her flag whipping smartly in the wind.

Live-aboards or no, Molly felt a surge of happiness at the thought of sailing *Fiona* again. The boat had been the locus of several adventures with Grandpa Emmett for Molly and her brother and sister, all intrepid sailors, though none of them was as skilled at sailing as their grandfather. During the past summer, she, her sister, Brianne, and her brother, Patrick, had accompanied their grandfather on a jaunt to Nova Scotia from his home in Maine. Although they'd been too concerned about Grandpa Emmett's increasing frailness to let him do much of the work, the trip, like all their previous ones, had been a great family experience.

But that was then. This was now, and it would be a different kind of voyage. Still, the trip was a break from job stress, and she could postpone shopping for a new winter coat to replace her old one, in which she'd recently discovered moth holes. Also, she'd recently broken up with Chuck the Cheese, alias Charles Stalnecky, and this vacation gave her something far more interesting to do than chowing down cold pizzas alone in her apartment every night. Grandpa Emmett's request to sign on as first mate on this trip—no, actually it qualified as a command—had seemed reasonable, appropriate, fitting.

Well, whatever. The morning's itinerary had involved a harrowing predawn succession of trains, planes and automobiles, and now Molly was ready to kick back and take it easy. She mounted the boarding stairs. Phoebe scrambled up right behind her as she clamped her fingers around the railing and made the transfer from stairs to boat.

"Hey, wait a minute. Be careful," Molly cautioned. One misstep and Phoebe would fall into the water, which was slightly choppy today.

Phoebe neatly negotiated the space between the stairs and the deck, though the gap widened perceptibly due to the motion of the waves. "It's okay. I do this all the time."

"You can swim?" Molly slowly descended the few steps to the cockpit and set her luggage on one of the benches along the sides.

"Sure. My dad says I swim like a champ. Oops, I forgot my vacuum cleaner. I'd better go get it." She prepared to climb back over the side of the boat, but Molly wasn't about to let this kid return herself to harm's way to retrieve something that didn't exist. As Phoebe prepared to make the leap, Molly seized Phoebe's shirttail and hauled her back.

"Wait a minute," Molly said. "I'll bet your vacuum will be perfectly happy on the dock for a while."

"You're probably right. What's that?" She pointed at Molly's harp case.

"That's my Irish harp."

"I saw someone playing a harp on TV once. It was big— real big."

"That was a pedal harp. This is a folk harp. Folk harps can come in any size, like the kind meant to be played in your lap, such as this one, or the kind that stand on the floor."

"Can you play it?"

"I certainly can. It's my hobby, like you and your vacuum cleaner."

Phoebe seemed to be considering this. She stared up at Molly. "Can you cook?" she asked.

Molly smiled. She was starting to like this kid. "I make a fantastic grilled-cheese sandwich."

Phoebe's face crinkled into a grin of delight. "I love grilled-cheese sandwiches. I used to call them sand *wishes,* you know. That's when I was little." She hollered down the open companionway. "Dad! Molly McBryde's here."

Molly massaged her sore knee and admired the sparkling blue water of Pamlico Sound, the pelicans wheeling overhead, the sails scudding in the distance. This was a far cry from Chicago, where at this very moment, people were enduring the first snowfall of the year. At least that was what Mrs. Brinkle, her treasured assistant, had informed her when Molly called the office to say that she'd arrived safely at her destination. That was before she'd fallen on the dock, of course. But then, there was no reason either Lorraine Brinkle or her boss, Francis X. O'Toole, needed to be informed of Molly's klutzier moments.

A tattered gray baseball cap emerged from belowdecks, followed by a high forehead bisected by a thatch of sandy hair, blue eyes and more beard stubble than was fashionable in her social circle. "I'm Eric Norvald," the man said, looking her up and down. The pungent aroma of diesel fuel accompanied him.

"Molly Kate McBryde," she said briskly, extending her hand.

"Sorry. I can't shake hands," he said, and she realized that he was wiping grease from his palms onto a filthy towel.

She let her hand drop. "I thought the repairs were finished. That's what my grandfather told me."

"They were. Things happen." He spoke gruffly, curtly. She didn't like the way he was staring at her, making her feel as if she were an insect mounted on a board. Suddenly she felt uncomfortable in her jeans, which she had discovered only yesterday were a shade too tight.

She drew herself up to her full height of five feet seven inches. "I expected everything to be in order."

"It isn't. I suggest you find yourself a comfortable hotel room and let me take care of the problems here." His voice sounded as though he'd roughed it up with sandpaper. He tucked the greasy rag into his back pocket, where it flapped in the breeze.

"Wait a minute," Molly said. "I'm staying on *Fiona*. I'm supposed to leave tomorrow."

"We'll leave on schedule."

"'We?'"

"You, me and Phoebe."

She stared at him in disbelief. "I'm expecting a licensed captain to help me sail *Fiona* to my grandfather's house in Fort Lauderdale."

"Emmett hired me himself. We became friends when he was down here supervising repairs to this boat a couple of months ago. Now, do you want to go on exchanging chitchat or shall I continue my work on this engine?"

"You mean *you're* the licensed captain?" This guy looked only one eye patch short of a pirate.

He tilted his cap to a more rakish angle and treated her to

a slow grin, maddening in its nonchalance. His teeth were very white. "If you care to see my certification, you'll have to come below. I'd better get back to work."

As he swiveled toward the ladder descending into the cabin, his forearm brushed hers. An unexpected shiver rippled across her skin. She jerked backward, earning a mildly surprised glance from those impossibly blue eyes. They caught and held hers, and it was all she could do not to be drawn into their warmth. She detected a glint of wry humor in their depths, and just as quickly as it had come, it disappeared.

With a cock of one eyebrow and an abrupt nod, he disappeared down the ladder. Molly rubbed her arm where his had touched it.

Phoebe leaned over the companionway. "Dad, Molly said she's going to make me a grilled-cheese sandwich. It's way past lunchtime." She slipped her hand into Molly's.

Though exasperated to the utmost, Molly didn't have the heart to pull her hand away. "I did not—"

Eric's drawl drifted up from the engine room. "If Ms. McBryde wants to take charge of the galley, it's all right with me." A clatter, a clang, a muffled curse, and then all was silence.

"I'll help you with the sandwiches." Phoebe's trusting eyes, blue like her father's, gazed up at her.

"Well," Molly said, suddenly feeling sorry for the child. Phoebe wore an air of neglect, and who knows if this Eric person took good care of her? If her clothes were any indication, he barely gave his daughter a passing thought.

"I like mustard on mine—do you?"

"Mustard. Hmm. I've never tried it. I like tomato and onion, though."

"We don't have those. There's lots of mustard."

Molly sighed. "Okay," she said, relinquishing her hopes of a quiet interlude with only herself for company.

"You go down first. Then me," directed Phoebe.

Molly climbed backward down the ladder, to encounter Eric's head crooked around the edge of the engine room door.

"Would you mind handing me that pair of pliers next to

the sink?" He jerked his head in that direction, but not before a quick and not very discreet assessment of her derriere.

Molly tossed him the pliers. "Thanks," he said offhandedly. "The mustard's on the shelf over the microwave. The bread's next to the toaster." He slammed the engine room door.

"Charming fellow," Molly muttered, as Phoebe's legs appeared and the rest of her followed.

Fortunately Phoebe didn't hear her. Molly peeked into the chart room and spotted a plaque leaning up against the polished teak paneling. Eric Norvald had been telling the truth— he was a licensed captain. Too bad, because she couldn't fire him on the grounds that he wasn't qualified. Mulling this over, she turned her attention to the galley.

At least the man kept things neat on *Fiona,* she thought as she moved around the familiar galley assembling ingredients and equipment. Everything was clean and in its proper place. The small stainless-steel sink was newly scrubbed; the refrigerator was well ordered. No spills marred the bright surface of the three-burner range, and the oven was spotless. The teak floors appeared freshly waxed.

"You still want a beer?" Phoebe asked, hoisting herself up on the counter and all but falling into the top-opening refrigerator as she retrieved a can of soda.

"No, I'll have what you're having."

"Not beer. It tastes like earwax." Phoebe climbed down again and popped the tabs on two soda cans.

Molly was pondering this startling answer when Eric opened the engine room door.

"I've already eaten, in case you're wondering," he informed her.

"I wasn't," Molly said.

"That's what I figured." He dug in a drawer, found a flashlight and aimed something that resembled a smile at her before retreating again to the engine room. Molly didn't like him. He was insolent. But she had to admit that there was a certain roguish attraction about him, unkempt though he was.

Phoebe found two small plates for their sandwiches and

set them on the table in the compact salon adjacent to the galley. She watched while Molly heated up the griddle.

"You do that different from Dad," she told Molly.

"Do what different?"

"Make grilled-cheese sandwiches. He doesn't put them together so neatly, and if they fall apart, he says a bad word. Then he usually burns himself on the frying pan or something and says another bad word. Then—"

"Phoebe!" came a stern voice from the engine room. "There are some things we don't discuss with strangers."

"This is Molly. She's not a stranger. Mr. Emmett told us all about her, remember?" Phoebe said patiently. She paused, and no comment came from the engine room. Instead the diesel engine roared to life, emitted a few metallic chugs, then quit abruptly amid a new outpouring of noxious fumes.

"Here's where Dad usually says a really bad word," Phoebe whispered, but the engine room remained ominously quiet.

Molly brought the sandwiches to the table.

"You know why I used to call them sand wishes?" Phoebe asked. "Because I thought I could make a wish while I was eating one and it would come true." She spoke wistfully.

"What wishes did you make?"

"To live in a house again. It hasn't happened so far, so maybe it's not really true about the sand wishes. Sometimes I still wish, but mostly for a mommy. My mommy died."

"I'm sorry, Phoebe. My mother died, too, but not until I was seventeen." Her adjustment to losing her mom at that rebellious age had been difficult, considering that her brother was already away at college. Molly, a senior in high school at the time, had been forced to assume most of the responsibility for Brianne, who at age eleven had been a handful. Molly's heart went out to Phoebe, who was so young to be left without a mother.

Phoebe waited for Molly to sit down, then went on talking. "I was four years old when Mommy died. I remember her, though. She wore blue a lot and liked to jog in the park. We had a dog named Cookie. My dad gave Cookie to the neighbors when we sold the house."

Molly detected a deep sadness in Phoebe's eyes, even though she delivered this information in a matter-of-fact manner.

"I bet you miss Cookie, don't you?" Molly noted distractedly that there had been no sound from the engine room for some time.

Phoebe nodded, her face solemn. "We're supposed to get Cookie back when we get another house, but I don't think that's ever going to happen."

The engine room door slammed open. Eric emerged, clearly annoyed. He addressed the air somewhere to the right of Molly's head. "I have to go to the marine hardware store for some bolts. Phoebe, you can come with me."

"We were just going to eat," Molly said.

"Yeah, Dad, she just made the sand wish—sandwiches."

Eric blew out a long breath. He treated Molly to a searching look. "Okay, Phoebe, you can stay here if Molly doesn't mind pulling baby-sitting duty," he said brusquely, as if he expected her to refuse.

"Of course I don't mind," Molly said quickly, taking perverse pleasure in the expression of surprise that flitted across Eric's face.

He afforded Molly a curt nod. "I'll be back in an hour and a half or so. Bye, Peanut."

He ruffled Phoebe's bangs before starting up the ladder, loose-hipped and long-limbed, and Molly forced herself not to look at his muscular legs working beneath the faded fabric of those tight jeans.

"I'm glad I can stay here with you," Phoebe confided, grinning up at her. "You know, I think this is a lucky day. We should both make wishes."

"I don't have a wish," Molly protested.

"Well, I do." Phoebe leaned toward her with an air of letting Molly in on a marvelous secret. "I'm wishing that you're going to be my new mommy."

Molly's jaw dropped at this unexpected pronouncement. "But I—"

"That's my wish, and you can't do a thing about it, Molly."

Molly, though reeling with astonishment, had the good sense to clamp her mouth shut. She never wanted to be a mother. After having guided Brianne through her turbulent teenage years, she was sure that motherhood was most definitely not her thing. Besides, she had a career, not to mention that she barely knew this child.

Phoebe picked up her sandwich, talking a mile a minute. "Now, listen, Molly, this is important. This is how you make a wish on a sandwich. You have to close your eyes, make your wish, say it out loud and take a bite." She demonstrated.

Bemused and amused, Molly listened as Phoebe made her wish. She didn't try to stop her, and she was so touched that she made no further comment. And in spite of herself, she found herself making a wish, too, though it was a silent one: *I wish I knew someone besides Eric Norvald to help me sail this boat to Florida.*

Never mind that Emmett had hired Eric himself. She was in a difficult situation here, and she'd better find a way out.

DESPITE HIS PROMISE to be back soon, Eric didn't return until after dark, whistling tunelessly as he came aboard, then tossing her duffel down the companionway ahead of him and carrying the case containing her harp.

"I'll take that," Molly said quickly, latching on to the harp case. For the past half hour she had been pacing the length of the salon, fuming at Eric's lack of responsibility, at his absence, and, since scruffy beards were a sore point with her, his appearance.

"What is it, anyway?" He was staring at the harp case.

"An Irish harp." She set it carefully on the lounge.

"I've never heard one."

"Maybe you never will," she said tartly.

He paused, pursing his lips. She thought she spotted the promise of a strong jaw and a firm chin under all the stubble, then wondered why she'd noticed.

"What are you trying to say?" he asked abruptly.

She drew a deep bolstering breath. "That my grandfather made a mistake hiring you to sail with me to Florida. I don't think we get along well enough to participate in a cooperative venture such as sailing this boat."

"How do you know that?" he asked.

"From the way you've acted ever since I climbed aboard," she said heatedly. "From your lack of responsibility. You've been gone for six hours—do you realize that?"

He ran a hand up the back of his neck, ruffling the hair that grew too long. "I'm fully aware of the time. I had to drive forty miles inland to get that special bolt, and when I got to the store, they only had two in stock. I had to wait for more to be brought in from Raleigh on a truck that broke down along the way. Believe me, I would rather have been here. Where's Phoebe?"

"She's asleep in there." She angled her head toward the smallest stateroom, barely big enough for two stacked bunks. "She heated us a can of hash before climbing into bed and singing her imaginary vacuum cleaner to sleep." Her tone was as accusatory as she could make it.

Eric opened the door, looked in on the sleeping Phoebe and shut the door again. His features softened, his voice, too. "Poor Phoebe. I should have been back in time to tuck her in," he said quietly, looking stricken.

"Don't you keep her on some kind of schedule?"

"Yes, when I'm not working night and day to get a boat ready," he shot back. "This engine can be a bitch to repair. It was made in Germany, hardly anyone in this country has parts to fit it and I've worked as hard as I can to meet the sailing date that Emmett set."

Molly knew from her grandfather's discussion of *Fiona*'s engine problems that what Eric said was true. Okay, so maybe she had overstepped her bounds. She forced herself to look him in the eye. "I'm sorry. I'm concerned about your daughter, that's all."

"Ah," he said. "Phoebe has all too few people to care about her. Thanks."

This man had given no indication of kindness or gentleness before this, and yet here it was. She made herself consider this situation from his point of view; the guy had lost his wife, after all, and it couldn't be easy to be a single father. She was considerably more calm when she finally spoke.

"Um, Eric. Can we start over?"

He shrugged. "Sure. There's work to do, but I'll have the boat ready by morning. We can leave early. According to the latest reports, we'll have an ideal weather window."

Now Molly realized that it was up to her to make a decision: Should she take a chance and fire Eric outright? And if she did, who would help her move *Fiona* to Fort Lauderdale? This was a sleepy little marina, and the nearby town wasn't even a dot on the map. It was unlikely that she'd find any qualified captains here. Her grandfather had specifically asked her to do the job, citing her brother Patrick's trip to Ireland, where he was working on a book about Irish folklore, and the fact that Brianne's job teaching photography in Australia wouldn't conclude for a couple more weeks. Emmett himself had mentioned medical tests as the reason that he couldn't accompany the refurbished and rebuilt *Fiona* to Florida as he usually did every fall.

Molly resigned herself to being stuck with Eric Norvald, like it or not. She supposed if he didn't work out, she could order him to pull into a larger marina somewhere down the coast where she'd be more likely to find another person qualified to sail *Fiona*.

"All right," she said wearily.

Eric seemed relieved. "Good. As for Phoebe, she's more resilient than you think. If she's ever in your way, holler and I'll see that she doesn't annoy you."

Molly nodded, surprised at this.

"By the way, how's Emmett? The last time I talked with him on the phone, he didn't sound too chipper."

The last thing she'd expected was for Eric to wax solicitous about her grandfather. "He's—he's as irascible as ever, eager to finish those tests he's having at the clinic in Minnesota, and looking forward to winter at his Florida house."

"Good. We'll have *Fiona* there when he arrives."

Before she could reply, Eric disappeared into the engine room, shutting the door firmly behind him.

Thoughtfully, Molly checked in on Phoebe, who was sleeping peacefully with her head pillowed on her hands, and then she went aft to stow her things in the built-in drawers of the master stateroom. Her grandfather occupied it when they sailed together, while she and Brianne shared the smallest stateroom and Patrick slept in the V berth in the bow. These quarters were bigger than her usual, and after she had finished settling in, she showered in the adjacent bathroom and climbed into the high queen-size bed. Over the bed were three lovely stained-glass windows, and the lights of the marina shining through them lent a soft glow to the room. It was good to be back on *Fiona,* good to be back where she'd so often had fun with her family.

Emmett would be traveling to the clinic from his home in Maine tomorrow, but he'd played down her concern about his health when she'd last talked to him.

"Oh, you know how it is," he'd said. "Doctors like to help out other doctors, so they're sending me to Minneapolis, where a new team of doctors will probably send me to some more doctors."

"Grandpa, you're scaring me."

"I hope I can scare off those doctors, as well. Say, Molly Kate, are you planning to enjoy your vacation from work?"

"Aren't I, though? And isn't my boss having trepidations about doing all my work himself?" At thirty-six, Francis X. O'Toole was only five years her senior, and she'd known him since she was a kid. She'd been a bridesmaid when he'd married Elise, who had been a college classmate of her brother.

"Don't worry about Frank, Molly Kate. He has the charming and efficient Mrs. Brinkle to run the office while you're away."

This was true. The effervescent Lorraine Brinkle of the short blond curls and flippy skirts had recently graduated from college with a B.A. in accounting at the age of forty-five, and despite her tendency to boogie down the hallways at the corporate offices singing reggae tunes, she was capable in the extreme. Which was why Molly should stop thinking about work.

After forcibly banning thoughts of McBryde Industries from her mind, Molly lay awake, listening to the waves slapping against *Fiona*'s hull. She'd always loved sleeping on the sailboat, lulled into peaceful dreams by its gentle rocking. But on this night, she was a long time falling asleep. The clang of metal against metal on the other side of the wall kept her awake as Eric worked on the diesel engine, and she kept expecting to hear the creak of the engine room door that would signal he was through for the night.

She never heard it. She fell asleep long before Eric's work was done. And she dreamed of a lanky man with bright blue eyes, though she never got a good view of his face. It was Eric Norvald, though. She'd bank on it.

Chapter Two

Eric rose from his berth in the bow of *Fiona* early the next morning before the fog had cleared from the Sound, checking on his sleeping daughter before brewing coffee as strong as he could make it. Her Majesty Molly Kate McBryde was sleeping in, no doubt, he thought wryly after a glance at the closed door to the master stateroom. It was probably just as well, since he had a checklist a yard long that needed attention before they could cast off.

He took his coffee up on deck and watched the sun rise over the water, inhaling deeply of the brine-scented mist. The sunrise was a pretty sight, one that never failed to please him.

That business about Phoebe last night and the fury in Molly's eyes when she all but accused him of being a father who shirked his duty—it was so unfair. He loved Phoebe wholeheartedly, more than he loved anyone else in the world. Who was Molly Kate McBryde to criticize him? She was a spoiled brat, heir to the McBryde millions, a dilettante who was free to leave her cushy job in the family manufacturing business for however long it took to ferry her grandfather's yacht to Fort Lauderdale. She wouldn't, couldn't understand what it would be like to walk a mile in his well-worn Docksiders.

He should have informed Emmett McBryde that he'd find his own first mate, thank you very much. He could have called his friend Tom, who in the past had often left his insurance business on the spur of the moment to go sailing. Or his brother, Lars, who needed a vacation from his family once in a while.

But would either of those options have worked? Tom's expanding business sapped most of his energy these days, and Lars's wife was expecting a baby soon. Maybe there was no one to call, no one he could rely on.

Only himself.

"Dad, I'm up!" said Phoebe, scrambling up the ladder. She catapulted herself into his arms, almost spilling his coffee.

"Wait a minute, Peanut," he said, setting his mug down carefully in the cupholder beside the ship's wheel. He wrapped his arms around his daughter, inhaling the fresh just-woke-up scent of her.

She pulled away. "You didn't come home until late last night," she said.

"It took me a long time to get the bolts," he explained. It seemed as if he was always explaining something to Phoebe, always trying to excuse himself.

"I waited and waited, but I couldn't stay awake. Are we leaving here today?"

"Yes, as soon as I finish my coffee."

Her face crumpled. "I was just getting to know Mrs. Knowles, the lady in the office. She makes really good oatmeal cookies. And she has a cat, Boots. He's going to have kittens."

"Boots is a she, Phoebe. *She's* going to have kittens."

"I won't get to see them," Phoebe said, disappointment evident in her tone.

Eric didn't know what to say about that.

"Well, one nice thing is that Molly is going with us. She said so," Phoebe said, perking up a bit.

"That's right." He drained the last bit of coffee and stood up. "Okay, kiddo, I set your Cocoa Krispies out in a bowl in the galley. You'd better eat before we get under way."

"I'll come up to eat with you," Phoebe said, climbing down the ladder.

Things might have been different by this time if he hadn't taken this job, Eric reflected as he proceeded through his checklist of things to do. Much as he liked Emmett McBryde, Eric hadn't wanted the task of sailing this big boat to Fort Lauderdale. But he'd bonded with the old guy during Emmett's visits to Tarheel Marina, and when Emmett had invited him to live aboard when he had to return home to Maine, Eric had accepted his offer. He figured that he'd feel good about helping Emmett out, and at the time he and Phoebe were staying on a trimaran whose owner had suddenly shown up and decided to go cruising to the Bahamas—and so here they were, living on *Fiona*.

Eric had meant his occupancy of Emmett's boat to be temporary before moving on to Thunderbolt, Georgia, where Steve, a buddy from his navy days, had invited him to work on a shrimp trawler. It sounded like a good deal. He and Phoebe could live in a camper trailer on Steve's property, and Phoebe would be able to play with Steve and Joyce's three kids and maybe be less lonely. Maybe quit playing with pretend vacuum cleaners, for Pete's sake.

He heard doors opening and closing below and turned around, expecting to see Phoebe.

"Good morning."

Damn! If it wasn't Queen Molly Kate McBryde, her hair as shiny as new copper pennies, her complexion all rosy from sleep. She peered up the companionway from the salon below, and she was wearing a robe that, from this angle, showed exactly the right amount of cleavage to whet his interest.

"Good morning," he said. "Help yourself to some coffee. You can fry yourself an egg if you want."

"Okay. Then I want to take a look at the charts."

"Go ahead." Eric wished that Molly had stayed in bed. Her presence on deck wouldn't be required until just before they actually left the dock, though he doubted that she would be much help even then. She didn't appear strong enough to haul in a sail, not that it would be necessary. *Fiona* had motorized winches. Eric doubted she'd know much about navigation, either. That was okay. He could handle it. It would be best if she'd limit her help to throwing a line now and then and confine her main attention to baby-sitting Phoebe. He'd feel better if two adults were keeping tabs on his daughter when they were under way.

Phoebe came up, balancing her cereal bowl carefully. "Guess what, Dad? Molly likes oatmeal. I told her to try Cocoa Krispies, but she only said, 'Yuck.' She offered to fix me an egg. I didn't want one, though."

"I'll cook eggs for you anytime you want," Eric told her. Something about Phoebe was different, but he couldn't figure out what it was. Still thinking about it, he made his way to the foredeck and studied the horizon. The Sound was calm today, and the wind was steady. Perhaps they could reach Trent's Cove by evening.

Phoebe had almost finished her cereal when he went back into the cockpit. "Molly gave me a headband to wear. She said she doesn't need it. She said I can keep it."

"Did you say thank-you?"

"Sure, I always say thank-you. Do you like it?"

Phoebe's bangs, which he usually trimmed with nail scissors, were neatly smoothed under some sort of elastic. "Maybe you should get a couple of those—what did you call it?"

"A headband. Can I get a red one?"

"Of course."

"Good. I like Molly, Dad. She read me a story last night, me and my vacuum cleaner."

Phoebe had a couple of tattered children's books that she'd carted everywhere they went. He'd always meant to get her some new ones, but there usually wasn't much room in their borrowed quarters.

"Great," he said without much enthusiasm. He wondered what story it had been. He wondered where you bought headbands.

"Molly sewed a button on my shirt, too. I think she should stay with us all the time, don't you?"

"I don't believe that's possible," he said, frowning.

"If she wanted to stay, you'd let her, right?"

This had gone far enough. "Phoebe, there are some things you need to understand," he said firmly.

At that moment, Molly came up the companionway and stepped into the cockpit. She was wearing a pair of khakis and a snug long-sleeved navy-blue T-shirt, and behind her, the newly risen sun set her red-gold hair on fire. After his first glance, he forced himself to look away from her breasts, thinking that she had big sails for such a small ship. As for the rest of her, well, he preferred a woman to have big breasts and narrow hips. Said woman had to have a perky derriere, and Molly Kate McBryde didn't disappoint.

"Dad, what were you saying?" asked Phoebe.

"Never mind. Time to be on our way. We have to get fuel first," he said, making himself focus on the task at hand, which wasn't easy, considering that this woman was gorgeous.

Molly looked down her sweetly upturned nose at him. "Fine. I'll handle the bowline if you like."

"That's good. Phoebe, you stay where you are, okay?"

"Can I go below? It's cold up here."

"Sure."

Phoebe departed, and Eric jumped across to the dock and pulled the line off its cleat, then tossed it to Molly before unwinding the line at the stern. By the time he was back on *Fiona*, Molly was efficiently coiling the bowline, a tumble of curls hiding her face. It was an exceptional face, he thought, with high cheekbones and none of the freckles he associated with redheads.

The engine started up right away. Molly stood beside him at the wheel, watching as the space between boat and dock widened. She had the greenest eyes he'd ever seen, greener than the shallows near the shore, greener than the sky when rain was on the way. He wanted to ask her if she wore tinted contact lenses, then realized that the color was natural. Emmett's eyes, though clouded now with age, were almost the same shade.

"We're going Outside, I take it?" she asked. Going Outside meant that they'd be heading out into the ocean instead of staying Inside in the protected waters of the Intracoastal Waterway.

He nodded. "I want to avoid using the engine as much as possible. We'll motor out of the marina, then raise the sails."

"You didn't get the engine repaired?"

"Oh, I did. Why gobble up expensive diesel fuel if you don't have to, that's all." He didn't add that he was worried about the temperamental fuel injector pump, which he hadn't been able to replace locally.

Molly didn't question his judgment. She only smiled, and in that smile was a whole world of enthusiasm. "It's looks like a great day for sailing. I'll be glad when we can cut the engine and let the wind take her away," she said.

But at the moment, he wasn't thinking about sailing. He was thinking about something else altogether, which was the lack of enthusiasm in his own life. He knew plenty about picking up and going on after a tragedy, but what he hadn't been able to do was regain his joy in simple things. Sometimes merely getting up in the morning and putting one foot in front of the other seemed like too much trouble. Yet he did it, mostly for Phoebe's sake. His love for his daughter sustained him, but no matter how hard he'd tried, he hadn't felt even one moment of true happiness since Heather died. He'd felt pleasure. He'd felt satisfaction in jobs well done. But that was about it.

In that moment, Eric wanted with all his heart to be able to look forward to something again. Almost as quickly, he discarded that possibility. It wouldn't happen. It couldn't happen. At least, it hadn't so far.

UNDER SAIL, they were able to achieve a speed of six knots, with calm seas and cooperative winds. *Fiona* made Trent's Cove by dusk, and they anchored around the point within sight of a desolate shore. By that time Eric was willing to admit, however grudgingly, that Queen Molly Kate McBryde was a pretty good sailor.

She knew port from starboard, and she didn't mind working. She knew when to pull in the mainsail and when to let it out; she understood when to tack and when to jibe. The main problem was that she didn't like to follow orders.

"It's not what you're asking me to do—it's your tone of voice," she'd informed him haughtily when he told her to go below and check their headings.

He didn't have much to say about that. He could have retorted that he didn't always have time to ask politely, and that when captaining a boat, he needed instant action from the crew in order to avoid mishaps. He could have reminded her that Emmett was paying him to be the captain of *Fiona* and that she had been foisted upon him as his first mate. He didn't say any of this, mostly because Molly's cheeks had been blazing with indignation, and he liked the way she looked with green fire sparking in her eyes.

Now he made sure that the anchor was firmly seated so that the boat wouldn't drift, and after that he followed Molly below and suggested that she cook their dinner. This seemed like a perfectly reasonable request. "Emmett left plenty of food stored behind the lounges in the salon," he told her.

He was unprepared for Molly to perch her hands on her hips and regard him with the disdain that she'd likely reserve for an invading army of cockroaches. "Let me get this straight, Eric. You expect *me* to cook dinner? And that would be *every* night, now?" she asked, her chin tilting up a notch as she spoke.

She had bound her hair, that riotous hair, back with a dark ribbon, and his fingers itched to untie it. He was sorely tempted to yank the ends of the ribbon and watch her hair tumble around her shoulders. Clenching his hands into fists at his sides, he stared back at her in the dim glow from the light fixture swinging above the dining table.

"I thought you'd want to cook," he said. "Since I'm not very good at it, as Phoebe has mentioned."

Molly tipped her head back so that she was gazing into his eyes. "What makes you think I'm any better at cooking than you are?"

This set him back a tad. He gazed out the porthole for a moment, noted that it was almost dark. "I—well, I assumed," he stammered, feeling like a fool for feeling like a fool.

"Grilled-cheese sandwiches are the extent of my cooking skills," she informed him. "Except for eggs and maybe a decent stew."

He stared at her. "We're in trouble, then. Don't you cook for yourself at home?"

"Rarely. If it comes to that, I usually open a can of soup."

He supposed he should have realized that Queen Molly wasn't in the habit of looking after herself. "All right, let's break out our supplies. We'll collaborate on meals, okay?" *Just trying to build a little team spirit here, okay?* he thought. *Just trying to get along.*

Going along to get along must have been in her mind, too, because she managed a tentative grin. "All right," she said.

Phoebe, listening to this conversation, said, "Why can't we have grilled-cheese sandwiches again?"

"Variety is the spice of life, my girl," Eric said, tweaking her nose as he pulled the cushions out of the lounge to expose the doors of the cabinets behind. He yanked one open and tossed a can to Molly, who caught it neatly.

"Baked beans," she said.

"Here's another."

She caught it, too. "Vienna sausages."

"Let's open a couple more of those. How about some corn?" He dug a can of Mexicorn out of a corner.

"I like Vienna sausages," Phoebe said, her eyes bright. "And can I have the baked-bean jar?"

"What for?" he asked.

"For my messages in a bottle," Phoebe said.

"What?" said Molly.

"She puts messages in bottles and throws them overboard. It's harmless enough."

"I'll wash out the jar for you," Molly told Phoebe after a moment's hesitation.

Molly opened the beans and sausages, and he took charge

of the corn. Phoebe arranged the sausages in a microwavable dish, and he and Molly shared the cramped space in front of the stove while everything heated up.

The deepening darkness outside lay about *Fiona* like soft velvet, and the fact that they were all alone in the cove made them seem encapsulated in the warmth and light of the boat. It was easy, when you were in this situation, to forget that there was a world out there, that somewhere people were driving home from work, picking up the kids at day care, planning an evening's entertainment. Phoebe, after consigning the Vienna sausages to the microwave oven, took the clean glass jar into the small chart room adjacent to the galley, where she sat intent on drawing yet another picture of a vacuum cleaner.

Molly seemed focused on her cooking chores, and every once in a while the motion of the boat rocking on the waves lurched him closer to her. She ignored him pointedly, but as they continued to work together to prepare the meal, he sensed a shift in her awareness. As the rocking of the boat grew stronger, he realized it was inevitable that they would eventually bump into each other. Sure enough, that happened twice in rapid succession. He said, "Excuse me" at each occurrence. The first time she replied, "That's okay," and the second time she colored slightly. Maybe that was because their hips touched. Or more accurately, her backside brushed the side of his thigh. It was something he didn't mind one bit.

After they heated up their simple meal, Phoebe pushed her drawing aside and insisted on sitting between them at the small oval table, keeping up a stream of chatter, so that he and Molly didn't have to talk. He treated himself to several covert glances when Molly was paying attention to something else. From what he could tell, under that shirt she had rock-solid abs. Long legs, long feet. He'd bet they were high arched and pale, adept at both walking and dancing. He'd like to get her on a dance floor sometime.

Ha! Fat chance. Queen Molly was barely tolerating him, though she'd warmed up a bit since last night when she'd confronted him about his shortcomings as a parent. How long would it take them to get *Fiona* to Fort Lauderdale? If he could stick it out, he'd be a few thousand dollars ahead, and he needed the money if he was ever to buy Phoebe the house she wanted in a community suitable for bringing up children.

None of which he cared to tell Molly, who sat across from him and carried on an animated conversation with Phoebe. His daughter's hair, tamed by the headband, looked better than it had in a long time. He had to admit that Molly had quickly wrought miracles in Phoebe's appearance.

They made short work of the dinner. "Not bad," he said, pushing back from the table after he finished eating.

"We can do better," Molly said, though he noticed she'd eaten all hers.

Well, the sea air made some people really hungry, and a hungry person wasn't usually particular.

"I'll clean up," Molly said after they all carried their dishes to the sink and Phoebe had trotted off to take a bath.

He figured Molly was volunteering for cleanup duty so that they wouldn't have to tango around each other again in the galley.

On a note of regret, he said, "Suit yourself." It came out sounding gruff and ungrateful, though that wasn't how he felt at all.

She merely shrugged. "Hand me the salt and pepper" was all she said. She stowed them in their proper place behind a rail in the galley, where they wouldn't slide across the cabinet tomorrow when they were under way.

"Guess I'll check the engine," he said, stretching elaborately.

She kept her eyes averted, rinsing the dishes. "Right," she said.

He went into the engine room and decided that the engine was holding up well. If only the blame thing would get them to Fort Lauderdale, he'd celebrate.

Phoebe came out of the forward bathroom. She was all clean and sweet-smelling from her bath and was wearing a warm cotton robe over her pajamas. "Dad, let's take cushions from the cockpit and lie down on the aft deck to look at the stars," she said. "After I throw my message in the bottle overboard, I mean."

Lying on the deck was what he and Phoebe did on many nights. He glanced at Molly to see if she was game.

"Oh, that sounds like fun," she said.

While he and Phoebe consigned her latest message bottle to the waves, Molly tossed pillows from the cockpit to the deck. "What's this message about, Peanut?" he asked, but she only grinned mysteriously. Once the bottle had floated away on the tide, Phoebe flopped down spread-eagled on her cushions and stared upward, and Molly, pulling a sweatshirt over her head, came on deck to join them. The sky overhead was spangled with stars trying to outshine the moon, and there wasn't a cloud in sight. *Fiona* rode easily on gentle waves; the air smelled of mists and marshes and places far away.

"I see the Milky Way," Phoebe said gleefully. "I see the Big Dipper."

"Point out the Little Dipper," Eric said, as Molly settled down beside him, arranging her cushions to her liking.

"It's right there."

"How about Pegasus?"

"There he is," Phoebe said, and added as an aside to Molly, "He's a flying horse."

"Phoebe, you're impressive," Molly said. "I bet most kids wouldn't be familiar with so many constellations."

"My dad taught me," she said, and Eric curved an arm around her.

He was proud of his daughter, of her considerable capabilities. She was as smart as they come, he was sure of that. He'd been home schooling her for the past year and a half.

"Can you find the Pleaides?" he prompted.

"Over there. They're stars, but they're called the Seven Sisters. I wish I had a sister." Phoebe yawned. Her voice kept getting sleepier and sleepier. "If you stay up until morning, you can see Jupiter. It's the biggest planet. You can see, oh, I don't know. Lots and lots. My mommy's up there, too. She's one of the brightest stars in heaven…" Her words trailed off, and when Eric glanced down at her a few moments later, Phoebe's eyes were closed. She had fallen asleep.

He wasn't sure what Molly had made of Phoebe's last statement. Once Phoebe had asked him what the stars were made of, and he'd told her that they were the souls of people who had died. She had wanted to know which one was her mother, and he had pointed out Vega, one of the brightest stars in the sky. Now he saw that Molly had turned her head and was looking at him inquiringly, and he thought that some explanation was called for.

He cleared his throat. "I, uh, told Phoebe that thing about her mom," he said.

"It's beautiful," Molly said quietly.

"I think so," he said. "It was easier than—well, just easier." Ever since she'd accepted that her mother was a star in the sky that she could see almost every night, Phoebe had been much less likely to ask him when Heather was coming back. Well, you did what you could in difficult situations, that was all.

They listened to a distant boat motor, to the wind singing in the rigging. Out of the corner of his eye, he could see that Molly seemed pensive, and he wondered what she thought about. Probably what all career-minded women thought about; themselves. Or at least that had been his experience in the old days before he'd opted out of the corporate world.

"What time do you want to leave in the morning?" Molly asked after a while.

"About the same as today," he told her.

She didn't speak again, and when he turned toward her, he saw that her eyes, too, were closed. Her features were cast in silver by the starlight, gentle in repose. He wondered what would happen if he reached out and tipped a finger across her lips, continued up toward her brow, threaded his fingers through that abundant mass of hair spilled across the cushion like rumpled silk. Would her eyes open in surprise, would she cry out, would she sit up and run below?

He was tempted to try it, but only for a moment. What was he thinking? He needed to clear his head, put a halt to wanting something that would never happen. She'd let him know that she didn't think much of him.

Moodily he turned his eyes back toward the heavens. He saw Vega now, glimmering and shimmering a brilliant blue-white, and for a moment, he wished that it were true, that it really was Heather up there looking down on them, shedding light on everything.

Molly stirred beside him, making a little purring noise like a kitten. She opened her eyes, stared blankly at him for several seconds, then sat up abruptly.

"What time is it? I almost fell asleep."

"'Bout nine o'clock."

"Time for bed." She yawned and stretched. "Do you need my help getting Phoebe below?"

He shook his head. "I'll carry her. I've done it before."

Molly hesitated. "She's a darling girl," she said.

"She is, isn't she? Thanks for saying so."

"You're—you're lucky to have her."

He gazed fondly down at Phoebe, whose chest was rising and falling with each breath. "I know."

For a moment it seemed as if Molly were going to say something else, but she must have thought better of it.

"Good night" was all she said, and then she was picking her way across the deck, avoiding the open hatches of the cabin below, reaching for the rigging so she wouldn't fall if the boat lurched. The breeze ruffled her hair and whipped her shirt and pants tight against her body, delineating every curve.

"Come on, Peanut," he murmured to Phoebe, who mumbled something and slid her arms up around his neck. He didn't carry her downstairs until he was sure that Molly had retired to her stateroom. He didn't want to have to press past Queen Molly in the dim light of the cabin, maybe coming too close, perhaps touching her without meaning to. If he had occasion to touch Molly Kate McBryde again during this voyage, he was pretty damn sure he would mean it.

Phoebe didn't resist when he tucked her tightly into her bunk. When he went to his own V berth in the bow of the ship, he punched his pillows every which way, but he couldn't get comfortable. Finally, he opened the hatch above him so that he could see Vega. That he had chosen this particular star to be Heather's, given the way it sparkled so blue, was fitting. Blue had been Heather's favorite color.

Eric had almost dozed off, when he heard the music coming from the aft stateroom. Harp music, soft and sweet.

Queen Molly's Irish harp. And she could play it very well. It sounded like the music of the angels.

He relaxed completely with that music echoing in his ears, imagining how Molly must look while playing her harp. She'd be sitting on the low bench beside the big bed in the master stateroom, the harp in her lap, her hair spilling across her lovely features. She'd be smiling gently. He'd be sprawled across the bed, perhaps fingering a silken sash that she wore around her waist. Every once in a while she'd glance over at him, a warm teasing light in her eyes. He'd smile back, and…

Unfortunately, he realized in the last few moments before he fell asleep, this was only fantasy. There was no room for him in this picture. None. And he'd better stop imagining that there was.

MESSAGE IN A BOTTLE

TO WHOM IT MAY CONCERN:

SHE'S HERE! MY NEW MOMMY! AT LEEST I'M WISHING THAT SHE'LL BE MY NEW MOM. SHE DIDNT MIND MY VACUME CLEANER AND SHE MADE A GOOD GRILLED CHEZE SAMWICH.

LUV FROM YORE GOOD FRIEND,
PHOEBE ANNE NORVALD
P.S. I HOPE YOU LIKE THIS NEW VACUME CLEANER PICTURE ITS THE ONE I DREW TODAY.

Chapter Three

"I liked hearing you play your harp last night," Eric said the next day.

They had left the cove shortly after dawn and were taking turns at the wheel. They'd raised the mainsail and the genoa, and the wind was blowing steadily from the northeast, bringing a chill with it so that Molly was wearing her windbreaker.

"I tried to play softly," Molly said. "I didn't want to disturb anyone."

"Hey, that was a compliment, not a criticism."

"I—well, thank you," she said, realizing as she said it that it was already too late to avoid an awkward moment.

"Where did you learn to play?"

This was something she felt comfortable discussing, at least. "Grandpa insisted I take lessons. My brother plays the guitar—my sister, the piano."

"Emmett was a big part of your upbringing?"

"Both my parents died when I was fairly young, Daddy first and then Mother. Grandpa took over the role of father in our lives when I was eight. He wasn't so good at making us practice our instruments, though. He traveled on business too much for that. I need practice. I could practice right now, in fact."

She started to get up to go below, but Eric said, "Whoa, not so fast. Sit back down." Then, amending it to a request after he saw her raised eyebrows, he said, "Please? I have something I want to talk over with you. About Phoebe."

That was what made her want to stay. She sat.

He kept his eyes on the horizon, where there was only one ship, a large freighter.

"I was thinking that maybe Phoebe should have music lessons. If she's left to herself, she'll be trying to play *Chopsticks* on her make-believe vacuum cleaner."

"Playing a musical instrument takes a lot of practice. I'm not sure a seven-year-old is into that. I didn't get serious about it until I was in my teens."

"How will I know if she's ready?"

Molly shrugged, not wanting to dismiss his question but unsure how to answer it. "Maybe you should ask a music teacher. I'm not exactly qualified to know, either as a musician or as an expert on children."

Eric's eyebrows lifted. "You seem so comfortable with Phoebe."

"She's—easy." Molly didn't know how else to describe Phoebe. It had taken a while to get past the quirky hair and mismatched socks, but she was an agreeable child who, so far, didn't seem disposed to temper tantrums or other diva tactics.

Eric chuckled. "You should see her when she gets her back up. It happens occasionally."

"Speaking of your daughter, she's awfully quiet down there." Earlier today Eric had assigned Phoebe a sheet of mathematics problems to do, and she had sat down at the table in the salon, bending over her paper and impervious to distractions.

"She likes to finish whatever she starts so she can move on to the next thing. She likes science best."

"Dad! Where's the pencil with the big eraser? I need it for my next message."

"Aren't you out of bottles?"

"No, I can use a soda bottle. If I drink the soda, I mean. Is that okay?"

Eric leaned over the companionway. "Sure, drink the soda if you want. And check the chart room for the pencil," he called down to her. A few minutes later he called, "Did you find it?"

"Uh-huh. Thanks, Dad."

During this exchange, Molly focused on a gray smudge beyond the distant freighter. She stood up for a better look. "Is that a squall I see on the horizon?" she asked.

Eric whipped out a pair of binoculars. "Could be."

"Let's see what it does," Molly said, keeping her eyes on the churning gray clouds. "It may stay to the east of us."

"Go down and break out the charts. I need to know—"

"Eric," Molly said with the utmost patience. "I don't mind consulting the charts. In fact, I'd like to do it. Would you mind asking courteously instead of ordering me around?"

Eric let out a long, exasperated sigh. "I thought we settled this yesterday. I can't issue courteous requests when we're sailing. There mostly isn't time."

"There is now," Molly said pointedly. "It's not as if you're telling me to throw a line to someone on the dock so they can pull us away from another boat as we're docking, or as if someone has fallen overboard." She tried to maintain a reasoning tone, which wasn't easy considering her passionate opinion on the subject, nor did she add that she wanted to stop feeling defensive all the time.

"What's the matter, you two?" Phoebe asked, poking her head up on deck.

"Nothing, Peanut," Eric said hastily at the same time that Molly said, "Your father—"

She stopped talking when she realized that she had no business dragging Phoebe into her argument with Eric.

Phoebe grinned. "Giving you a hard time, is he? He can be like that. Dad, have you seen the pencil sharpener?"

"In the forward stateroom next to the bed. And don't make a mistake and stick your little finger in it instead of the pencil."

Phoebe giggled. "He always says that," she told Molly. She disappeared below.

Molly ducked her head and shot Eric a look. "Sorry," she said.

"So am I." He hesitated. Then he grinned at her. "I'll try

to do better, okay? Now, are you going to check those charts or not?"

"Aye aye, Captain," Molly said, sending him a smart salute, and as she climbed down the ladder, Eric was laughing.

"You see," said Phoebe, settling down in the salon with her freshly sharpened pencil. "He's not so bad."

"No, he's not," Molly said with some surprise as she spread out the charts. "He's not at all."

She was beginning to think that maybe, just maybe, she might get along with Eric long enough to get *Fiona* to Fort Lauderdale as planned.

As IT TURNED OUT, the squall did head their way, and as soon as they realized that it wasn't going to bypass them, Eric ordered the dropping of *Fiona*'s sails and headed for the closest inlet.

"We'll have to take the Intracoastal," he shouted over the rising wind. "There's no point in fighting this."

Molly zipped up the side curtains of the cockpit and braced herself for rough waters. Eric started *Fiona*'s engine before they began their transition into the calmer waters, and though he looked worried and was clearly listening for the diesel to begin making unusual noises, he didn't seem to hear any.

Once they had reached the inland waterway, Molly complimented him on his expert seamanship.

"I know that inlet well," he said.

The way he said it made her swivel her head. "Why is that?"

"Used to live near here," he said, the words barely more than grunts.

She narrowed her eyes, trying to figure out if she'd touched a nerve. "Was that when you were a boy?" she ventured.

"After," he replied succinctly. Then he excused himself to take care of a flapping halyard on deck. He worked quickly and efficiently, refusing to let the wind slow his progress.

You seem to be one good sailor, Eric Norvald, Molly said silently. *And you don't give anything away, do you?*

She never would have dared to say anything of the sort to him. But she was beginning to see him as more than a boat bum. He was definitely a man of mystery. And not as unappealing as she had originally thought.

THE INCLEMENT WEATHER decided to stick around for a while, keeping them confined mostly to the cabin and cockpit and under engine instead of sail.

"One thing about the Intracoastal is good," Phoebe said as Molly sudsed out some clothes in the galley sink. "If we're on the Intracoastal, the television set will pick up signals better. Dad might even be able to watch *Jeopardy!* That means he'll be in a better mood most of the time."

"You're joking, right?"

"Nuh-uh. You'll see. I mean, if we can get *Jeopardy!* And if we always have Chunky Monkey ice cream on board. Otherwise, he'll go on being Mr. Grumpy."

Molly let the water out of the sink. "Is that what you call your dad? Mr. Grumpy?" Privately, she found this amusing.

"I don't tell him I call him Mr. Grumpy. Just like I don't tell you that he calls you Queen Molly—" Phoebe clapped a hand over her mouth. "I wasn't supposed to say that."

"So Eric calls me Queen Molly? Great jumping Jehosaphat," Molly muttered, not allowing a stronger epithet to escape her lips because of Phoebe's big ears and tender age.

"Great jumping who?"

"Jehosaphat."

"Is that what you're going to call my dad?" Phoebe appeared ready to burst into giggles.

"Only if he's lucky, because I could think of other names," she said darkly. She carried the underwear she'd just washed to her stateroom.

Phoebe followed. "Where are you going with those? Aren't you going to hang them on deck?"

"No, in the shower where they can drip dry." She pushed aside the shower curtain and began to drape her clothes over the line that she'd rigged earlier. Molly wasn't about to tell Phoebe that she didn't want to hang her underwear where Eric could see it.

"We always hang our wet laundry on deck. The wind dries it real fast," Phoebe said, standing by the bed and running her hand over the glowing pale wood of Molly's harp in its open case. The instrument was delicately painted with a design of intertwined thistles and shamrocks, intricate and elegant.

Phoebe climbed up on the bed. "Molly, when are you going to play your harp?"

"When I get some free time," Molly said. She was still smarting at the news that Eric was calling her Queen Molly behind her back.

"When is that?"

Molly lifted the instrument and strummed the strings. Unlike many other string instruments, the Irish harp was meant to be played with the fingernails. Her fingernails had been too short, bitten to the quick; she'd been biting them ever since she'd started work at McBryde Industries. Now they were almost grown out enough to play, but so far she'd had no time for it. When she wasn't taking over some cooking chore or another, she was cleaning the galley or coiling lines or helping Mr. Grumpy with the myriad tasks that went with sailing a boat like *Fiona*.

"Maybe I'll play for you tonight," she told Phoebe.

"Oh, awesome," Phoebe said before running off to present her day's schoolwork to Eric for his approval.

When Molly joined Eric in the cockpit, she sat down on one of the long benches flanking the ship's wheel where Eric stood to steer the boat. Each side of the waterway was lined with sumptuous homes, and palmetto trees had begun to be part of the scenery. Molly closed her eyes and let the sun hit her full in the face. It felt so good, that sun. She didn't regret coming on this trip, not one bit.

"Hey, Molly, what have you heard from Emmett lately?" Eric asked.

She opened her eyes. "Not much. I need to call him, find out what's going on at the clinic."

"He's a nice old fellow. We got along great."

"Grandpa gets along with everyone."

"A guy like that, it's not surprising."

When Molly had talked with Emmett on her cell phone the morning after she came aboard *Fiona*, he'd spoken of Eric in glowing terms. "Eric's to be trusted completely," he'd told her. "I grew fond of him on those many long evenings spent on *Fiona* when I was in North Carolina, and I like the fellow. I don't want you giving him any trouble at all, at all."

"And am I giving him any? Aren't I doing my best to get along with him?" Molly had replied, thinking it was a good thing that Emmett didn't know how close she'd come to firing Eric.

"You'd better," Emmett had huffed, and that had been the end of the conversation.

Emmett wasn't feeling well. He didn't want any flack from his granddaughter, that was for sure.

Now, she realized, Eric was making an effort to be agreeable. "Grandpa liked you, too," she said.

Eric gave her a sly look. "Better than you do, no doubt," he said.

"I think I'll check the food supplies and see what we can throw together for dinner," she said hastily. She didn't intend to be baited, and she didn't care to engage in a conversation that could get out of hand.

As it turned out, dinner was tuna sandwiches and a garbanzo salad, both of which Molly managed to figure out how to make on her own. Afterward, Phoebe got out the chess pieces and board, insisting that Eric continue teaching her how to play. At first he resisted, but finally he gave in. Molly, feeling distinctly left out of this close-knit little family, went to see if her clothes that she'd hung in the shower earlier were dry. She put the dry ones away, swept out her stateroom and tried to call Grandpa Emmett, only to find that her cell phone was out of range. By the time she returned to the salon carrying her harp, Eric was winding up the chess lesson.

"Wow, Dad, you sure know a lot about chess," Phoebe said

as she gathered up rooks and pawns, kings and queens, and stashed them carefully in their box.

"Which is why I'm the smartest guy in the universe, right?"

"You might be the smartest guy on Earth, but I don't know about Jupiter, Pluto and all the other planets," Phoebe said seriously.

"Hey, give me a break here," Eric said pleadingly. "I'm your dad."

Phoebe pretended to consider this. "All right, you can be the smartest guy in our whole solar system—but I'm not sure about the universe."

"Kids," Eric said as he turned to Molly. "You do everything you can for them, but you get no respect."

Determined to remain noncommittal, Molly sat down across from them and began to tune her harp. "I'm not taking sides," she warned. "It wouldn't be right."

"You'd be on my side if you did," Phoebe said. "After all, we're the only girls. What's that hanging out of your pocket, Molly?"

Molly looked down blankly at the bit of pink nylon protruding from the side pocket of her jeans. She plucked at it and held it up, then felt her cheeks starting to color.

"Um, it's—"

Eric was staring, a slow smile spreading across his face, igniting his eyes devilishly. She felt like an idiot, because the pink thing was a thong that had dried before the other underclothes that she had hung in the shower.

"I think," Eric said succinctly, "that's something private. Something that you and I, Phoebe, aren't supposed to see."

"Oh," Phoebe said, interested—until Eric suggested ice cream.

Bundling the wisp of pink into a tight wad in her fist, Molly got up and slunk back into her stateroom, not as embarrassed about her gaffe as she might have been if Eric hadn't been so tactful. He could have laughed, or he could have made a bawdy comment, but he hadn't. He deserved points for that.

She lingered in her stateroom to straighten the clothes in

the few drawers, turn the bed down for later, even to brush her teeth unnecessarily—passing as much time as possible in an attempt to make sure that her cheeks were no longer red with embarrassment when she went back to the salon.

If only she hadn't promised Phoebe, she'd make some excuse to get herself off the hook. But when she opened the door to the salon, all was normal.

She started by strumming a few chords and soon commenced playing a song that she thought Phoebe would like, singing along with the harp as she hadn't done in a long time. Phoebe clapped loudly at the end.

"Play more," she begged.

Molly couldn't help noticing that Eric was staring at her, and she avoided his eyes. "Here's one about Ireland," she said, tossing her hair back and making herself concentrate on the song. This time she played a chord wrong at the beginning and had to start over, but Eric didn't comment. It was a plaintive song, one of Emmett's favorites, and it always put her in a contemplative mood.

"Well, now," she said when she'd finished. "Isn't it about time for everyone to start thinking about bed?" Sometimes when she played the harp, she slipped into an Irish way of speaking, like Emmett, and this was one of those times.

"Isn't it, though?" Eric said, flashing those white teeth of his.

She might have thought he meant something indecent by that statement if he hadn't scooped Phoebe into his arms and carried her off for a bath.

"I'M GETTING TIRED OF THIS," Phoebe had said after a few days. "I like being out on the ocean, not in this narrow little Intracoastal."

"So do I," Molly had told her fervently. As she had often remarked to her grandfather and brother and sister, a sailboat should sail. Period. She didn't like using the engine any more than Eric did, and he made it clear that he didn't like it much.

Fiona was capable of traveling only seven or eight miles per hour, so it was slow going. But this gave Molly the opportunity to see some of the small towns along the way: Southport, North Carolina. Beaufort, South Carolina. Brunswick, Georgia.

"It sounds wonderful," said Mrs. Brinkle when Molly checked in at her office by phone in midweek. "What are the people like in those places?" Mrs. Brinkle had never been anyplace outside of Chicago except Milwaukee, where she sometimes visited relatives.

"We only stop to get fuel," Molly told her. "I don't get a chance to meet anyone."

"Well, enjoy" was the reply. "I sure wish I could be there on *Fiona*. Do you know how cold it is here today? Twenty-seven degrees."

"I don't miss the cold—but am I missing anything else? Anything important?"

"Your grandfather called from the clinic."

"How did he sound?"

"Like always, and with that Irish brogue of his. Flirting shamelessly. Teasing me about wanting your job. Don't worry, though—I'm looking into a promotion to Legal."

Molly felt a prickle of apprehension. She didn't want to lose Lorraine Brinkle and her many skills.

"Oh, don't threaten me with Legal. We need you in Accounting."

"Mmm-hmm. But now that I've got my college degree, I'm ready for bigger and better things. That's what your grandfather says, anyway."

Molly could imagine Mrs. Brinkle rolling her eyes.

"I'll have to speak to him about undermining our department. What's Frank doing?"

"He's working on the annual report. We're busy little bees with you gone, Molly. I'm juggling five hundred things and loving every minute."

"Great," Molly told her, wondering why she didn't feel the slightest tug of emotion pulling her back to work. The fact was that McBryde Industries seemed so far removed from her life at the moment, she could hardly picture the skyscraper building, her office, or even her desk.

"Don't you worry about anything, Molly dear. Anything at all."

"I won't," Molly assured her.

"I mean it," Mrs. Brinkle said.

"So do I," Molly replied.

THE SLOW PROGRESS of *Fiona* down the Intracoastal Waterway didn't bother Eric. He liked it. Sometimes he even sat on the bench behind the wheel and steered the boat with his feet.

When she saw him doing this, Molly narrowed her eyes. "Is that proper procedure for a licensed captain?" she asked.

Eric stayed right where he was. "You can try it if you like."

"Never mind," she said quickly. She sat down, but not too close. She watched the birds following a nearby fishing boat, hoping for cast-offs. "You had to study to become a captain, I take it."

He focused on the same birds. "Right," he said. A stiff breeze was whipping into the cockpit, making him thirsty. He supposed it would be too much to ask Molly to bring him a beer from the galley below.

"Just wondering."

"You thinking of becoming a captain yourself?"

She stared at him. "I have an M.B.A. I'll have to go back to my job as a corporate accountant when this is over."

Was he mistaken, or was that a tinge of regret in her tone? He took his time answering. "I have an M.B.A. too, but one thing I'm not going to do is give up this life for one I didn't like much in the first place."

He thought her jaw started to drop, and he enjoyed watching her recover from what he figured must be something of a shock. "I—well, I didn't realize that you—" She stopped talking.

"That I had an education?" he asked.

"Something like that."

He chuckled. "I guess that might surprise a lot of people."

She didn't say anything, and after he'd looked away, he glanced back and caught her staring at his beard. Self-consciously he ran a hand over the stubble. He hadn't shaved for, what, a month? Maybe more?

Her gaze was assessing, not critical. He raised his eyebrows, but she didn't comment.

He removed his feet from the steering wheel, stood up and stretched. "How about taking over while I go check on Phoebe, get a beer?"

"Okay," she said. She stood and positioned herself behind the wheel.

He went below, approved Phoebe's completed social studies assignment and cadged a beer out of the fridge. Before he climbed back up the ladder, he ducked into the forward bathroom and took a glimpse of himself in the mirror over the sink. The crosshatching and fine lines around his eyes made him look older than his thirty-five years, and then there was the beard growth that emphasized rather than diminished the grooves at the sides of his mouth.

"It's definitely been more than a month," he said to himself, rubbing his beard again. It was starting to itch, but he'd thought it was well past that stage.

He set the beer down on the edge of the sink. "What the hell," he muttered, and then he reached for his razor.

Chapter Four

That night they anchored off a marina near Jacksonville, Florida. After dinner, Molly gave Phoebe a manicure while they all watched *Jeopardy!* together. Eric proved to be a trivia expert, calling out most of the questions before the on-screen contestants even buzzed in. He was in a good mood afterward, teasing Phoebe about her Cinnabar Red nail polish.

"I love it," Phoebe said, holding her fingers this way and that to admire them before climbing into her bunk. "It makes me feel grown up and girly."

"You're my best girly," Eric told her before kissing her and turning out the light.

After Phoebe was in bed, Molly and Eric went up to the cockpit so that their conversation, if any, wouldn't keep Phoebe awake. Eric rolled up the clear vinyl side curtains to admit a balmy breeze, and Molly busied herself sorting sheet music into folders that she'd brought along. The radio played soft music, and the faint laughter of folks at the marina floated across the water.

Eric seemed to be studying her, and she was doing her best to remain aloof and nonchalant. She had been surprised this afternoon when he had suddenly shaved off his beard, appearing in the cockpit without his baseball cap, for once, and freshly showered. As she'd suspected, he did have a strong chin, and moreover, there was a cleft in the middle.

She cast around for some safe topic of conversation. "How's the engine holding up?" she asked.

"Okay, I hope," he said cautiously.

She sent him a covert look from under her lashes, trying to come up with small talk.

"What are you gawking at?" he demanded abruptly and with mock outrage.

She wished she didn't have a tendency to blush. "Nothing," she said.

"Is it because I shaved?" he asked, treating her to an impish grin.

"Maybe it's the clean clothes. Or because you're not wearing a hat," she shot back, but she couldn't restrain the smile that turned up the corners of her mouth.

"It has to be because I shaved. I could be mistaken, though, right?"

"You *have* made mistakes about a lot of things so far," she said.

"Like what?"

"Well, there was the Queen Molly mistake."

His eyes widened perceptibly. "You know about that?"

"Phoebe told me. Don't be angry with her," she said hastily. "She was only repeating what you said."

He rolled his eyes and stared up at the canvas canopy for a moment. "She say anything else?"

"Not about that. I don't think I'm royalty, by the way. A goddess, maybe. But not royalty." She barely suppressed a smile.

Eric threw back his head and laughed. "I was miffed when you waltzed aboard *Fiona* with your talk of firing me and how you don't cook and—"

She waved her hand in dismissal. "Please. The past few days have changed my mind. I didn't think much of you, either, to tell the truth."

"And now?"

"I've learned that you're a fine sailor." She paused, then continued. "Also a caring father."

"Thanks," he said thoughtfully. "Praise coming from you is sweet."

"Mmm," she said, wishing he would stop looking at her like that. She stuck a few more sheets of music in her folder and stood up. At that moment, the radio began to play a slow song with a throbbing beat, one she recognized from her teenage years. In those days, she'd been a true romantic, and she recalled dancing with her boyfriend to that same tune at her high school's sophomore hop.

To her surprise, Eric stood, too. "One more thing, Molly Kate McBryde, before you go below." He paused as if to assess her mood.

"I—" As she backed away, the folder fell from her hands and the sheet music scattered across the floor of the cockpit. "I'd better pick those up," she said.

"Not yet," Eric murmured, taking her hand in his.

Then, somehow, her other hand came up to rest on his shoulder. He pulled her closer. She tried to take a deep breath, but the air seemed to have grown thinner, the space between them more electric.

"May I have this dance, Queen Molly Kate McBryde?" he asked, his lips so close to her ear that his breath disturbed the wispy tendrils there.

"I never dance," she murmured.

"But you have music in your soul," he said.

"I can play the harp. That's all."

"And you can dance," he said as her feet began to move. "Don't tell me you never learned."

"It was long ago," she said helplessly as her temple came to rest against his cheek.

The song had already awakened memories of a time when she'd been in love with her first boyfriend. Now she felt a stirring of something that she hadn't felt in a long time—nostalgia, perhaps, or maybe it was the lingering regret that she had sometimes felt in the past after love had gone. Whatever it was, it was a bittersweet emotion, and she cautioned herself not to read too much into the way Eric was slowly massaging her back as they danced. Or the way he held her, so carefully, as though she would break.

Another song began as soon as that one ended, and Eric didn't release her. Instead they segued effortlessly into the new rhythm, which was slower than the last one. Around them, the night seemed to pulse with starlight, shimmer with moonlight, the water below them reflecting myriad possibilities, one of which was that she wouldn't mind kissing Eric Norvald, who most definitely was not her type.

She pulled away. "Eric, I really should get some sleep. I need to pack in a few more zees before—"

He refused to release her hand. "Before you do something you'll regret?" he shot back, his eyes gleaming in the moonlight.

"Yes," she whispered. She fled down the companionway, stopped outside Phoebe's room to check on her, and realized that her heart was thudding crazily against her rib cage.

She didn't remember until she was behind the closed door of the master stateroom that she had left her sheet music scattered all over the floor of the cockpit. For a moment, she debated whether to go back up there to get it, then finally decided that Eric would think her reappearance was a capitulation. So she crawled into bed, pushing aside the thought that sleeping would be far more pleasant if she didn't have to sleep alone.

When she woke up the next morning, the folder containing the sheets of music had been slipped beneath her door. Attached to it was a brief note: *Take a look at the top sheet of music,* it said. *A prophecy of things to come?*

The title of the piece was *First Kiss.*

FIONA'S UNPREDICTABLE ENGINE began to make ominous noises somewhere south of St. Augustine.

Eric pulled panels out of the floor in the salon, spent time in the engine room cursing at the engine and soon admitted defeat. "There are a couple of things wrong, and I can fix all except one. It looks like the fuel injector pump is shot, and it will have to be specially ordered from Germany. In half an hour or so, we'll pull into a little marina at a small town called Greensea Springs. I can check things over more carefully there."

Molly had never heard of the place. "Shouldn't we try to go a little farther? There might be better repair facilities farther south," she said anxiously.

"I'd rather stop before the engine quits altogether" was Eric's terse reply.

"You can't talk with him when he gets in this kind of mood," Phoebe said sagely after Eric returned to the cockpit. "The best thing is to feed him some Chunky Monkey ice cream."

"He can get his own ice cream," said Molly, tired of riding out Eric's moods. Phoebe's mouth formed into a surprised O, and Molly regretted her sharp tone. She looked around the salon for something to do. "What do you say I fix us some sandwiches?"

"It's only ten o'clock," Phoebe reminded her.

"Hmm. What would be fun for you?"

"I know," Phoebe said, brightening. "Maybe you could wash my hair and blow-dry it."

"I'll teach you to do it yourself," Molly said.

"Could I, do you think?"

"Of course."

Phoebe followed her back to her stateroom. "You and I could take our sandwiches ashore and have a picnic when we get to Greensea Springs," she said.

Molly could only imagine how it felt to be a child confined to a boat, for days at a time unable to run and play on dry land. "Good idea," she said warmly, as Phoebe draped a towel over her shoulders and leaned over the tub.

Later, after Molly's hands-on blow-dryer lesson, Phoebe admired her own reflection in the mirror. "I like my hair better this way than the way my dad does it," she said. "I'll be glad when you're really my mommy."

"Don't hold your breath," Molly murmured.

"What?"

"Don't get your hopes up," Molly amended, hurrying into the galley and opening the cabinet where they kept the peanut butter.

Phoebe hiked herself up on the table and swung her legs while Molly prepared the sandwiches. "Don't you like my dad?" she asked.

"Of course I do. You have to like someone quite a lot for what you're suggesting."

"He likes you a bunch."

Molly stopped spreading peanut butter and looked askance at Phoebe. "You'd better jump down off that table. Your dad will be annoyed if he comes down and sees you there. How do you know how much he likes me?"

"He shaved off his beard. He wants to be handsome for you. Do you think he's handsome?"

"Um, yes. Do you want jelly on your sandwich?"

"No, and why don't you want to talk about my dad?"

"Because I'm busy, and besides, you ask too many questions."

Phoebe hopped off the table. "That's what he says."

She climbed the ladder to the cockpit and Molly exhaled a long sigh of relief. She shuddered to think of the conversations that Phoebe must have been having with Eric on the same subject.

Eric greeted Phoebe heartily when she came on deck. "I like your hair that way, Peanut," he said. It was fluffy, not spiked, and the bangs fell softly across her forehead.

"Molly is teaching me to do it myself."

"Good. I don't know much about little girls' hairdos," he said, noting that the Greensea Springs marina was coming up on their starboard side, Bottlenose Island to port.

"Molly knows lots of useful things. Hey, Dad, I believe she really likes you."

"How do you know that?"

"She said she thinks you're handsome."

"She said that?" Good thing he'd shaved off his beard.

"Uh-huh. I told her I think you're handsome, too."

Eric tried to see if there was a big enough slip at the marina for *Fiona;* otherwise they'd have to anchor out and dinghy into the marina, which would be a big nuisance. Too soon to tell; they were still too far away.

"I'm the most handsome fellow on this boat, anyway," he said distractedly, and Phoebe laughed at that.

"You're the only fellow on this boat," she said.

"And how," Eric said under his breath, as Molly started up the companionway wearing a shirt with a scoop neck, which showed off a couple of her ample female attributes.

"You can help me dock," he said to her, hoping she'd notice that he'd given up barking out orders and was making an effort to soften his commands.

"I'm going to vacuum your room," Phoebe said, looking pleased with herself. She disappeared down the ladder, leaving the two of them alone.

"That kid," Eric said to Molly. "Her make-believe vacuums are driving me crazy."

"Did you ever consider that maybe if she could live in a house and have a real vacuum, she might get over this phase?" Molly asked.

"You said you're not qualified to give advice about children," he said. "So what's with that?"

"Sorry," Molly mumbled, swinging up and out of the cockpit onto the deck in preparation for docking.

The last thing Eric wanted at the moment was parenting advice from someone who had never been one. Unless he asked for it, that is.

THE GREENSEA SPRINGS MARINA was, as Eric had said, small and looked slightly run-down, but the biggest slip was available and adequate for docking *Fiona*. Bottlenose Island, one of a string of barrier islands between the Intracoastal Waterway and the Atlantic Ocean, provided protection from rough weather. The other boat people at the marina were friendly, running out to help them dock and lingering afterward to tell them where to find laundry facilities and a nearby grocery store.

"Molly and I can stop to buy food on the way back from our picnic," Phoebe said, bouncing up and down on one foot in front of the chart room where he sat.

"What picnic?" Eric said, looking up from *Fiona*'s log-book.

"The one where we're going to eat our peanut butter sandwiches," Phoebe informed him.

Eric shot a questioning glance at Molly.

She shrugged. "You're welcome to join us," she said.

"I need to have a talk with the dockmaster, see if there are any mechanics around here who can advise me about this engine," Eric said as he closed the log. "You two go on."

They left Eric topping off *Fiona*'s water tanks. "Have a good time," he called after them, and Molly had the distinct impression that he regretted not being able to go along. When she glanced over her shoulder, he was gazing after them wistfully.

Phoebe skipped alongside Molly all the way up the dock. A couple of curious pelicans did an inquisitive fly-by as they passed the marina office, then settled on two pilings and tucked their big bills down into their chests. A scruffy dog ran up and followed them to the street, sitting down beside a bench to watch while they crossed to the other side.

"What's that funny smell in the air?" Phoebe asked, wrinkling her nose.

"That's sulfur," Molly said, consulting the town map that the dockmaster had given Eric when he checked them in. "There's a spring here where people from the north used to visit in the winter. Drinking the water was supposed to be beneficial to their health, but it certainly doesn't smell good."

"I like it," Phoebe said as she took Molly's hand. "It smells friendly."

Molly laughed. "If you say so" was all she said. "Look up there, Phoebe. That's the Plumosa Hotel. According to the notes on the map, it was a major tourist attraction around the turn of the century."

The large rambling building, which occupied the center of a city square, was embellished with cupolas, porches and gingerbread trim. Although part of it appeared close to falling down, scaffolding stood against the side nearest them. A man was diligently painting the worn and weathered clapboard a bright sparkling white. Behind the hotel was a park—Springs Park, according to the map.

"They're fixing up the building," Phoebe said. "When they finish with it, it's going to look like the world's biggest birthday cake."

Molly agreed, but there was more to see than the hotel. They were passing beneath enormous live oak trees whose leafy branches arched over the brick street. Water Street was flanked by small stores—a chichi boutique, a hardware store, a café. The windows gleamed with wide expanses of glass, and the signs were uniform in size and noticeably deficient in garish neon. Tiny patches of grass edging the sidewalks were free of litter and neatly clipped and trimmed. Planters containing bright flowers were spaced every ten feet or so beside decorative wrought-iron benches. All in all, the effect was of a town that had wandered off a Disney stage set.

Phoebe seemed entranced by their surroundings and began to talk nonstop. "I like Greensea Springs, don't you, Molly? I hope we get to stay a while. Maybe they have a McDonald's. Do you like McDonald's? I could go to school here instead of getting home schooled. Is that a good idea, Molly? My aunt said I'm not being socialized properly. What does that mean? Oh, a vacuum cleaner shop!" Phoebe ran up to the window under a sign that said A Perfect Vacuum and peered in. "And they have a Robo-Kleen! It's a robot vacuum cleaner like I told you about! Please can we go inside? Please?"

The Robo-Kleen in the window was going busily about its work, and amazingly, it was avoiding a chair and a footstool that had been set up to demonstrate the vacuum cleaner's self-steering capabilities. Molly found the machine mildly interesting, and before she could give Phoebe permission, the child disappeared inside the shop. Molly followed, figuring that it couldn't hurt to learn more about vacuum cleaners. It wasn't an area of expertise that had ever interested her, but she had to admit that maybe she had missed something important.

The proprietor of the shop was talking with a young mother who was there with her three children. He looked like Santa Claus.

"Thanks for stopping in, Dee," he said, chucking the baby under the chin. "I think those bags will work fine on your canister vacuum."

"We'll see you at Art in the Park in a few weeks," the woman said. "Come along, Lexie. Did you thank Mr. Whister for the lollipop? Corduroy? Let's go, son."

But her son, a self-possessed sort who wore thick glasses, a ready grin, and had a wild thatch of white-blond hair, was already talking with Phoebe, who was explaining how the Robo-Kleen worked.

"And it's real lightweight," Phoebe said. "Even we could pick it up." She started to lift the immobile one on display, but Molly stopped her.

"Phoebe, you'd better not," she interjected hastily.

Mr. Whister laughed, a jolly ho-ho-ho. "It's okay. I'll show her how," he said to Molly. He strode to where Phoebe and the boy were standing. "You hold it by this handle. Then you won't do it any harm," he said, demonstrating. Phoebe lifted it up first, then the boy did so.

"It's real nice," the boy said admiringly.

"I have a Model 440 Hoovasonic Sweeper of my very own," Phoebe was saying.

Oh, great, thought Molly. The pretend vacuum cleaner again. "Phoebe, come along," Molly said firmly, prepared to shepherd her small charge out of the shop.

"We only have a Model 320," said the boy, sounding impressed. "My name's Corduroy. What's yours?"

"Phoebe Anne Norvald. I'm seven and a half years old and I live on a boat."

"A boat? Really? Wow!"

The mother, who balanced a baby on her hip and held her older daughter's hand, moved closer to Molly. "Our children seem to have struck up an acquaintance. We're going to the park for a picnic. Would you like to join us for peanut butter and jelly sandwiches?"

Molly held up the brown sack she carried. "We brought our own, and yes, we were going to the park. It would be fun to go together."

"I'm Dee Farrell. This is Jada," she said, jiggling the baby. "My other daughter is Lexie."

"I'm nine," said Lexie. "My brother's dumb. He likes horseshoe crabs."

Clearly this statement needed more explanation, but that would have to wait. Before Dee and Molly had even left the shop, Phoebe, Lexie and Corduroy were already racing through the ornate iron gates of Springs Park.

Molly and Dee followed at a more sedate pace, past a shallow pond where children were wading and sailing their boats. "You're new here, aren't you?" Dee asked. She was short, with a mop of shiny brown hair and glasses that couldn't hide a lively curiosity about the world.

"We just got in last night," Molly told her. "We're on *Fiona* at the marina."

"What brings you to Greensea Springs?"

"We were moving *Fiona* to Fort Lauderdale and stopped here for repairs," Molly said.

"I hope you get to stay a while," Dee said. "Our kids are having a great time."

They passed a fenced area where dog owners could unleash their dogs and let them run free. By the time Molly and Dee reached the picnic tables in a grove of live oaks, the three older children were exploring a nearby play pirate ship complete with the Jolly Roger flying overhead. Phoebe was hanging from her knees on one of the bars, and Corduroy was clambering up the mast. Lexie had assumed the role of captain on the foredeck.

"They do seem to get along well," Molly murmured. "But Phoebe's not my daughter."

Dee's eyes widened. "I'm sorry," she said. "I assumed she was."

Molly launched into an explanation of how she happened to be with Phoebe, and Dee evinced interest in what it was like to live on a boat. Then the children interrupted, and Dee's attention was diverted when Lexie stubbed her toe on the picnic bench.

While all this was going on, Molly considered for a moment what her life might be like if she really was Phoebe's mommy and they really were going to stay in Greensea Springs.

The idea rattled around in her mind, settled in and felt uncomfortable. She adjusted it: What if Phoebe's most cherished wish came true? If she and Eric fell in love and got married and they all lived happily ever after?

No. It could never happen. She knew that. She had a job in Chicago and a life of her own, and she didn't want to be a mother, ever.

Only, she couldn't shake the idea as easily as that. As she watched Phoebe playing so happily in the playground with the other children, as Dee discreetly began to nurse baby Jada by her side, an unfamiliar yearning washed over Molly, and she felt a twinge of longing for a life that she would never know, the life of a wife and mother. Eric's face came to mind, his blue eyes, his impudent grin. And two words flashed through her mind, two words full of unlimited possibility: What if…

MESSAGE IN A BOTTLE

TO SOMEBODDY:

I THINK THEY LIKE EACH OTHER. MOLLY AND MY DAD, I MEAN. HE HASNT BEEN MR. GRUMPY FOR A LONG TIME AND HE'S ONLY WATCHED JEPPARDY ONCE. I WILL LET YOU NO WHAT HAPPENS. I SENT NO VACUME CLEANER PICTURE TODAY BECAUSE I DID NOT DRAW ONE. I WENT TO THE PARK INSTEAD.

YORE FRIEND,
PHOEBE ANNE NORVALD

Chapter Five

"It's like this," Eric said the next morning when they were eating breakfast on deck. "I'm waiting to hear from the factory in Germany about ordering the new fuel injector pump. We may be stuck here in Greensea Springs for a while."

"Goody!" shouted Phoebe.

"Oh, no," said Molly, making a grab for Phoebe's cereal bowl, which almost flew from her lap.

Phoebe accepted the bowl from Molly, dismay written all over her face. "I thought you liked it here, Molly."

"I do, but we need to get *Fiona* to Fort Lauderdale."

"We'll get her there," Eric said. "Don't worry about that."

"I'm worried about work," Molly said, thinking about Frank and Mrs. Brinkle handling things at the office all by themselves.

"Don't," Phoebe said consolingly. "Work's not important." She started spooning up Cocoa Krispies and milk, totally unconcerned.

"Not to you, maybe, but it certainly is to my boss," Molly said.

Eric stood up and looked out over the marina. Down the dock, a man was hosing off his cabin cruiser, and a dog on one of the boats began barking at something unseen. "Have you heard that they have open mike night at the Plumosa Hotel a couple of times a week?" he asked abruptly. "I thought about you and your harp."

Molly recognized a diversionary tactic when she heard one. "How did you find out about that?" Dee hadn't mentioned it when she'd briefed Molly about what to expect while living in Greensea Springs, but then, most of their talk had centered around the kids.

"I heard it from Mickey, the dockmaster here, who is someone I know from way back."

Molly detected a thread of discomfort in his words, wondered about it for a moment, then dismissed it.

"According to Mickey, there's work for me here if I want it. A couple of people might need boat repairs while we wait for the engine part."

"I don't want to delay our trip because you've found other work," Molly said, the words sharper than she intended.

He looked surprised. "Hey, don't worry. *Fiona* is my first priority. Speaking of which, I'd better go up to the captain's lounge and make a few phone calls to Germany."

"You can use my cell phone," Molly said. "That might be more convenient." She reached into her pocket and handed it to him.

He stared at it for a moment before accepting it. "Thanks. I gave up my cell phone a long time ago. They're handy things to have, I'll grant you that." He started down the ladder to the cabin. "Say, why don't you girls do something fun today."

Phoebe spoke up. "We're going to find McDonald's. Corduroy's mother said it was just a few blocks from the park. I'm going to get a Happy Meal. You could go with us, Dad."

"Oh, I don't know," he said, looking straight at Molly.

"It would be fun if the three of us went," Phoebe said eagerly. "Wouldn't it, Molly?"

"Well," Molly said, wanting Eric to go with them but not in the mood to say so.

"I'm supposed to check with Mickey this morning, get the names of the boat owners who need work done," Eric said. He paused, assessing Molly's expression. "How about if I let you know?"

"Fine," Molly said brusquely, standing and brushing biscuit crumbs off her lap. Eric had made biscuits, or rather he'd taken them out of a can and baked them. He'd also fried sausage and squeezed fresh orange juice from the fruit that Molly and Phoebe had bought yesterday at the grocery store.

"What shall we do now?" Phoebe asked.

"I want to practice my harp," Molly told her.

"I could do my schoolwork right away and be all done with it before lunchtime. Then maybe Dad will take me to the office to see Mickey," Phoebe said.

She hurried down the ladder, and Molly heard her talking with Eric about her assignments. Molly sat on deck, raising her face to the warm sunshine. It was nine o'clock, and a couple of boats were heading out for a day of fishing. The air was scented with tar and brine, an odor peculiar to all the marinas she'd ever visited. She felt at home here, on *Fiona,* with the sea air caressing her cheeks as gently as a lover might.

Only, she didn't have a lover, and she didn't want one. Men could be a lot of trouble. They got in the way, often tried to control and generally made nuisances of themselves. She'd had enough of that with Charles Stalnecky, the guy she broke up with last summer. She didn't miss him, not one bit.

After Phoebe seemed to have settled down in the salon with her schoolwork and Eric was talking on the phone to someone in Germany, she went to her cabin to get her harp.

If she was going to play at open mike night, she'd need to practice.

"I'LL HAVE A BIG MAC with fries," Molly told the girl at the counter.

"Same here," Eric said.

"I can't recall the last time I ate a Big Mac," Molly confessed.

Eric grinned at her. "You poor deprived soul," he said soothingly.

When they reached their table, which had a view of the McDonald's slide and gym, Phoebe was busily vacuuming the carpet in the vicinity with her make-believe Hoovasonic. Eric aimed a stern look at her. "Honey, don't do that," he said as he deposited her Happy Meal at her place.

She pretended to switch off the vacuum cleaner and wind its cord, which Molly found amusing. Eric apparently didn't.

"Phoebe, as of now, you are forbidden to take your vacuum cleaner off the boat," he said.

Phoebe rolled her eyes and sat down. "My dad hates my vacuum cleaners," she said to Molly. "One time he wouldn't even let me say the words for a couple of years."

"It was more like a couple of months," Eric said. "I got tired of hearing them, that's all."

"You'd think he didn't like vacuum cleaners," Phoebe said. "I like them. Don't you, Molly?"

Molly, her mouth full of food, nodded.

"It's not that I have anything against vacuum cleaners," Eric explained, dunking a French fry in ketchup. "There are better things for a seven-year-old girl to do."

"That's why he's teaching me to play chess," Phoebe confided. "He says it's cerebral. That means something to do with the brain."

Eric grinned at her, and Phoebe grinned back. "How about eating your Happy Meal, which would require doing something with your mouth," he suggested.

Phoebe giggled and turned to Molly. "My dad's pretty funny, wouldn't you say?"

Molly, her mouth full again, shrugged elaborately and took a pass on that one, too.

Fortunately, Phoebe decided to concentrate on her meal, and she finished in record time. She wadded up her hamburger wrappers and threw them in a nearby trash can, then started to fidget.

"You can go out and play, Phoebe, if you'd like," Eric told her.

She slid off her chair. "That'll be fun. Then you and Molly can talk to each other."

Molly blinked at that, amazed at Phoebe's ability to notice everything that went on around her. True, she and Eric hadn't spoken since they sat down, but to her way of thinking, it was okay.

"Don't leave the playground," Eric cautioned his daughter, "and try to stay where I can see you."

"My dad always wants to know exactly where I am," Phoebe told Molly. "He doesn't like me wandering off."

"That's the way parents are," Molly replied.

"Uh-huh," Phoebe said before skipping away.

That left Eric and Molly facing each other across the narrow Formica table.

"I guess all this kid stuff is new to you," he said. "The vacuum cleaner obsession and everything."

She wished his eyes weren't so blue; thinking was hard when he looked at her the way he was at the moment, all earnestness and boyish vulnerability, a quality that hadn't shone through the scruffy beard that he'd finally had the good sense to shave off.

"I'm not up on child psychology, but I doubt that her interest in vacuum cleaners is unhealthy," she said. "The pictures she draws of them are rich in detail and well thought out."

"She's artistic, that's for sure. It's just—" He rolled his eyes. "I don't understand kids sometimes."

Molly had heard enough about Frank's adventures in fatherhood to know that this was normal, and she told him so. "Most parents are at a loss when dealing with their kids. You're not the only one who gets confused about child rearing. Anyway, being around a child is fun," she added.

His eyebrows flew up, and she decided to elaborate.

"Seeing the world through Phoebe's eyes makes everything seem new," she said. "When we become adults, it's easy to be self-absorbed. Children take us out of ourselves, force us to become like them, to some extent. It's—it's enriching." She stopped talking when she realized that he was nodding in agreement.

His expression softened. "Without Phoebe, I'd be jaded and world-weary, especially after…" His words trailed off, and he bit his lip. "Molly, does it bother you if I talk about Heather once in a while?"

She shook her head, touched by his openness. "Of course not."

Eric focused for a moment on Phoebe playing outside the window. "After my wife died, I found that I wanted to talk about her often. I wasn't maudlin about it, but just mentioning her to someone else kept her memory fresh in my mind. People backed off, and I could see the uncertainty in their eyes—they were uncomfortable when I brought up Heather's name. So I stopped talking about her. But she was always in my thoughts."

"I understand," Molly said quietly. "It was that way for me when my mother died."

His eyes bored into hers. "I guess I should say I'm glad you know what I'm talking about, but maybe that would be the equivalent of saying that I'm glad your mother died. I'm not, though. I'm sorry that happened to you."

"Everyone is sorry," she told him. "They haven't figured out what to say, that's all."

"Yeah. They have no idea that grief is as painful as sinew tearing away from bone. Or that you've been lying awake all night aching inside because when you stretch your hand across to the other side of the bed, you touch…emptiness. And that the emptiness hollows out your very soul."

He smiled bitterly, and she caught a glimpse of a harrowing sadness behind his eyes.

"Sorry. I shouldn't run on like that."

His unexpected revelations about himself had thrown her off balance, and for a moment she sat frozen, not sure how to respond. She was having a hard time breathing, seemed to have forgotten how, and suddenly she was daring to reach across the table to him, was covering his hand with hers. Never mind that she had a spot of ketchup on her thumb or that her fingers were greasy. Never mind that her touch might be unwelcome.

"I don't mind if you talk about it," she said. "If it helps."

"Can anything?" he said, but he didn't sound bitter now, only lost.

Molly glanced out the window. Outside, Phoebe was emerging from the round opening of the yellow tube slide, landing with a thump and a grin before rushing around to slide again. Her hair flopped over her forehead despite the head-band, and she had a smudge of dirt on one cheek.

"Phoebe helps," she said. "You said so." She gave his hand a little squeeze before folding her own hands in her lap.

A moment passed before Eric spoke. "You're right," he said softly. "I tell myself that every day."

"Just don't stop reminding yourself," Molly said.

His gaze, when it met hers, was grateful. "I won't. Especially with you to remind me, too." His tentative grin banished some of the bleakness from his expression.

"Talk about Heather whenever you like," she said.

"I—well." He stared off into the distance. "Maybe I won't have to talk about Heather so much," he said. "Now that you're here."

Molly was rocked by the feelings that his words engendered. There was gratification, and warmth, and a certain amount of panic. And awareness of the need for caution.

She'd recently broken off with one man who posed problems. She was wary of taking on another. And now that she'd seen this serious side of Eric, she thought that things might have been easier between them when he'd been his old devil-may-care self.

THE CAPTAIN'S LOUNGE at the marina, which was adjacent to the marina office and laundry room, contained a book exchange and Internet connections for people who were passing through. That evening after dinner Molly went to find a book to read to Phoebe and was disappointed that the library contained no children's books. An adult mystery with a bright cover caught her eye, and thinking that she could use some reading material, she began to skim its back cover. When she was halfway through the cover copy, a cheerful round-faced blonde with a ponytail stuck her head in the door.

"Oh!" she said. "You're Molly, Eric Norvald's girlfriend."

Molly set the book down. "I'm not his girlfriend. We're delivering my grandfather's boat to Fort Lauderdale."

"Sorry," said the woman, looking embarrassed. "I just assumed that you're together. I'm Micki, Eric's friend from Angler's Spit."

"*You're* Mickey? I thought you were a guy," Molly said, liking her right away. "And where is Angler's Spit?"

"That's where Eric used to live before he lost Heather. And it's Micki with an *i*, short for Michaela." Her eyes sparkled when she smiled.

"Actually, Eric and I met only a few days ago," Molly confessed.

"Oh, he's a great guy. My husband and I used to hang out with Eric and Heather and a few other couples on weekends, most of them military from the nearby Air Force base. Eventually, my husband got sent to Afghanistan and I took a job as dockmaster here. That way I could be close to my brother and sister-in-law. I worked at a marina in Angler's Spit, so it was a natural progression. I live on *Fair Warning*. It's the catamaran at the end of Dock B."

"Have you been here long?"

"About a year, and was I ever surprised to see Eric when he arrived on *Fiona*! I told him I have work for him around the marina if that's what he wants. Gee, it's funny. In our Angler's Spit days, I remember Eric going off to the office wearing a suit and carrying a briefcase. Angler's Spit is a paper-mill town, and he was a manager at the mill. Brilliant, according to some. It was a shock when he quit."

"I can imagine," Molly said. She was inordinately curious about Eric's past life. She told herself that this was because of her interest in Phoebe, but a niggling little voice somewhere in the back of her mind whispered that this wasn't entirely true.

"Some of us told him that living a vagabond life wasn't the

best way to raise a child, but Eric wouldn't listen. Phoebe's a charmer, by the way. She was always so cute and so bright, even as a baby. Well, I've bent your ear long enough," Micki told her. "I'd better go back to work. I told Eric that the four of us should get together sometime if you're going to be at the marina for a while. I also mentioned that I'm available to baby-sit anytime. And, Molly, if you ever need anything, call on me."

"Thanks, I will."

"By the way, I've read that mystery you were studying when I walked in. It's wonderful, a real page-turner. You might like it."

Molly picked up the book again. "I'll give it a try," she said.

As she walked down the dock back to *Fiona,* Molly was pensive. She recalled that Eric had brushed off her inquiry during the first days of her trip when he'd mentioned someplace that he used to live as they were sailing down the coast. He clearly hadn't wanted to discuss it. If that was where he'd lived when Heather died, the place was probably full of painful memories.

When she boarded *Fiona,* Molly saw Phoebe in her pajamas, lugging the cushions from the cockpit onto the foredeck.

"We're going to do some stargazing tonight, remember?" Phoebe asked.

"Right," Molly said.

"I have an idea about what we can do tomorrow, too," Phoebe told her.

"What?"

"I could have a makeover. I saw a program on television this afternoon, and they get a person all new clothes and makeup so they are really beautiful. You could do that for me, couldn't you? Tomorrow?"

"I don't know, Phoebe," Molly said. "Makeup might be a bit more than you need."

"How about clothes? All mine are worn out or too small."

Eric climbed the ladder to the cockpit. "Did I hear someone talking about a makeover?"

"Me, me, me!" said Phoebe. "I want Molly to take me shopping and to get my eyebrow pierced."

"Wait a minute," Molly said. "I didn't agree to any piercings. Nothing like that's going to happen on my watch."

"Thank goodness," Eric said under his breath. "Phoebe, no body piercings. And that's that."

"Corduroy would think it's cool," Phoebe said. She stood back, surveying the cushions she'd set out. "Dad, did you bring the popcorn?"

Eric turned his back to Phoebe so she'd be unlikely to hear him. "Who is this Corduroy kid? He doesn't sound like a good influence on my daughter," he said indignantly on his way down the companionway.

"Corduroy seemed like a normal boy," Molly told him when he reemerged with the bowl of popcorn.

"That's a normal kind of name?"

"Dee told me it's a nickname, after the bear in a children's book."

This earned her an elaborate lift of the eyebrows from Eric.

"All ready," Phoebe said with satisfaction. "You can come up on deck now."

Molly treated Eric to an equally elaborate shrug and followed him to the aft deck.

"You're over there," Phoebe said. "I'm on this end, and Dad is in the middle."

The last time they'd done their stargazing on deck, Phoebe had been between them. Molly was all set to object, but Eric was already lowering himself to the middle cushion.

"First, why don't you tell us the story about Nut, the sky goddess. It's one of my favorites," Phoebe said as she cuddled close to Eric.

"She's really into mythology," Eric said to Molly.

"I'd like to hear the story, too," Molly said.

Eric settled back on his cushion. "Different cultures made up different stories to explain the things they saw in the sky," he said. "There are Norse myths about the constellations, and

African myths, and Greek and Roman myths. The myth about Nut is Egyptian."

"She was a naked giant woman," Phoebe said. "I mean, she was *enormous*." She held her hands out to demonstrate.

"Bigger than that," Eric said. "Nut supported the whole heavens on her back."

"And she was blue," supplied Phoebe. "And she was covered all over with stars. The constellations would have been like these humongous shiny tattoos all over her. I want to get a tattoo in the shape of Pegasus."

"Let's not talk about tattoos," Eric said hastily, and Molly suppressed a grin. "All right, now for the story. Nut fell in love with the earth god, Geb. She married him without asking permission of the sun god, Re, who was very powerful. Re was unhappy that Nut didn't ask his permission, so he decided to punish her."

"Like if I do something without asking Dad if it's okay, Dad will punish me. Usually he doesn't let me play with my vacuum cleaner for a while."

Eric cleared his throat. "The punishment for Nut was slightly more serious. Re said that she would not be allowed to have children in any month of the year. Nut was sad because she wanted children. She had a friend named Thoth, who was the divine scribe."

"That means he wrote letters for the gods and goddesses. They couldn't write because they were so busy being divine."

"I know the feeling," Molly said. "Since I'm a goddess and all."

Eric raised his eyebrows. "You mean you're not the queen of *Fiona*?"

"Dad," said Phoebe with the utmost patience. "If Molly says she's a goddess, then she is. Keep telling about Thoth."

"Thoth," Eric said, resuming the story, "asked the Moon to play a game with him, and the winner's prize was the Moon's light."

"I bet it was chess," Phoebe said. "They probably used the

earth for a chessboard and people who were real bishops and knights."

"That's not exactly the approved version of the story," Eric said.

"But it could have happened."

"Maybe. What we do know is that Thoth won light from the Moon, so much of it that the Moon had to add five new days to the official calendar. Thus Nut could finally bear her four children."

"Tell us their names, Dad," Phoebe said. She was starting to sound sleepy.

"Yeah, Dad." Molly poked him with an elbow.

"Their names were Osiris, Seth, Isis and Nephthys."

"You sound pretty sure of that."

"You can look it up."

"I'm tired," Phoebe said with a wide yawn. "I can't wait to get my makeover. Dad, I wish you'd come with us."

"I might," he said consideringly.

Molly risked a glance in his direction. His head was turned toward her, and he grinned.

"Would it make you angry if I accompanied the two of you, Goddess Molly McBryde? You might have something to teach me about the care and feeding of little girls. I'm not much on wardrobe coordination or beauty secrets."

"You can come if you like." She started to sit up.

Eric's arm drew her back. "Please," he said. "Don't go. It's so pretty up here. *You're* so pretty."

She sank back against the soft cushion. "Eric," she began, but he had rolled his shoulder out from under the now-sleeping Phoebe's head on the other side of him and propped himself on his elbow to peer down at her in the bright moonlight. Her breath caught in her throat, and she tried not to let her attraction to this man show.

She could have stopped him, but for some reason she hesitated. Maybe it was those eyes, so deep and unfathomable, or the way his face was illuminated by moonlight. Or perhaps it was his finger, which had moved to her eyebrow and was feathering its way down her nose, then pressing against her mouth.

"When Emmett first told me about you back at the marina in North Carolina, I thought he was blathering. It was 'Molly Kate can do this,' or 'Molly Kate did that,' and I was thoroughly sick of hearing about you before I ever laid eyes on you. Now I'm glad I paid attention, because everything Emmett said about you was true."

"What kinds of things did he say?" she asked, as his hand cupped her cheek, caressed it briefly and worked its way under her hair.

"That you were beautiful. That you were intelligent. That you were dependable, and thoughtful, and that you made a really good grilled-cheese sandwich."

"He said that about the sandwich?"

"No, I was kidding about that. The other comments—he said them, all right. I wonder if I should have asked him whether you were good at…other things."

Molly stared up at him, her heart beating so hard that she was sure he could hear it. "Like—like what?" she asked, though she was sure of the answer.

"Like kissing," Eric said, his voice a mere whisper stirring the tendrils lying against her neck.

"Why don't you find out for yourself," she said, the words coming out in a rush.

"I intend to, sweet Molly."

His face descended toward hers, filled her field of vision and blotted out the wide starry sky, the shiny disk of the moon. In that moment, he was all she wanted to see, all she wanted to feel, and she reached up and curved her hand around the back of his neck. For a long time, they only gazed at each other, the waves splashing against the hull of the boat, the sounds of the marina fading away from their consciousness as they were captured in a net of emotion that excluded anything outside themselves.

And then the spell shattered and they moved toward each other at exactly the same instant, both of the same mind.

Their lips touched, tentative at first, then sure. It was a deep satisfying kiss, one that had been a long time coming.

A boat entered the marina, chugging too fast toward its slip and churning a wide wake. The sound made her open her eyes, and as the wake reached *Fiona,* the big sailboat began to roll on the waves and strain against the lines holding her to the dock.

Phoebe stirred beside Eric. "Daddy, I want to go to bed now," she said sleepily, and Eric drew back from Molly.

"So do I," he said with a meaningful and regretful look back at Molly. "I'll take Phoebe below," he said. "After that—"

She silenced him with a hand pressed against his lips. He kissed it, but she pulled away and shook her head.

He stared at her for a moment. "A shame" was all he said.

Molly lurched to her feet, grabbing the jib for support as *Fiona* gradually stopped rolling.

"I'm sorry, Eric."

"So am I," he said evenly. He turned to pick up Phoebe, and Molly fled.

That was stupid of me, she told herself. She knew enough not to get a man aroused unless she intended to follow through. But in that case, she'd better be sure that's what she wanted.

The truth was that right now she was still trying to figure out what was going on between Eric and her. And until she did, she'd better not make any foolish mistakes.

Chapter Six

"Okay, Frank, so what do your kids like to read?"

"*Harry Potter* books," her boss said without hesitation. "When do you think you'll come back to work?"

"Not yet," Molly hedged, flicking a curious chameleon off her shoe. She sat talking on her cell phone near the marina office, beneath an arbor covered with a profusion of bougainvillea blossoms. The chameleon twitched his head and gazed at her with his beady eyes before sprinting toward the street.

"Mrs. Brinkle and I are handling things here rather well," Frank said. "Just between you and me, Molly, I'm glad she's busy. It keeps her from pursuing an alternative destiny in the Legal Department until I can figure out a way to promote her to a job in this department that's more in keeping with her many capabilities. Besides, you should see how she's organized the file room."

"Can't wait," Molly said, wishing she meant it. "I need a book I can read to Phoebe. Would a *Harry Potter* book be suitable?"

"Sure. My four oldest loved the last one. Who's Phoebe, anyway?"

"A child I've learned to like a lot."

"*Harry Potter* will probably be perfect, but in case it isn't, I could advise you about other books. My in-home research team will be happy to assist."

"Put them on the case, and I'll call you next week."

"You mean I'll have to wait that long before I hear from you again?"

"'Fraid so, Frank."

"Molly, how's your grandfather doing?"

"He's terrorizing everyone at that clinic. I talked to him a few minutes ago."

"I hope he'll be able to travel to Fort Lauderdale soon."

"So do I." Emmett had sounded in good spirits but admitted that he felt weak. Molly wasn't sure how seriously to take him.

"All right, Molls. We're getting along without you here at the office, but we miss you. By the way, bring back some fresh tangelos, will you? The kids love them."

"You've got it. I miss all of you, too, but not the weather. It's in the seventies and sunny here in beautiful downtown Greensea Springs."

"Sounds like heaven. Bye, Molly."

"Goodbye, Frank. Give Elise and the kids my love."

"Will do."

Molly hung up and sat pensively watching the boats in the marina for a few minutes. Eric and Phoebe were on *Fiona*, and Eric was supervising Phoebe's studies. As soon as Phoebe was through for the day, they were leaving in the marina van, on loan from Micki the dockmaster because they'd promised to run errands for her at the mall. Phoebe had been delighted that her father was going to participate in her makeover.

Molly stood and decided to stroll down Water Street to the bookstore at the end of the block. Perhaps she could pick up a copy of the latest Harry Potter book there, in which case she would start reading it to Phoebe tonight.

Better to plan something to do in the evenings so she wouldn't have so much time on her hands with which to get herself into trouble if she didn't stay on guard.

"WHICH ONE DO YOU LIKE, Dad, the yellow one or the red one?" Phoebe held up the yellow dress, eyeing it dubiously.

"How about you, Molly?" Eric asked.

Molly tilted her head and studied the dresses. "I think the red one looks best with Phoebe's coloring," she said. "It brings out the pink in her cheeks."

"I'll go with the red, too," Eric said. They'd driven to a mall on the outskirts of town and were shopping in one of the big department stores, an outing he'd discovered that he was enjoying immensely.

"Red is my very favorite color. How about if I try on a couple more pairs of shorts and shirts?" Phoebe said.

"Go ahead, Peanut. We'll be waiting right here." He sat down on the bench outside the dressing room next to Molly, and she scooted over to make more room for him.

"Let me know if you need any help, Phoebe," Molly called over the partition for the dressing area.

"Okay."

"Thanks for taking this on today," Eric said. "Phoebe has mostly had to make do with hand-me-downs from my nieces and nephews, and I guess she's getting too grown up and too style conscious for that."

"It's fun," Molly said.

She leafed through a magazine that she'd brought along, and Eric wished she'd stop it and pay more attention to him. After their torrid kisses last night, he knew lots of things he'd like to discuss with her. For instance, the curve of her lower lip, which was so damn sexy. Or the tiny freckle at the edge of her left eye, which wasn't noticeable until you got really close.

"I found the latest *Harry Potter* book for Phoebe this morning," she said. "I'll start reading it to her tonight."

"I'll reimburse you," he said quickly. "I've been meaning to get her some more reading material for a long time."

"It's a gift," Molly said, returning her attention to the magazine. "Oh, and I ran into the guy who owns the vacuum cleaner shop. His name is Ralph Whister and he's head of the committee that is turning the Plumosa Hotel into an arts center. He told me about art classes that Phoebe might like to attend."

"Maybe they'd teach her to draw what other kids do," Eric said with a touch of irony. "Like kittens and bunny rabbits."

"Rabbits are *bor*-ing," Phoebe called over the partition. "They don't even make an interesting noise. I can't draw kittens at all."

Molly shot Eric a meaningful look, implying, he was sure, that they should keep their voices down. "I could go with her tomorrow morning to register her for the first class and inquire about open mike night at the Blossom Cabaret."

"Good for you," Eric told her. Molly would be a big hit with her soulful voice, sweeter than any he'd ever heard, and all that hair falling over her face as she strummed her harp.

"We've also been invited to a cookout tonight," Molly said. "Dee—that's Corduroy's mother—belongs to a supper club where they take turns eating at one another's houses twice a month. She asked us to come because it's at their house, and she thought Phoebe might enjoy playing with Lexie and Corduroy. Everyone brings their kids, and they eat early so they can put the children to bed at a reasonable hour. I told her I didn't know if we could be there."

Eric considered this. He'd belonged to such a group back in Angler's Spit, and he and Heather had thoroughly enjoyed it. Hanging out with young married couples now, though, might bring back painful memories, and he wasn't sure he was ready for that. Yet these wouldn't be the people from his past, and this was a different town. Maybe it would be all right after all.

Molly evidently realized that he needed convincing. "I thought it would be good for Phoebe. She lights up when she sees Corduroy. She gets to be around other kids so seldom."

That was what decided him—Phoebe's well-being. He didn't want his daughter to grow up a social misfit. She should have the company of other children, everyone said so. He'd detected an element of scolding in Molly's tone, too.

"All right, we'll go. Just so you'll know, I make an effort for her to be with other kids as often as she can. The way we've been living, moving from place to place, it's not that easy."

"I understand, Eric, but don't you understand how much she longs to settle down?"

"This lifestyle is only a passing thing. It'll be over soon enough."

"Not soon enough for Phoebe," Molly muttered.

Eric bit back an irritated retort, just as Phoebe came out of the dressing room.

"Everything fits," she announced. "Can I have all these shorts?"

"Sure, and we'll take the matching shirts, too," Eric said, still discomfited over Molly's reprimand. "Let's go pay for them now."

Molly said nothing more, only got involved in a spirited discussion with Phoebe about whether the child required a new pair of sneakers.

Yet Molly's criticism stung. He knew that he'd have to find a home for the two of them, himself and Phoebe, eventually, but no one realized better that he did that his homemaking skills were still kind of patchy, and he'd always found it heartbreaking to contemplate going to work and coming home to a house without Heather.

When they were finished in the store, the three of them walked to the parking lot together, Molly and Phoebe several feet ahead of him. His daughter was holding Molly's hand and talking enthusiastically about clothes. Molly responded in kind, and the two of them laughed about something.

Eric felt excluded. He would have liked to barge in on their girl talk, to insert himself into the conversation, but he hung back, worried that either one or both of them would resent it. Finally Phoebe glanced back over her shoulder.

"Hurry up, Dad," she said.

He walked a bit faster, and when Phoebe ran ahead to the van, Molly shot him a glance.

"I'm sorry if I overstepped my bounds back there," she said. "It's so obvious that Phoebe longs for a real home, that's all. I should mind my own business."

"Maybe not," he said. "It's not a bad idea for someone to bring me up short now and then."

Molly stared back at him in surprise, but she didn't reply.

"I want to sit in the back seat," Phoebe said. On the way to the mall, she'd sat in front next to him.

Eric installed Phoebe in back, where she started going through their purchases with little exclamations of delight, and Molly climbed into the front beside him.

"Hey," he said, aiming what he hoped was a jaunty grin in her direction before turning onto the road in front of the mall. "I'm just a plain old garden-variety single father, trying my best to get along on my own. I make mistakes now and then, okay?"

"You don't make many," she conceded. "You're a decent guy, Eric."

He would have preferred that she said he was a *sexy* guy, or a *brilliant* guy, or a *good-looking* guy. But he'd take "decent" from Goddess Molly Kate McBryde, grudgingly though she'd bestowed that word. "Decent" was pretty damn good, now that he thought of it. And a "decent" father was exactly what he was trying to be.

THE FARRELLS LIVED about four blocks from the park, in a small tidy pink house with a Spanish tile roof. The street was quiet and shady, lined with candy-colored homes similar in price and design to theirs. Dee welcomed the three of them at her door, baby Jada draped over her shoulder and drooling onto a folded cloth diaper. "Come in, Molly. Eric, I'm so glad to meet you. Phoebe is a special person to Corduroy and Lexie, even though they've only known each other for a few days."

The house had a bright airy floor plan, and all rooms opened to the pool area. Dee's husband, Craig, stocky and gregarious, met them at the door and immediately offered Eric a beer. The men wandered out to the backyard, where steaks and hamburgers were cooking on a grill. Molly had brought a bean salad, which she'd feverishly concocted from a recipe on one of the cans of beans she'd dug out from their storage place in the salon. Eric had smiled at her concentration as she measured out oil and vinegar, splashing some on the floor. After she'd combined the ingredients and put the salad in the refrigerator, she'd periodically hauled the plastic container up and out so she could stir it. It was her first stab at preparing anything for a potluck supper, she'd said.

He looked around for her now, but she was nowhere to be seen, so he tried to pay more attention to the conversation around him.

"I guess we'll have to buy bunk beds for the boys' room," said one of the guys, Linc, who had been introduced as a neighbor of Craig's. "With Steffie expecting another boy, I mean." He seemed pleased to be announcing that he had fathered another son; Eric understood that Linc already had one son and two daughters.

"Yeah," Craig said. "Lexie was eight when Jada was born. Dee was adamant that the two girls not share a room because of the difference in their ages. So we added a nursery in the garage for the baby, which meant that my truck has to stay outside." He shrugged. "It doesn't matter. Babies are more important than trucks." He laughed and took a long pull on his beer.

The conversation continued, and though Eric found himself smiling and nodding, he felt out of it. He hadn't been part of this scene for a long time, had forgotten how domestic issues took precedence over anything else when you had a real family. This gave him pause; he considered Phoebe and himself as a real family, though a small one. But were they? Or was he merely a "decent" father who did his best but could do better by his daughter if he tried, and she a little girl who felt out of the loop where other kids were concerned?

He searched the group of children for Phoebe. There she was, swinging on the gym set beside Lexie, who was pumping herself higher and higher. Behind them, Molly gave each one a push now and then.

"I'm Pegasus," Phoebe yelled. "I'm flying!" She was wearing one of her new pairs of shorts and a matching shirt, her hair confined by a yellow headband. Her cheeks were rosy, her eyes bright. She was a beautiful child, and he would think so even if he were not her father.

His gaze locked with Molly's. She was wearing a T-shirt that showed off her considerable assets, and if she wore a bra, it was a minimal one that didn't obscure her nipples. Mesmerized, he watched as her breasts shifted under her shirt, putting him in mind of how long and lonely the past few nights had been. He wanted her so much, wanted to make love to her.

"Here's another beer," Linc said, pressing a cold, damp can into his hand. "Say, I don't believe I've met your wife. What's her name?"

Eric looked at him blankly, uncomprehendingly. *Heather,* he wanted to say, but there was Molly in his field of vision, Molly whose allure caused her to be regarded with admiration by every man present, and that was who Linc meant.

"Oh," Eric said, embarrassed. "Molly's not my wife."

Linc seemed surprised. "Sorry, Eric. I thought—"

"We're delivering a boat to Fort Lauderdale. I met her only a few days ago."

"Oh, a boat babe," Linc said knowingly. "Lucky you."

Eric felt a rise of indignation. Boat babes were bimbos who hung out at marinas up and down the coast, waiting to hitch rides with guys who would, for a time, supply food, transportation, lodging and often sex.

"It's not like that," Eric said quickly, earning a skeptical frown. "I mean, Molly's crewing for me, but her grandfather owns the boat. She's a corporate accountant in the family business, McBryde Industries. They make plastic parts for industrial components."

"Even better," Linc said.

There was no convincing this guy; it was pointless to try. Eric shrugged. "Yeah," Eric said, as Molly took the two girls by their hands and led them into the house. "I guess it is." He didn't want Molly tossed into the boat babe category, but there seemed to be nothing he could say to change Linc's opinion.

Yet Linc had sown seeds of speculation in his own mind, because for the rest of the evening, he couldn't shake the idea of Molly as his wife.

The whole idea was ridiculous. Molly had made it abundantly clear that she didn't care for him in that way.

But for a second or two, he couldn't help wishing that she did.

DEE HANDED MOLLY a stack of plastic plates. "Please put these on the table," she said.

Molly checked the table as she set out the plates. "I think we need a few more forks."

"Here they are," said Dee's friend Selena, who was helping them put the food out.

"Your little girl gets along great with Corduroy and Lexie," Selena said conversationally as they arranged the dishes and platters for easy access. "She's adorable."

Phoebe was holding hands with Lexie as they ran shrieking from Corduroy and some of the other boys, who were pretending to be sharks chasing other fish.

"Oh, Phoebe's not my daughter," Molly said hastily. "She's Eric's."

"A second marriage, right?"

Molly shifted uncomfortably and positioned the mustard and relish close to the hamburger buns. "Actually, no. We're not married."

Selena was taken aback. "I'm sorry," she said. "I thought I overheard Phoebe referring to you as her mom when she was talking to the other kids."

"Oh…" Molly said, her voice trailing off. "Um, maybe she did."

Selena touched her arm. "Please don't get the idea that I disapprove of living together before you're married. I moved in with my Ben six months before we tied the knot." She started to go back into the kitchen.

Molly cleared her throat. "Eric and I aren't living together. I hardly know him."

Selena flushed. "Sorry again."

Molly quickly explained that she and Eric were taking *Fiona* to Fort Lauderdale.

"That's cool," Selena said.

"Phoebe and I are having a lot of fun together," Molly added. She almost said that she wished Phoebe were her daughter, which, right this very minute, was the surprising truth. She was bowled over by the unexpectedness of her emotions. "Anyone would be fortunate to have a daughter like Phoebe," she finished lamely, meaning every word.

"Yes," Selena said a bit too brightly before tripping back into the kitchen. Through the window, Molly saw her whisper something to Dee, and Dee seemed to brush it off. Dee shook her head and moved out of Molly's line of sight.

Molly, not wanting to return to the kitchen just yet, hesitated beside the table and watched one of the men lighting the tiki torches around the pool. Phoebe and her new friends were chasing one another in and out of the bushes, squealing and laughing in delight. An occasional riff of male laughter drifted back to the porch along with the scent of charcoal smoke, and inside, the smaller children were parked in front of the Farrells' TV.

This was Middle America, which to Molly had been as mythical and mysterious a place as one from her brother's Irish folklore. To her, accustomed as she was to entertaining and being entertained in restaurants or clubs, it seemed every bit as exotic. She had warmed to the casually offered friendship of Dee and her friends, had taken pleasure in the sweet smiles of the babies and become interested in the relationships of Phoebe and the other children. She had never been part of a young-married set, and if she had been asked if she missed that kind of social setting, she would have replied that you couldn't miss something you'd never had.

"Molly, would you prefer to put your bean salad in a bowl or leave it in the plastic container?" Dee was standing in the door to the kitchen, and she beckoned Molly to join her.

"The plastic container is okay unless it's not elegant enough for our table," Molly told her.

Dee chuckled. "We're not exactly what I'd call elegant," she scoffed. "We're just ordinary."

Molly followed her back into the kitchen, but she didn't agree. There was nothing ordinary about these people. They might be what was sometimes referred to as the salt of the earth, and the rapport that they had for one another and the interest they had in their children were special. It was extraordinary, and Molly was glad to be, even so briefly, a part of it.

LATER THAT NIGHT, Eric spent time to making sure *Fiona*'s lines were secure before he went to bed. They had stayed at the Farrells' house until eight o'clock, then the guests had begun to disperse.

Phoebe was ecstatic about being asked to spend the night with Lexie some weekend. When she'd relayed the invitation, Eric hadn't had the heart to tell her that they might not be in Greensea Springs long enough for that to happen.

After he'd finished his chores on deck, he descended the ladder. All was dark in the salon except for the wedge of light cast on the teak floor through the partly closed door of Phoebe's stateroom. He heard Molly's voice rising and falling in a pleasant ripple of sound, and Phoebe, sounding sleepy, interrupted once and subsided. Neither of them had noticed that he was there.

Molly was reading to Phoebe from the new *Harry Potter* book, the bunk light casting a mellow glow across his attentive daughter's face. The two of them were curled up on Phoebe's bed, which was too narrow to afford much space. Phoebe was under the blanket, her head resting trustingly on Molly's arm in a position where she could see the pages, and Molly's head was bent over Phoebe's dark one. Molly, reading, seemed totally caught up in the story, as was Phoebe.

Eric started to speak, then held back. Something told him not to interrupt this tableau even as he felt a stab of something that could pass for jealousy. Molly had clearly gained a foothold in his daughter's affections, and he was pleased about that. He considered her a wonderful influence. But he'd been working his tail off to provide for Phoebe, was accustomed to filling her every need, and here was someone who didn't have to do much of anything at all to make Phoebe hang on her every word, include her in every plan.

That he was jealous of Molly—if he was jealous, that is—shocked him. He had been thinking about how attracted he was to her, how much he wanted to make love to her, and he hadn't until now considered that her presence had upset the balance of his relationship with Phoebe.

He crept past the door, unwilling to draw attention to himself. In his cabin, he lay down on the V berth and rested his hand over his eyes. After a while, the rise and fall of Molly's voice stopped, and he heard her telling Phoebe good-night, sleep tight and don't let the bedbugs bite.

That was what his parents had always said to him and his brother at bedtime, but he had forgotten about it. He'd never said that to Phoebe, not even once. Why hadn't he thought of it?

"Dad?" Phoebe called. "Are you here?"

"Sure, I'll come tuck you in," he said, swinging his feet off the bed.

"That's okay. Molly already did."

"Good night, Eric," Molly said from the other end of the boat.

"Good night," he replied. He sat there for a moment, giving her time to disappear into her stateroom and close the door.

Then he got up and went to tuck Phoebe in anyway.

MESSAGE IN A BOTTLE

DEAR PERSON OUT THERE,

I SAW DAD KISS MOLLY!!! THEY DIDN'T KNOW I SAW! IT WAS THE NIGHT DAD TOLD US THE STORY ABOUT NUT HOLDING UP THE WORLD. THE NEXT DAY WE WENT SHOPPING AND I GOT NEW ~~CLOTHS~~ CLOTHES. THEN WE WENT TO A PARTY WITH OUR FRIENDS.

    I LIKE MY NEW MOM JUST FINE. HOW MANY SAND WISHES WILL IT TAKE FOR DAD TO FIND OUT THAT SHE'S THE ONE?

LUV FROM PHOEBE ANNE NORVALD

Chapter Seven

On Saturday morning, Molly regarded Eric over the rim of her coffee mug and didn't even try to keep the disappointment out of her voice. "I thought *I* was going to register Phoebe for her art class," she said.

"I want to," Eric said stubbornly, removing his feet from their prop on the ship's wheel. "She and I need to spend some time together." He drained his mug and stood up.

"Oh," Molly said. "I understand." She wasn't sure she did, though.

"You can come with us," Eric offered, but his heart didn't seem to be in it.

"I may go over there later," she said. "To check on open mike night."

"You should," Eric said with false heartiness.

For the life of her, Molly couldn't figure out what his problem was this morning.

"Phoebe!" Eric called. "Are you ready?"

Phoebe appeared at the top of the ladder. She was carrying a big sketch pad and a couple of pencils. "Let's go," she said.

"See you later," Molly said, as offhandedly as possible.

"Aren't you going with us?" Phoebe asked, clearly dismayed.

"Not this time."

"Come along, Peanut."

"I want Molly, too," Phoebe stated, planting her feet firmly on the deck.

"Sorry, Phoebe, I have things to do," Molly said, realizing her brusque tone only after the words were out.

Phoebe didn't say anything, only gaped at her in surprise.

"Let's not be late," Eric said, turning to wait for her before making the move from boat to dock.

Hugging her sketch pad to her chest, Phoebe, all big eyes and hurt feelings, followed wordlessly. Molly continued down the ladder to the salon. She didn't see how she could have contradicted Eric, and in the end he *had* invited her to go along. But the way Phoebe had looked at her when she said she wasn't going with them had made her feel guilty, and she didn't know why.

Thoroughly disgruntled by the whole upsetting scene, she went below and tried to practice her harp, but decided it was a waste of time when she was in this mood. Instead she left *Fiona*, planning that she'd do some window shopping along Water Street.

"Molly! How are you?"

Molly swiveled and saw Micki coming out of the marina office, carrying an armload of mail.

"Fine," she said.

Micki studied her face. "I don't think so," she said. "What's up?"

"Not much. Well, I take that back."

Micki tsk-tsked and drew her into the office. "How about a couple of doughnuts and some coffee? You can tell Mama Micki all about it."

The office was furnished in discount-store style, but it had a frill of cheery cotton fabric over windows framing the marina and waterway. Molly perched on a tall stool at the counter, and Micki poured the coffee.

"It's not easy living elbow-to-elbow on a boat," Micki soothed. "I can relate, since my husband and I lived on a houseboat with my in-laws when we were first married. Believe me, I couldn't wait until we got our own place."

"That's part of it, I guess. I'm not used to living with any-one else, much less a man and his daughter. Even though

Phoebe is a nice kid." Molly sipped at her coffee and gloomily wondered whether to choose a chocolate-frosted doughnut or a powdered one.

"Eric's a great guy, don't get me wrong, but something changed in him after Heather died," Micki said. She shook the extra sugar from her powdered doughnut back into the box.

"What was he like before?" Molly asked, with more interest than she thought prudent to show.

"Buttoned-down, cheerful, kind of into himself. Everyone liked him. He and Heather had a happy marriage as far as anyone knew."

"Did he and Phoebe have a special relationship right from the get-go?"

"He was crazy about her, that's for sure. You have to remember that Phoebe was a little kid, so I don't know how much attention he paid her. Eric probably worked such long hours that he wasn't around."

"Hmm," Molly said. She took a bite of a chocolate-frosted doughnut and decided it was exactly what she needed. She finished it off in short order.

"Eric and Phoebe headed down Water Street a while ago. Phoebe didn't seem too happy."

"She should be," Molly said. "She was on the way to starting an art class at the Plumosa Hotel."

Micki's eyes were kind. "Did something happen this morning, Molly? Is that why you're so down?"

Molly couldn't help it. She poured out the story of how she'd planned to take Phoebe to her art class and how Eric had insisted that he be the one.

"Oh, dear. It sounds as if Eric resents your spending so much time with Phoebe."

"He certainly encouraged it in the beginning," Molly said helplessly.

Micki tightened her lips and got up to remove an incoming fax out of the machine. "That was before Phoebe stopped paying attention to him. When he brought her in here yesterday, that child talked about 'Molly this, Molly that.'"

"I didn't realize that," Molly said in bewilderment.

"You ready for some advice? It's free of charge."

Molly managed a wry smile. "Sure, why not?"

"Give both of them a lot of space."

"That's what I've been doing," Molly said unhappily. "He's been keeping Phoebe close by when he works, and I've done my own thing all week."

"Whose idea was that?"

"I thought it was mine. I—I hoped to keep Eric at arm's length so that he wouldn't think that—well, you know."

Micki studied her face. "I guess there's a problem, huh?"

"Nothing I can't handle," Molly said with more certainty than she felt.

If Micki doubted her, she didn't say anything. "I've got a two-person kayak—let's go kayaking some day, or we could do a movie if you're up to a little girlfriend fun. My guess is that Eric will be upset once you've backed off."

"Why? If he wants to spend time alone with Phoebe, he won't care. He'll be glad I'm busy elsewhere."

"Don't bet on it. I've heard a lot of single fathers say that nothing is going to come between them and their kids, but any redblooded man eventually gets bored hanging out with seven-year-olds. If you ask me, Eric's half in love with you, and you've already captured Phoebe's heart completely."

Molly laughed at that. "I'm not eager for Eric to be in love with me."

"What are you, girl, crazy? Why not?"

Molly couldn't answer.

AFTER SHE LEFT THE MARINA, Molly did her window shopping and continued on to the Plumosa Hotel. Not because she intended to check up on Eric and Phoebe, she told herself, but because she wanted to find out more about open mike night.

The hotel's spacious lobby, still resplendent with antique wicker furniture and terra-cotta tile floors, had lately been converted into an operations command point where visitors could see a model of what the hotel would look like once restored to its former glory. Molly picked up a flyer about open mike night and lingered there, taking in the spacious grounds, which included Springs Park, where she and Dee had gone with the children to play on their first day here. When she learned that visitors were encouraged to walk along the breezeway that stretched from the hotel to the enclosed warm sulfur pool, she set out in that direction.

According to a brochure she found on a table outside the glass enclosure, the pool had been a popular attraction with winter visitors around the turn of the century. It was still maintained as though people swam there, and Molly went inside the enclosure to study the frescoes on the only solid wall. The pictures showed men and women dressed in bathing costumes of the early 1900s, the styles quaint, even amusing. The temperature of the spring, Molly read on a small sign near the door, held at a steady seventy-two degrees Fahrenheit all year long.

The sulfur odor—some might call it a stench, though Molly wasn't willing to go quite that far—permeated the pool enclosure. Runoff from the indoor pool coursed down a small waterfall through an opening in the wall and was carried away by an underground culvert to the park. There it collected in the wide pond where Molly had seen children sailing boats on that first day. Large sconces that had once held candles adorned the marble pillars.

On her way back to the hotel lobby she encountered a man sweeping the breezeway. "Excuse me," she asked, "but why isn't swimming allowed in the pool?"

"People today don't like to swim in sulfur water," he replied, leaning on his broom for a moment. "They most likely go to the municipal swimming pool over on the other side of town. The days of moonlight swims by candlelight are over except for a couple of times a year when the chamber of commerce holds a party."

"A pity," she said. "This pool is so picturesque."

The man laughed. "It is that. You'll want to check with the chamber of commerce, buy you a ticket for the next big do. Might be a couple of months."

"Thanks," Molly said, but she knew that *Fiona* would be long gone by then.

Out of curiosity, Molly detoured through the corridors of the hotel. A sign explained that they had been constructed so wide because hotel guests in the late 1800s and early 1900s had customarily arrived with huge steamer trunks, which were stored in the hallways. At the end of one such corridor, she interrupted workmen on their way out for a lunch break.

"Are you here about the puppet theater?" one of them asked.

"No, I'm not," Molly said, peering around them into a large room with what appeared to be a stage at one end.

"Sorry, we thought you were the lady over to measure for curtains. If you see her, tell her to go ahead. We'll be back in an hour."

"Would you mind if I have a look?"

"Nope, please do." One man stayed behind the others. He opened the double doors for a better view. "The stage is almost finished. We're building benches in a semicircle for kids to sit on, and we'll put a light panel up there." He gestured overhead. "This used to be a parlor, and now it will be put to use to entertain the children of the community."

"How wonderful," Molly murmured.

"We think so, too. We'll have several productions a year, hold classes in puppetry, teach kids to paint scenery for the shows and make puppet costumes. A PBS station has already contacted us to film a documentary about the process."

"That's pretty neat."

"This will be something for us to be proud of when we're finished. Make yourself at home. You might want to get involved." He afforded Molly a cordial nod and left.

Molly let the doors swing closed behind her as she made her way up the wide space that was going to be an aisle. The sunlight beaming through the tall window swam with dust

motes, and the framework for the stage smelled of newly sawn pine. A breeze from an open bay window ruffled a set of architect's plans spread out on a door mounted between two sawhorses. Shelves, presumably to hold puppets and stage props, lined the walls backstage, and a poster asking for donations to build the theater was stapled to a closet door.

She stood for a moment on the stage facing the audience area, smiling at the memories that rushed at her from the past. Emmett had loved puppets, had built a small puppet theater in the playhouse in his big backyard in Lake Forest, the upscale suburb outside Chicago where he'd lived when he was actively involved in the running of McBryde Industries. He'd bought them hand puppets, and her mother had helped her and her brother and sister construct furniture out of cylindrical potato chip cans with Barbie doll accessories for props. They'd made up their own stories and performed them for neighborhood children, who always sat enthralled while Molly, Patrick and Brianne put on their plays.

Molly credited the puppet theater with nurturing her brother's interest in Irish folklore, which he'd researched when he was eleven or twelve in preparation for a show about leprechauns. It had been one of their best, complete with a wailing banshee and a renegade leprechaun who hated the color green.

"Excuse me—oh, Molly, is that you?" A woman stepped into the room, carrying a retractable tape measure and a sheaf of folders. It was Selena, whom she'd met at Dee's cookout.

"It is, and I'll bet you're the one who is going to measure for curtains," Molly said, jumping down from the stage.

"That's why I'm here—and would you mind helping me? I need to get this done before I pick up my Amy from the art class upstairs. I volunteered to make the curtains, but don't ask me why. Sometimes I rue the day that I let anyone in Greensea Springs know that I can sew."

"I'll be glad to hold the tape measure," Molly told her.

"Great! How did you happen to be here?"

"Exploring. I stopped to see the indoor swimming pool and was fascinated by it. A custodian told me that it's only used for swimming a couple of times a year. I suppose that's why they haven't boarded up the glass enclosure."

"It's one reason, but if you're concerned about vandals, don't worry. We haven't much of a problem with them in Greensea Springs, and that's good because our budget doesn't allow for a watchman anymore. How'd you get from the pool to the puppet theater? Did the custodian tell you about us?"

Molly shook her head. "I took it upon myself to look around and was pleased to find this place. My brother and sister and I used to put on our own puppet shows when we were growing up. It was so much fun, and I'm glad that there's going to be a puppet theater in the new art center."

"It's been an uphill battle," Selena said, jotting numbers in her notebook. "Some people weren't convinced that puppets are art. Others thought the money would be better spent on something for adults."

Molly nodded toward the poster. "You've raised some money for the puppet theater, haven't you?"

"Not nearly enough." Selena stretched out the ruler again. "Construction costs were more than we thought they'd be. The cost of the lighting system went way over budget. We'd hoped to pay a puppet expert to come in and explain how to teach the children, but we won't be able to do that until our second season, if then."

"That's a shame," Molly said. "You'll still be able to put on some shows, right?"

"Yes, because we have plenty of volunteer help. There, that takes care of it. Thanks, Molly. Would you like to walk up to the art class with me? They should be getting out about now."

Molly shook her head. "I'm going back to the boat to practice my harp for open mike night."

"Oh, you're a harp player! Wonderful, because we've been inundated with poetry readers lately, and a harp's something new. Will you be there tonight?"

"Maybe," Molly said.

"Great! Good luck, and I hope I'll catch your performance." With that, Selena took off at a trot toward the stairs.

That was where Eric would be, Molly thought glumly. He'd pick up Phoebe, and they'd go somewhere fun without her. She wished she could get over this morning's rejection. After all, she'd gotten along fine before she ever met the Norvalds. Why did she feel so lonely? Did she want to be part of everything they did?

The answer was an emphatic no.

MOLLY WAS IN HER STATEROOM, playing her harp when Eric and Phoebe arrived back. She heard Phoebe arguing with her father as they walked down the dock, and she stopped playing as the child stomped across the deck.

"Don't walk away from me, young lady, when I'm talking to you," Eric said. He sounded angry.

The footsteps stopped, and Molly could imagine Phoebe turning on her heel and planting her hands on her hips as she faced off with her dad.

"All I was trying to say," Eric said in a reasoning tone, "is that I'm glad you drew a picture of something besides a vacuum cleaner at art class. You could be interested in a lot of other things."

. "Well, Dad, I'm real interested in a house, and that's why I drew a picture of the Farrells', but I don't think we're ever going to have our own as long as I live."

Molly sensed real distress in Phoebe's voice.

"Peanut, we will eventually."

"Everyone in the whole world has their own house and their own dog and their own vacuum cleaner. You're never going to get us a house. You might as well admit it."

Heavy footsteps thudded across the cockpit. Eric was probably sitting down on the long bench that ran the length of it. "Come over here, Peanut. Sit on your daddy's lap and we'll talk it over."

"All you do is talk. You never do anything, and I'm getting tired of it." Molly heard Phoebe scramble down the ladder, march across the salon and go into her room. She slammed the door, hard.

Molly didn't dare breathe. She halfway hoped that neither of them knew she was aboard, but they'd probably heard her playing her harp.

At any rate, she was out of the mood to practice. She set her harp carefully in its case and snapped it shut.

It occurred to her that this would be a good time to wash clothes, so she stuffed a few more things in the canvas bag hanging from a hook in the bathroom and opened her stateroom door. It squeaked. That scratched any hope she might have had for a quiet escape.

"Molly?" Eric stood at the top of the ladder. He looked tired, exhausted and discouraged.

She waited until he'd moved aside before she climbed the ladder. He eyed her laundry bag and then flung himself down on the bench.

"I'm on my way to the laundry room," she said unnecessarily.

"Could I convince you to stop and drink a beer with me?"

"No, Eric," she said.

He ran a hand through his hair, tousling it so that it looked particularly attractive.

"You heard," he said. It was a statement, not a question.

"Yes."

"You're on Phoebe's side."

"It doesn't matter whose side I'm on, Eric. I'm not involved."

"Aren't you?" His eyes were steady upon her face.

"What do you mean by that?"

"You've been talking up a house, you might as well admit it."

"I never said anything to Phoebe," Molly said furiously. When the expression of dismay flitted across his features, she regretted speaking so sharply.

"Sorry," he muttered. "I assumed the two of you had been dad-trashing."

"Eric, I would never run you down. Never." She was horrified that he'd even think so.

"I believe you," he said heavily. "I'm sorry. Now it seems that I've got two women angry with me instead of only one. Not a good thing."

"Eric—"

"Forget about the beer. Go on to wherever you're going."

"Could we please keep our voices low so that Phoebe doesn't hear?"

"She won't, because this discussion is over." His brows were drawn into a straight line, as was his mouth.

All of a sudden, Molly realized that she didn't want to let the opportunity pass to tell Eric how she felt about his insistence on living an uprooted life. He was already angry with her, so what did it matter what she liked to say now? As her grandfather always said, in for a penny, in for a pound. And she had accumulated a pound of irritation over the issue that Phoebe seemed to be so unhappy about.

"Your daughter let you know exactly how she feels about not having a real home. And what did you do, Eric? You put her off, evidently not for the first time. She's a delightful girl who wants a set of friends, the support of a community, her dog, Cookie. She wants her own house, probably so she can have those friends over to play and ride bikes and, yes, admire her very own vacuum cleaner. Okay, so that's a little odd, but it shows that she has an imagination. An imagination, Eric, that makes her able to experience all those wonderful things in her own mind. Maybe she magnifies them out of proportion. Maybe, if she had the life she so desperately wants to lead, it wouldn't live up to her expectations. But she deserves to find that out for herself. She deserves the best you can give her, Eric Norvald, and the life of a boat bum isn't it."

A stunned Eric gazed at her openmouthed throughout this diatribe, and when she stopped, she inhaled a deep breath. "I'm going out," she said. She hauled her laundry bag off the seat and climbed out of the cockpit. When she stepped from the edge of the deck onto the stairs leading down to the dock, she saw Eric still staring after her.

She set off down the dock at a fast clip, refusing to look

back. It might not have any effect on what Eric did, but she certainly felt a lot better for hauling off and giving him a piece of her mind.

BY THE TIME SHE RETURNED to *Fiona*, Eric and Phoebe were gone. They hadn't left a note saying when they'd be back, so she ate a solitary supper of canned soup and crackers, discovering that she didn't like eating alone. Solitary mealtimes certainly hadn't been a problem back in Chicago, but now she was accustomed to the spirited byplay between Phoebe and Eric as they all prepared dinner, and to discussion of Phoebe's schoolwork and other sundry items, followed by watching *Jeopardy!* She missed the easy companionship.

Later, in keeping with her resolution to establish a life of her own in Greensea Springs, she took her harp and walked to the Plumosa Hotel, where she was assigned a number. Before the show, she enjoyed talking with the other performers—a reader of poetry, a man who played spoons and an amateur opera singer.

As she sat in the wings waiting for the comedian preceding her in the entertainment lineup to finish telling a few lame jokes, she peeked through the curtain at the audience. Its ranks were swollen with tourists who had driven over from nearby St. Augustine, a historic city and one that ranked high on many tourists' lists of must-see Florida attractions. She spotted Selena and her husband in the center section, and she thought she recognized a couple who lived at the marina sitting in the front row. The room was so crowded that there were even a few people standing in back.

When her turn came, Molly walked briskly to the chair provided for her onstage and adjusted the mike. She was aware of an expectant hush when people saw her harp; it was the promise of something different, she knew from performing at local clubs when she attended college in Boston.

She'd worn her usual jeans and a V-necked T-shirt tucked in at the waist. A spotlight zeroed in on her, making it hard to see the audience. It was better that way, since if she couldn't

see them, she didn't feel self-conscious. As for stage fright, performing in Emmett's puppet shows when she was a kid had pretty much solved that problem.

She began to strum the harp and sing, an old Irish revolutionary song full of fiery passion about a cause, and she followed it with another one about heartbreak and remorse. That was all she had planned, but when the last chord had shimmered and faded away, the audience erupted into applause that seemed way out of proportion to her performance.

Or maybe it just seemed that way because of the acoustics of the room, which occupied the old solarium of the hotel. The people standing in the back shifted as she stood and took her bow, and someone in the front row yelled, "More! We want to hear more!"

"That's all for tonight," she said before she started to walk offstage, and that was when the spotlight switched off and she spied a lanky figure detach itself from the others in the back of the room and slink out the door.

Eric. No one else held his head at just that angle, no one else was that tall and slim. No one else had the ability to make her heart leap to her throat at the sight of him.

And why did her heart do that? Why, indeed? Because she was being stupid, was investing her relationship with him with more importance than it deserved. Which she shouldn't do, considering her last, ill-fated romance.

She rethought. It couldn't have been Eric standing in the back of the room. By this time of night, he would be with Phoebe back on *Fiona*, and besides, there was no way he would have followed her to the Plumosa Hotel after their last interaction, which she was beginning to regret. She shouldn't have told him off. She'd been way out of line.

Instead of staying to watch the other performers, she set out walking toward the marina. The streets were quiet and well lit, and the scent of some unidentifiable tropical flower wafted in the air. It was a good opportunity for reflection and thought, and who she thought about was Charles Stalnecky, alias Chuck the Cheese.

They'd met at a conference for accountants where she'd given a speech, the topic of which escaped her now. He'd sauntered up to her afterward, smiled engagingly and asked her out for a drink. He was so appealing in contrast to the others in that stodgy group that she hadn't said no, even though his charm alone should have set off warning bells in her head.

He'd courted her shamelessly for two months, when she'd finally capitulated. She'd been ready, too, of course, but he was a disappointing lover. However, she'd become so enmeshed by then that it seemed like more trouble than it was worth to break up with him, plus she enjoyed having a ready escort who was adept in social situations. They'd fallen into a regular routine, because Chuck was all about schedules. In fact, they never did anything spontaneous. She'd been bored almost from the beginning.

Still, he was considered a catch by the other single women she knew. He earned an income almost as high as hers, and his grandparents had left him a trust fund. He belonged to the right clubs. He gave Molly presents, sent a dozen roses to the office every month on the anniversary of their meeting, called faithfully every night. Except later she found out that some of those phone calls had been made from his assistant's apartment after she'd fallen asleep. The assistant, that is. Chuck kept himself awake after making love to her so that he could call Molly and tell her he loved her.

When she caught him at it, Chuck seemed sheepish and said apologetically that he didn't love the assistant, a little dumpling of a blonde whose name was Rhonda Wettingfeld. Rhonda, he claimed while making puppy-dog eyes at Molly, was a convenience. Nevertheless, after sneaking a peek at Chuck's PDA, Molly learned that Rhonda was a planned convenience, just like her. She'd allowed Chuck five minutes to clear his things out of her apartment, and afterward she'd tossed his forgotten favorite sweater into a Salvation Army barrel.

Goodbye, Chuck the Cheese. She'd never regretted kicking him out of her life. But she'd never found a replacement for him, either, because trusting anyone after such a disheartening experience was difficult.

And yet...and yet, Eric was different. Was he different enough to risk losing her heart? Or her mind, or anything at all?

The very fact that she was asking herself such questions about Eric Norvald was enough reason for her to cut and run back to Chicago as fast as she could. She had a good job there, and she worked with people who liked her as much as she liked them. She didn't like hassles, didn't need another guy who was going to turn into a problem.

But there was Phoebe. Phoebe, who missed her mother and her dog and longed for nothing so much as a sense of permanence in her life. She'd taken to Molly right away, and Molly, though she didn't like to admit it, was smitten with the child. She sympathized with her. She didn't want to make Phoebe's life any harder than it already was.

So sure, she could hightail it back to Chicago and resume her life where she had left off. She could continue to go out with a succession of uninteresting men and meet her girlfriends at Starbucks for coffee and visit Frank and his family on holidays. She could settle back into her comfortable, decorator-designed high-rise apartment overlooking Lake Michigan and never think about Eric and Phoebe Norvald again.

But she knew she wouldn't be able to shut Phoebe out of her mind. It was easier, she decided helplessly, to banish a man from her thoughts than an adorable child whose welfare mattered to her more than she had dreamed possible.

So she wouldn't go back to Chicago yet. McBryde Industries didn't need her nearly as much as Phoebe did. Molly would stay in Greensea Springs, and maybe she'd make some progress in convincing Eric to stop this nonsense of dragging his daughter all over the place in search of who knows what. Maybe the things she'd said this afternoon had impressed him in some small way, and maybe they hadn't. But if Molly left, she'd never find out if her input had helped.

When she got back to *Fiona*, all was quiet and dark. Phoebe was asleep in her bunk with the door open, and the door to Eric's stateroom was securely closed. He would never leave Phoebe alone on *Fiona* or anywhere else, Molly was certain of that. So it couldn't have been Eric who rushed out of the Blossom Cabaret right after Molly's performance. That had only been Molly's imagination working overtime.

She went back up on deck and stared for a long time at the reflections on the water. She wasn't sleepy at all. She was wide awake and aware of the ramifications of staying on *Fiona*. But she'd come to terms with the reality that she wasn't, at this point, capable of leaving.

Chapter Eight

"I'll be working on *Miss Take* in slip 22 today," Eric told Molly without preamble when she appeared on deck the next morning. "Phoebe can come with me."

Phoebe, though she looked rebellious, said nothing.

Molly cleared her throat. "If that's what you want, fine," she said evenly.

"It's not what *I* want," Phoebe said. "I need a new pad of paper for art class so I can get started on my assignment. The teacher told us the kind to buy. The store's on Water Street, and I was thinking I could go there this morning."

"It's Sunday, honey. The store won't be open."

"My teacher said it would be. He said it's a drugstore."

"Well, Harold Pauling is expecting me to show up on time to assess the problems on his boat. He's planning a fishing trip soon, and he's eager for *Miss Take* to be ready."

"Molly and I could go get the paper," Phoebe suggested.

Eric sighed and pushed his hat back on his head. "Molly? What say you?"

"Sure," Molly said, holding her breath. Eric might still be on his kick of wanting exclusive rights to Phoebe. On the other hand, maybe this week's extended togetherness was wearing thin. In the past few days, he and Phoebe had gone on a bird-watching expedition, to a children's story hour at the library and to buy groceries, all without her.

Eric hesitated, but he finally gave his grudging permission.

"All right. Far be it from me to stifle the work of a budding artist. Draw me a picture of yourself, will you, Peanut?"

"Oh, Dad, I'm not much good at drawing people."

"Then why am I paying for this art course, huh?" He grinned at his daughter.

"So I'll be a happy camper, right?"

"Yeah, right. We hope to have only happy campers around here." He sneaked a glance at Molly.

Molly only raised her brows. Truth be told, she didn't like being left out, but she and Micki had gone to a movie one night, and she'd gone for several long walks around town.

Eric, still waiting for Molly to speak, drained the coffee from his mug. When she didn't say anything, he seemed chastened and dug deep into his pocket, withdrawing a wad of bills. "Here, Molly. This is to pay for Phoebe's paper."

"I don't—"

He pressed it into her hand. "We're not a charity."

"I didn't mean that," she said.

"I pay our way, Molly. That's how I want it."

She accepted the money, and Eric swung up onto the deck. "See you around three, Phoebe." With one last unreadable glance back at Molly, he hurried down the dock.

"Did my dad give you a lot of money?" Phoebe asked with interest.

"Enough to pay for your paper and a bit extra."

"Will you keep the extra?"

"Of course not. I don't need it." Molly stuffed the bills into the pocket of her jeans.

"My dad says you have lots. He says you're an air mattress."

"He says I'm a *what?*"

"An air mattress. It means you're going to inherit a whole bunch of money."

Laughter bubbled up in Molly's throat, but she didn't want to hurt Phoebe's feelings, so she held it back.

"I believe he meant that I'm an *heiress.*" She never thought of herself that way; she'd always worked for a living. But she and her siblings would inherit Emmett's considerable fortune someday.

"That's the word. Are you rich, Molly?"

"No, Phoebe, but I have a very good job in my family's company. I hope it will be a long, long time before I inherit any money. Now, how about if we head below and get ready to go buy that paper?"

"Okay," Phoebe said obediently, hopping down off the bench.

Molly followed her, wondering how much Eric knew about her inheritance. It wasn't something she'd ever brought up, but maybe Emmett had let the information drop when he and Eric became friendly in North Carolina.

As THEY RETURNED from the drugstore after buying Phoebe's paper, they detoured past A Perfect Vacuum so that Phoebe could study the Robo-Kleen in the window.

"Well, Miss Phoebe, what can I do for you?" Ralph Whister, the jovial vacuum-cleaner shop owner, grinned at them from his shop's front stoop, where he was sweeping cobwebs away from the overhead light.

"I came to see the Robo-Kleen," Phoebe said, gazing up at him wide-eyed. "I want to draw it in art class."

"Oh, Phoebe," Molly said, "maybe you should draw something else. Remember what your dad said."

Phoebe pursed her lips. "I might draw trees and flowers and stuff to keep him from bugging me, but I'm still going to draw vacuum cleaners," she said stubbornly.

"Say, if that's what you like to do, how about drawing me some? I'll let you put them on my bulletin board," said Mr. Whister.

"Could I? You mean it?" Phoebe's eyes sparkled in delight.

"Of course. Join me inside, I want to show you something."

"Oh, we couldn't," Molly said. "It's Sunday."

"No problem. I went to an early church service today and thought I'd stop by here and handle the maintenance chores."

Once inside, he led them behind the counter and gestured at a bulletin board on the wall. "See, I tacked up photos of some of the prettiest vacuums, but I don't have any drawings."

"That's a crowded bulletin board," Phoebe said doubtfully. "I don't see much room for anything else."

"I'll get rid of a few things. Like this article about the vacuum cleaner competitions in Jacksonville next month." He unpinned the scrap of paper.

"Could I have that? I've never been to a vacuum cleaner competition," Phoebe said.

"I manage to get to this one every year. All kinds of vacuum cleaners enter, and people compete to see whose vacuum can pick up the most dirt."

"I wish I could go," Phoebe said wistfully, taking in the article and the pictures that went with it.

"Someday I'm going to enter my old Sweep-O-Lator. It's a 1920s vacuum that I'm restoring, and there aren't many of those left."

"You have a Sweep-O-Lator? No kidding."

"Yep, I sure do. I'll bring it to my shop and let you run it sometime."

"I'd like that!" Phoebe grinned ear to ear.

Molly sighed. Even though she knew better than to try to come between Phoebe and any vacuum cleaner, she was bored with this topic and ready to move on. She thought she'd caught a glimpse of Corduroy's white-blond head in the park down the street.

Phoebe accepted the article that Mr. Whister passed across the counter and stared at it for a moment before stuffing it into the pocket of her shorts. "A competition must be so much fun! My dad sometimes tells me not to talk about vacuum cleaners 'cause he gets tired of it. That's why I'm sure he'll never take me to a competition. Isn't Jacksonville near here? I think we passed it on the way to Greensea Springs."

"It's only an hour's drive by car. I'll have to talk to your dad about it." Mr. Whister winked at Molly.

"I wouldn't do that if I were you," Phoebe warned. "Dad

turns into Mr. Grumpy real fast when you bring up *anything* to do with vacuums."

Mr. Whister shot Molly a puzzled look, and when no further information was forthcoming, he let out a jolly ho-ho-ho. "Tell you what, Phoebe," he said. "I'll display your best picture in our special children's exhibit area at Art in the Park in a couple of weeks."

Phoebe brightened at this offer. "Cool! I love my art class. My dad enrolled me in it last Saturday."

"That's great."

"If I'm going to draw a picture of that robotic vacuum, I'd better study it."

"Be my guest," Mr. Whister said, and Phoebe moved on to the display area near the other wall.

"I'm the chairman of Art in the Park," he told Molly. "We always encourage children to participate. Say, Molly, I was at the Blossom Cabaret for open mike last night. You were wonderful."

"Thanks, but I hadn't performed in a long time," Molly said, waving away his praise. "I'm a little rusty—lack of practice."

"I wouldn't have guessed it, and we certainly hope you'll be back."

"Uh, well, maybe," she said, keeping an eye on Phoebe, who was studying the robotic vacuum from every angle.

"In fact, Selena told me that she saw you in the puppet theater. She's my daughter, you know."

"No, I didn't. I loved the puppet theater, though. It reminded me of the one that my grandfather built for my brother and sister and me when we were growing up near Chicago."

He appeared interested. "Hey, if you ever want to get involved with our arts center, please tell me."

Molly hastened to set him straight. "I'm only here for a while. We're waiting for an engine part for our boat to be shipped from Germany, and then we'll be on our way."

His face fell, but he grinned anyway. "That's too bad. Greensea Springs needs people like you. And Phoebe, of course."

Phoebe, hearing her name, bounded over. "I love it here, Mr. Whister. I wish we could stay forever and ever."

"So do I. You're a neat kid. I was something like you once upon a time," he said.

"Really? My dad says there's no other kid in the world like me."

Mr. Whister laughed. "He's right. There's never anyone with the same amount of talent or imagination or creativity as anyone else. I meant that I loved vacuum cleaners from the first time I ever saw one. I became an engineer, worked on the space program at Canaveral for NASA. Got tired of it, didn't fit anyone's cookie-cutter image of what an engineer should be. I quit and opened A Perfect Vacuum ten years ago. Joined the local arts community and became a pretty good watercolor artist. Believe me, I've never been happier."

"What a great story," Molly murmured. She'd always, in theory, been in favor of people doing what they really wanted. In her life, she had begun to realize, things hadn't worked out that way.

"Okay, Molly, I'm finished studying the Robo-Kleen. Bye, Mr. Whister. I'll bring you a vacuum cleaner picture as soon as I draw one."

"I can't wait." Mr. Whister walked them to the door. "Come back again soon. I get lonely sometimes now that I have to leave Brewster home."

"Brewster?" Phoebe repeated with an air of puzzlement.

"My golden retriever. He recently had an operation on his hip, but he'll be back as good as new before long. You'll have to meet him."

"I'd love that," Phoebe said.

Molly smiled her thanks for his hospitality, and they went out into the warm humid air. "Let's go to the park. I have an idea your friends are there," Molly said.

Phoebe raced ahead while Molly followed, walking slowly. Ralph Whister had given her reason to think about her life, and so far, she wasn't entirely pleased with the state of it.

WHEN THEY GOT BACK to *Fiona* after spending time at the park with the Farrells, Eric was coiling lines on deck, his head down. He glanced up as they came onboard, regarding them with an expression that was not a scowl but definitely not a welcome. Molly was still trying to figure it out as Phoebe ran up to him.

"Guess what, Dad! We saw Corduroy and Lexie at Springs Park, and we're invited to Thanksgiving with them and their whole family! And they want us to go on a picnic the day afterward! We're going to Bottlenose Island in Mr. Farrell's boat and we have to take something. Can we bake cookies? Huh? Can we?"

Eric glanced at Molly as if to ask if she'd given her approval for this outing, and she replied with a slight lift and fall of her shoulders that it wasn't her call. She wouldn't be a bit surprised if Eric cut her out of the excursion, considering his present mind-set.

"Well…we might be able to do that," Eric said cautiously. "Can't we just *buy* cookies, though?"

"They have to be homemade. You don't take bought cookies on a picnic," Phoebe said with great finality. "We can get the dough in a package at the grocery store. You only have to slice it and bake it. Let's go get it now, okay?"

Eric stepped into the cockpit. "All right, we'll go to the market. I could pick up one of their lemon-pepper roasted chickens for dinner, if that's agreeable to you," he said to Molly.

"Sounds wonderful," Molly said, still self-conscious around him.

Phoebe went below, and Eric leaned on the wheel, studying her. She started to follow Phoebe, but he said, "Just a minute. What's this about Thanksgiving?"

"It's on Thursday of this week. Dee's making the traditional turkey and trimmings, and she wants us to come." She didn't mean to emphasize the "us," but that's how it came out.

"I'd forgotten about the holiday. How could I let it slip my mind?" Eric didn't seem to be asking her, but she answered anyway.

"You have a lot to think about, what with the work you're doing on *Miss Take* and worrying about when that part's going to arrive from Germany, and—"

"Don't make excuses for me, Molly," he said, and she realized that he'd moved closer. "Thanksgiving should be a big deal for kids, and I hadn't made any plans. Maybe we'd better go to the Farrells'. Phoebe would like that."

"'We'? You mean I'm going, too?"

He stared at her as if she'd lost her mind. "Did you say they invited all of us?"

"I guess I thought that—oh, I don't know. That you and Phoebe would want to celebrate alone."

He drew a deep breath and cocked his head sideways, assessing her. "It wouldn't feel right without you there," he said slowly.

At first she thought it was a failed attempt at sarcasm, but she caught an unmistakable sincerity in his tone.

"I mean it, Molly. You've noticed that lately I've spent extra time alone with Phoebe, and that's only right and good, but—" He threw his hands out in a gesture of exasperation, and for some reason, Molly recalled what Micki had said—that men eventually got tired of togetherness with their young children.

She decided against taking him to task for excluding her the past several days. Instead, she only smiled. "I know," she said soothingly, which provoked surprise from him. "It's okay, Eric. Really." With that, she brushed his hand with her own and continued down the companionway ladder, leaving him staring at her with a perplexed expression on his face.

She'd have to tell Micki that she'd been on the button with her male psychology lesson. And she'd ask Dee if she could bring her bean salad as a contribution to Thanksgiving dinner. Girlfriends, she reminded herself, had to stick together.

THANKSGIVING DINNER WENT OFF without a hitch. The Farrells were hospitable hosts, Molly's salad was a hit, and Phoebe began teaching Lexie and Corduroy to play chess. At various times during the afternoon, Molly caught Eric eyeing her with the ghost of a smile, and when they came close together, the air seemed to scintillate between them. At such moments, she was luxuriously aware of him, of his strong, clean features and sheer male vitality. Facing him across the table, she grew fascinated with the neatly honed edge of his chin, so much so that when Dee asked her to pass the gravy, she didn't hear until she'd been asked twice.

Bemused, she avoided Eric after dinner, remaining in the kitchen entertaining Jada in her lap while Dee loaded the dishwasher, and later playing horseshoes with the kids outside as it grew dark.

Walking back to the marina after dinner, she and Eric and Phoebe passed houses with lots of cars parked in front because relatives were visiting. Molly thought about Emmett all by himself in Minneapolis and her brother and sister being out of the country. She felt a pang of guilt for having such a wonderful Thanksgiving, a day that should be spent with family. She'd never given a thought to her family being so far-flung, but after participating in the Farrells' Thanksgiving, she felt wistful that the McBrydes were no longer as close as they once had been.

Back on *Fiona*, she helped Phoebe prepare for bedtime. Eric hung back, watching but not interfering. In a way she was glad; she liked supervising Phoebe's bath and story.

"Tomorrow we go to Bottlenose Island," Phoebe said as she climbed into her bunk. "I can hardly wait."

After Eric kissed his daughter good-night, he dug a gallon of ice cream out of the freezer, and before he could ask her if she wanted some, Molly made the excuse that she was tired and needed to get some sleep. She felt his eyes on her back as she went to her stateroom.

She heard Eric rattling around in the galley, making more noise than she thought was strictly necessary when dishing out ice cream. If he was trying to get her attention, he had succeeded. But then, he'd had her attention from day one.

Now she also knew she had his.

THE WESTERN SHORE of Bottlenose Island was a tangle of
mangroves on the Intracoastal Waterway, and the ocean side
was bordered by a spectacular pink-sand beach. Craig's jon
boat deposited them at an opening in the mangroves around
ten o'clock the next morning, and Molly and Eric helped the
children with their inner tubes, snorkels and towels as they
slogged through the shallows to the shore. Once there, they
began to climb the winding path toward the ocean side.

Dee and Jada had backed out at the last minute due to a
skin rash that Jada had developed overnight. Dee didn't believe it was serious, but she wanted to check with the pedia-
trician and was reluctant to take the baby out into the hot sun
out of concern that Jada might be developing a fever. Molly
thought it was unfortunate that she wouldn't be seeing her
friend, but watching Phoebe playing with Lexie and Corduroy more than made up for her disappointment.

Craig, getting into the spirit of the outing, pretended to be
Lizard Man, chasing Lexie and Corduroy along the path, hiding in the sea-grape bushes and jumping out to bellow at
them as they shrieked with glee. Eric swung Phoebe up for a
piggyback ride, and Molly gamely trudging along behind,
under a heap of beach paraphernalia that the kids had abandoned in favor of fun and games.

"I see the ocean!" Corduroy yelled, and then Phoebe
begged to be let down so that she could run with the others
and bellyflop onto inner tubes in the gentle waves lapping on
the shore.

"I'd better keep an eye on the children," Craig said, heading toward the water.

"We'll spread the blankets and set up the umbrella," Eric
called after him.

Far down the beach, a man threw sticks for his dog, who
chased them into the frothy waves. The air smelled of salt and
the scent of sun-dried seaweed. After pausing for a moment
to take it all in, Molly busied herself with planting the picnic
cooler in the shade beneath the umbrella, while Eric dumped
all the swimming gear on one of the large towels.

By the time they had finished organizing things, Molly was ready to cool off with a swim. She divested herself of her beach cover-up, tugging the bottom of her bikini down self-consciously.

A short distance from shore, the waves reared green and glassy before tumbling over themselves on the sand. Once in the water, Molly walked out as far as she could, then dived in and swam for a long way underwater before breaking the surface to catch a breath of air. She floated on the gentle swells and observed the action closer to shore. Craig had linked the three children and was playing tugboat as he towed them along. Phoebe's hair was drenched, and she giggled with glee every time Craig whipped them around.

Eric was swimming toward her with swift sure strokes. "Look," he said, stopping to tread water and pointing out to sea. "A flying fish."

Molly had seen them before, of course, these small fish of warmer climes that glide above the waves, often to escape predators. This one managed to ride an air current for sixty feet or more before slipping beneath the water's surface again. "There's another," she said, and they watched until it, too, disappeared.

"This is the life," Eric said with conviction. "This is living."

Molly considered this and decided that he had a point. Lolling in the ocean was a whole lot better than navigating slushy Chicago streets or trying to protect herself against frostbite as she walked to work.

"Race you to the point!" Eric said suddenly, and he began to swim to a rocky outcrop where the island jutted into the sea.

Molly had no intention of letting him best her at anything, so she struck out in his wake, sure that she could catch him.

She was swamped in his backwash for a minute or two before she pulled clear. Then they were neck and neck, and Molly was tiring rapidly as her feet found the rocks that lay on the ocean floor. Gasping, she propelled herself forward, threw herself on the warm sand and realized that the race had ended in a tie.

"Hey," he said, "you're pretty fast. I didn't know you were such a strong swimmer."

"I swam freestyle and backstroke in college competition," she said, rolling over on her back on a bed of tiny shells. They ranged in shading from pink to mauve, the colors soft against the background of pale sand. She squinted up at the puffy white clouds sailing across a luminous blue sky, then closed her eyes against the brilliance.

She didn't know how much time had passed, and maybe she even dozed for a few minutes, but then she became aware of Eric's shadow falling across her face.

She sat up abruptly. "I almost fell asleep," she said. "We'd better get back."

"Craig and the kids are still playing in the water," he said, but he stood when she did.

Keeping her eyes on the little group in the water, she began to walk briskly up the beach, skirting mounds of dead seaweed and driftwood at the high-tide line. Eric strode silently beside her, focusing straight ahead. She was surprised when he spoke.

"About the time when you lit into me about not settling anywhere," he said. "Remember, last Saturday after Phoebe and I came back from her art class...?"

That wasn't a conversation she was likely to forget. She frowned slightly, on the verge of asking why he'd raised a subject that was better forgotten.

"I'm sorry I accused you of fomenting Phoebe's rebellion," he said. "It wasn't right. I guess that in my mind, the only thing that had changed in our lives lately was that you're on the scene, and it made you suspect. I mean, she's always been such a tractable child, easy to manage. Lately—well, you heard her that day."

"I wish I hadn't," Molly said, keeping her eyes focused forward.

"I was so concerned about the things she was saying that I couldn't think straight. I should have seen that Phoebe is getting older and wiser. She's seen for herself that her friends live differently than we do. It's only natural that she would want a life like Lexie and Corduroy's—the dancing lessons, the big yard to play in, a safe street where she could ride a bike. I shouldn't have been so quick to accuse."

"So, um, this is an apology?" Molly said.

"I hope you'll accept it as one," Eric added in a rush.

A glance at him told her that he was truly contrite. "Of course. As long as you understand that I never want to come between you and your daughter."

"I realize that. I'm sorry, Molly."

"*Goddess* Molly," she corrected.

He grinned. "Okay, Goddess Molly. Are we friends again?"

"We always were," she said as she waved to Phoebe, who, from her inner tube close to shore, had spied them walking up the beach.

He shot her an exuberant smile. "This makes me really happy," he said. "I've been agonizing over the whole thing ever since. That's part of the reason I pulled back, avoided you, didn't include you when Phoebe and I found interesting things to do. That's over now, Molly."

"All right, let's not talk about it."

He held his hand up, and after a moment's hesitation, she slapped him a high-five.

"Are you kids hungry?" Eric called, a question that provoked three emphatic yeses and one thumbs-up from Craig.

"We'll have lunch ready in a few minutes," Molly said, and the kids all shouted their enthusiasm.

Molly and Eric worked together to set out the turkey, pimiento cheese and peanut butter sandwiches, as well as potato chips, apple slices and cookies. Molly almost remarked about how well they pulled in tandem, but then thought better of it. She didn't want Eric to take a casual remark to mean something more, and so she kept her mouth shut.

But they did excel at anticipating each other's moves, at staying out of each other's way and filling in when the other didn't think of something that needed to be done. It was a skill that they had learned while jockeying around each other in *Fiona*'s small galley, and Molly hadn't understood until now that the ability translated to other tasks and other places.

When Eric beckoned the others to the picnic, she remained quiet, thinking about this new discovery and its ramifications. If she and Eric meshed so well in one way, could they also become good partners in other ways?

AFTER LUNCH, Molly slathered on a thick layer of coconut-scented sunscreen and settled herself on a big green towel under the umbrella. Near the water's edge, Eric and the others were sculpting a huge sand sculpture of a shark, complete with seashells for teeth. She had opted out of the exercise, reserving some time alone in which to call her grandfather, but no one had answered the phone in his room at the clinic.

Molly was sure that Emmett was undergoing more tests, but it rankled that no one kept her abreast of what was happening, least of all him. Emmett bristled every time she asked about his health, sometimes retreating into abrupt retorts sounding like "mmpfh." The last time they'd chatted, the only information she'd pried out of him was the news that her sister Brianne was due back any day from Australia.

As Molly watched, Eric left the group in the sand and strode toward her. Once in the shade of the umbrella, he stood looming over her for a moment, and the breeze flung drops of seawater on her skin, where they quivered and shimmered like so many jewels.

"I didn't mean to do that," he said apologetically before spreading his towel beside hers. He sat down and tipped a rainbow droplet from her forearm with his finger.

"It's okay. You cooled me off. Want some lemonade?"

He shook his head. "Not at this moment." He picked up the sunscreen.

Molly flipped over on her stomach and rested her head on her arms. "We'll be leaving soon, right?"

"Once the shark is finished."

"It seems a shame. Sculpting something so special and losing it to the next high tide."

"The thing is to enjoy it while you can. Like relationships."

She opened her eyes. "Want to explain that?"

"You spend a lot of time on them, then something comes along and washes away the whole edifice that you've built so carefully."

"You're speaking of you and Heather?"

He shook his head and glanced down at her. "Not entirely. I'm talking about the two of us, you and me."

Molly rolled her eyes and rested her head on her arms again. "Maybe you shouldn't go there."

"Shouldn't I, Molly?" he asked softly. She felt his hand, smooth and cool from the water, brush her shoulder as he slid his arm around her. She lifted her head and blinked, surprised that he had moved so close; another couple of inches and their lips would touch.

"Eric—"

"Don't talk," he said, and then his lips covered hers.

They were warm and salty and pliant, and her lips surrendered without a struggle, tasting the tang of the sea and the indefinable essence that was Eric. He prolonged the kiss when she would have twisted away, and then she no longer wanted to end it but to go on kissing him until the tide washed them away. Like the sand-sculpture shark, which was now finished, as evidenced by the three children whooping their way up the slope from the ocean.

"I guess that's that," Eric said under his breath when he finally released her, and they both inserted a proper space between them. Molly thought that Phoebe, who was first to reach them, gave them both an overly curious once-over, but then the others arrived and started talking.

"We're going to the other side of the island to hunt for horseshoe crabs," Corduroy said with an air of self-importance. "My dad said we could."

"Have you ever seen a horseshoe crab, Dad?" Phoebe asked. "Corduroy knows everything about them."

"Not everything," Corduroy protested. "But almost."

"My dad knows everything because he watches *Jeopardy!*" Phoebe declared, prompting Eric to deny it.

"I bet he doesn't know much about horseshoe crabs," Corduroy said. "Did you know that they've been around since prehistoric times? And they're not really crabs? And the biomedical industry uses them to detect toxins in intravenous medicine?"

"They're also smelly and ugly," Lexie insisted, whereupon Corduroy chased her, shrieking, up the beach.

"Okay, let's get going," Phoebe said, clearly excited at the prospect of finding out exactly what was so great about horseshoe crabs anyway.

Molly stood up and began to toss things into her beach bag. Craig deputized Lexie and Phoebe to police the area for trash, and Corduroy helped fold the beach umbrella. Soon they were traipsing toward the dune path leading to the other side of the island.

Phoebe and the other children sprinted ahead with Craig, who kept up steady warnings to watch out for Lizard Man. Molly waited for Eric, now lagging behind because he had lingered to make sure that no one left anything on the beach.

"I wish you'd relax about us," he told her as he drew abreast. "Let nature take its course."

"You make it sound so simple," she said. "As if there aren't other considerations." She aimed a meaningful glance toward Phoebe, who was directly ahead of them.

"It doesn't have to be difficult," he pointed out. "Not when the foundation of this relationship is based on caring, understanding and mutual respect."

So that he wouldn't be able to read her expression, she pulled ahead of him on the path. And because she didn't allow them to be cut off from the others for the rest of the outing, the topic was effectively squelched.

MESSAGE IN A BOTTLE

HI THERE,

I DON'T NO WHAT IS GOING ON. I SAW DAD AND MOLLY LYING REAL CLOSE TOGETHER ON THE BEACH. THEY LOOKED IMBARRASED. DOES THAT MEAN THEY ARE IN LUV?? I LIKE MY NEW FRIENDS. I GOT TO SEE A HORSHUE CRAB. IT LOOKS A LOT LIKE A ROBO-KLEEN ONLY IT HAS A LONG STRATE TAIL. IT IS PRETTY UGLY BUT I DID NOT SAY THAT TO CORDROY.
    I WANT TO STAY IN GREENSEE SPRINGS FOR-EVER. IF YOU CHANGE TWO LETTERS IN MOLLY'S NAME, IT SPELLS MOMMY. I HOPE SHE WANTS TO BE MINE.

LUV FROM PHOEBE ANNE NORVALD

Chapter Nine

The next morning, Eric was gone before Phoebe and Molly woke up. He left a note saying that he would be working on *Miss Take* and to not expect him back for lunch.

"It's Saturday. That means we can do something fun."

"Don't you have your art class?" Molly asked absently. She stirred sugar into the contents of her mug and sat down on the lounge in the salon beside Phoebe.

"No, because it's Thanksgiving weekend. I know—we could take the beach towel back to the Farrells." When the families had been separating their belongings at the boat launch after they came back from Bottlenose, Phoebe had somehow ended up with a towel belonging to Lexie.

"Hey, good idea," Molly told her, her spirits spiraling an upward turn at the idea of seeing Dee. "I'd like to find out how Jada is doing. I hope she's over the rash."

"Me, too. I like babies, don't you?"

"I guess so," Molly said slowly, not adding that she hadn't been acquainted with too many.

"I mean, Jada's so cute. I'd like a baby sister just like her. No, a baby brother."

"Mmm," Molly said, not wanting to encourage this line of thought. Still, she wondered what it would be like to have a baby. To nurture another human being inside her body, to give birth to it, to hold it in her arms and, most of all, to love it.

"If I have a baby brother, I want to name it Thoth," announced Phoebe. She produced one of her new headbands from under the seat of the lounge. "Will you help me with my hair, Molly?"

"Why would you want to call a baby brother Thoth?" Molly asked.

"Don't you remember? He was the big blue goddess Nut's scribe. I like the way the name sounds."

"It's suitable for a character in a myth, but people don't usually name their children Thoth." Molly tried not to laugh, but it wasn't easy to keep her expression neutral.

"People don't usually call their boys Corduroy, but it's still a nice name," Phoebe countered, standing still so Molly could begin brushing her hair.

"I guess you've got a point," Molly said, but the conversation made her think about what she'd name a baby if she had one. She'd always loved the names Nicholas for a boy and Emma Kate for a girl, the Emma in honor of her grandfather.

Of course, such a choice depended on the baby's surname. A child's name should have a pleasant flow to it and be composed of euphonious sounds. And if Molly's last name happened to be Norvald, either Nicholas or Emma would be lovely.

"WE'RE GOING OVER to the Farrells'," Molly called down into the cabin of *Miss Take*. "We'll see you when we get back."

Eric's head appeared in the opening above the ladder. Cobwebs stuck to his black T-shirt, and he carried a wrench. He reached up and pushed his baseball cap farther back on his head. "Are you sure that's a good idea? Jada was sick yesterday."

"I spoke to Dee on the phone a few minutes ago, and she said it was only diaper rash. Jada's fine."

"That's good." His glance was admiring as it skimmed her figure. "You got a bit of sunburn, didn't you."

"I should have worn more sunscreen." That he was examining her so carefully embarrassed Molly. She was wearing khaki shorts and a jade-green jersey top, plus sandals. She'd clapped a wide-brimmed hat on her head to ward off the sun and bundled her hair up into it.

"You look wonderful," he said warmly. "Your hair's too pretty to cover, though."

"Thanks." The compliment left her feeling awkward. "We'd better get going," she said. "I left Phoebe over by *Fiona*, making friends with a couple who just arrived. They have a dachshund."

"Wait, I'll walk up the dock with you. I have to use the phone in the office."

"You can use my cell," she said, unclipping it from her belt.

Eric accepted the phone from Molly. "I'd better go below and find Harold's number. I wrote it on a piece of paper." He started down the ladder.

While Molly waited, she perched on the deck rail. Out in the river, someone was trying to sailboard. He managed to pull himself upright but soon fell into the water. He was having fun, Molly thought. She'd like to try it sometime.

Suddenly she heard the distinctive three-tone ring of her cell phone. "Eric?" she called.

"Mind if I answer it?" He grinned up at her from below.

"No, of course not. Go ahead."

Knowing that most calls she received while she was on vacation weren't urgent and work-related was a relief. She settled against the railing again and observed with interest as the sailboarder resurrected himself from his dunking. Soon he was aloft again, and she could think of nothing more pleasant than sitting here on this yacht, keeping her eye on Phoebe as she petted the new dog at the marina and letting someone else take her calls.

ERIC, TRYING TO MAKE HIMSELF comfortable amid the clutter of various engine parts, fumbled with the unfamiliar phone until his fingers found the right button.

"Hello?"

A long pause, so long that he thought there was no one

there. "Molly?" said a deep voice. A cautious male voice, in fact, and it wasn't her grandfather.

"Eric here." He spoke briskly, trying to sound businesslike.

Another pause. "Oh. May I speak to Molly?" The voice had taken on a guarded tone and came across as less than friendly.

He pushed the mute button. "Molly, it's for you," he yelled up to her. He heard her talking with Phoebe, who had evidently just walked up. Molly interrupted their conversation to speak to him.

"Eric, ask who it is so I can return the call."

He unmuted the phone. "She said she'll phone you back."

"You can tell her Chuck called. She has my number," the man said succinctly.

Is that so? Eric thought with a degree of bewilderment. Molly had given him the impression that she was unattached, yet this Chuck person projected an unmistakable proprietary air.

"It was Chuck," he called to Molly after the man hung up. Absolute silence greeted this announcement.

"Chuck?" she repeated after a moment.

"Right. He didn't think it was necessary to leave his number, he said." He avoided infusing his tone with any meaning whatsoever, tried to remain nonchalant.

An audible sigh. "Okay. Say, Eric, keep the phone as long as you want it. I won't need it anyway."

"You're not going to return his call?" He couldn't help being curious.

"No, and Phoebe and I are eager to get going." Molly stood up, her tall figure blocking the bit of sunshine that made it down the companionway.

He peered up at her. "Okay, if you're sure you don't mind." Her lips were set in a tight line, and she looked annoyed.

"I'm sure. Phoebe, let's roll."

He heard the two of them giggling as they started up the dock and thought what a pleasure it was to hear them enjoying each other's company. He had never considered how Phoebe needed the gentle influence of a woman in her life after her mother died. She'd made no secret of the fact that she wanted a mother, but for a long time he'd thought that there wasn't anything he could do about that.

Now maybe there was.

But. Who was this man, Chuck? And what did he mean to Molly Kate McBryde? The only way to find out was to ask her, but he didn't have any real reason to do that.

Well, maybe he could find one. He hoisted his wrench and got back to work, trying to think of how to broach the subject. After turning the situation over in his mind, he realized that perhaps if he made her feel comfortable enough with him to trade confidences, she might tell him what he wanted to know.

Unfortunately, to foster the kind of atmosphere that was conducive to such revelations, he'd have to open up to her himself.

And that, he realized with a certain amount of amazement, he really wouldn't mind.

"DAD! DAD! GUESS WHAT I'm going to do!" Phoebe flung herself at him as soon as she stepped over the gunwales of *Fiona*, almost knocking the magazine out of his hands.

"Hold on, Peanut," he cautioned as he righted himself. "You almost knocked me overboard." He set the magazine, the latest issue of *Small Business Journal*, aside and took in the glorious spectacle of Molly's long legs as she climbed aboard. This was the kind of scenery he could appreciate, and in his opinion, it was even better than the sight of Bottlenose Island in the distance or the Atlantic Ocean beyond.

"I'm invited to spend the night with Lexie. We're going to camp out in the backyard. Can I go, Dad? Please?"

Eric looked at Molly. She was nodding slightly, and he recognized this as a signal that it would be okay.

"Sure," he told Phoebe. He and Craig had discussed this possibility on the way back from the beach yesterday.

"Goody! I'll have to figure out what to pack. See you later,

Dad. Oh, and they want me to come early enough for dinner. That's okay, isn't it?"

"Yes, if that's what you'd like."

"Oh, would I! Thanks, Dad." Phoebe went below, humming to herself.

Molly picked up the magazine and studied it for a moment. "Do you subscribe to this?" she asked curiously.

"No, I found this copy in the marina office, but I used to. That was back in the old days, when I thought the way to get off the corporate treadmill was to start my own business."

Molly sat down and studied his face.

"Why didn't you do it?"

"I had no heart for it after Heather died, because she was my number-one cheerleader. She thought I could do anything, and with her, I could. I left the corporate fast track, all right, but I fell back on something else that I knew well. Boats."

"How'd you pick up that knowledge?"

"Oh, I had my ways," he said with a twinkle.

"Seriously, Eric," she said.

"I was around boats when I was growing up. My dad was from the Midwest and was stationed in Norfolk, Virginia, when he was a career officer in the navy. He taught my brother and me to sail when we were little kids, and he made sure we were good swimmers so we wouldn't drown if we fell overboard. I picked up engine mechanics around the marina where we kept our boat. I always liked working with my hands, but I majored in business in college. It seemed like a wise choice at the time."

"You must have liked the field, since you bothered to get an M.B.A."

"My advanced degree got me a great job at Carolina Novelties, a paper-and-plastics packaging company near the coast. Unfortunately, I became disillusioned by the time I'd worked there for a few years and I didn't have confidence in upper management after they brought in a hatchet man from out of state to get rid of good, loyal workers who had devoted their lives to making the company grow. How could I aspire to that level of management when I no longer respected it?"

"Some people might say that you should have stayed and tried to change policy," Molly pointed out.

"I decided that would be impossible when dealing with managers who didn't give a damn about the company and were only concerned with racking up huge bonuses and stock options," he retorted. He immediately regretted his sharp tone, but Molly didn't blink.

"I understand," she said with great certainty. "I'd hate working for people like that."

He relaxed. For a moment he'd forgotten that she would have more than a rudimentary understanding of corporate politics. "Tell me about McBryde Industries," he said. He understood something about the company from his lengthy talks with Emmett, but he wanted to hear Molly's slant on things.

She leaned back and clasped her hands around her knees. "Grandpa started the company, as he probably told you. It was strictly a hands-on operation until a few years ago when he retired."

"Did the company change then?" At Carolina Novelties, morale had started on a steep and steady downward slide after old Mr. Thaxter, the grandson of the company's founder, died.

"Not much. Of course, my grandfather installed his relatives at every level of the company, and he made sure they all had a good grounding in business. My cousin David, a Harvard graduate, is president now. His sister Lynn has responsibility for the sales department. I'm in Accounting, Grandpa's youngest brother is in charge of research, my boss, Frank, is the son of one of Grandpa's neighbors in Lake Forest and so on."

"A real empire," Eric said.

"Yes, it is. When we were growing up, we all realized that there would be jobs waiting for us when we graduated from college. Not that we all availed ourselves of them." She laughed lightly. "My brother insisted on studying Irish folklore. My sister became a crackerjack photographer and presently teaches courses in the Australian Outback. I'm the only one of us who stepped up to the plate at McBryde Industries." Her smile faded. "I wonder if that was such a good idea," she added, looking more serious.

"Come on, Molly. You have a great job," he said.

She gazed off into the distance, duly chastened. "Yes," she said quietly. "I do. Only sometimes when I'm exhausted at night from attending too many meetings, or when I'm sitting in a stuffy airplane waiting to take off on another business trip, I think how fantastic it would have been to pursue music as a career."

This surprised him. "Is that what you planned to do?"

When she spoke, her tone carried a hint of wistfulness. "I wanted to please Grandpa. My brother had already turned down a position at McBryde, and my grandfather was so hurt. I thought I should make it up to him. So—" she shrugged "—I was a dutiful granddaughter. I put away my harp and I buckled down."

He was touched by her sense of obligation. "You seem so regretful," he said.

"Since I've been here in Greensea Springs, I've realized that everyone doesn't live at the frenetic pace that I do. The locals have time for recreational pursuits, enjoying nature, being with friends, putting family first. It's made me think that— Oh, but I shouldn't be talking about it." She stood abruptly.

He rose to his feet also, uncomfortable with the shadow that flitted across her features. Even so, he understood what she was feeling. Similar thoughts had set him upon his present career path—or lack of it—a few years back.

All of a sudden he wanted to take advantage of Phoebe's overnight absence to be alone with Molly. Impulsively, he said, "Molly, let's go to dinner tonight. It would be good for us to get off the boat."

She hesitated, as if she couldn't make up her mind. Then, to his immense relief, she looked him straight in the eye.

"I'd like that," she said. She frowned. "I've already signed up to participate in open mike night at the Blossom Cabaret again tonight. That means we should go to dinner early. Is that a problem?"

"Not at all."

"Six o' clock?"

"Six o'clock is good. That will give me a chance to walk Phoebe over to the Farrells' house and come back for you. We could eat at that restaurant in the big old two-story house on the corner of Vendue Lane, near the grocery store."

"I'll be ready," she said. "And now I'd better see if Phoebe needs any help." She smiled at him before she headed down the ladder.

WHEN SHE WAS PACKING for this jaunt, Molly had included one dress. A simple sundress, it was constructed of a gauzy material in shades from peach to coral to russet; the skirt was short but full and swirled around her thighs when she walked. She wore it with no bra, because the top fit snugly enough to provide ample support, and when the light was behind her, the outline of her legs was barely visible. It was one of her favorite dresses for warm weather, and it had a matching fringed shawl for cool evenings.

When she was ready, she stood in front of the narrow mirror in her stateroom and studied her reflection. She'd braided the two strands of hair on either side of her face and drawn them together in the back, where she'd clipped them with one of Phoebe's barrettes. Her earrings were simple, three pearls and a small diamond; they'd belonged to her mother. Her only other jewelry was a watch.

Eric, recently returned from taking Phoebe to the Farrells', was waiting on deck when she emerged from her stateroom, carrying her harp in its case. "Give that to me," he said, reaching down for it.

She did, and after he'd set it aside, he gave her a helping hand. She was grateful, since she was wearing flimsy sandals that made it hard for her feet to get a grip on the ladder.

"You look great," he said, and there was no mistaking his admiration.

"Thank you," she said, feeling suddenly formal. They stood staring at each other for several moments. Molly took in his neatly pressed chinos, the way his white shirt contrasted with his dark tan. He smiled tentatively, and she smiled back.

"It seems odd to go somewhere together without Phoebe," she said, mostly to fill the silence.

"Yes, Molly, but maybe we should do it more often," he replied.

Maybe we should, she thought, but she didn't say the words. Past experience had made her cautious about letting men think that she was more interested than she was.

THE PLUMOSA HOTEL WAS SHROUDED in shadows behind its curtains of Spanish moss. As she and Eric walked past on their way to the restaurant, she saw that he was studying the glassed-in pool enclosure.

"When I was exploring here last week, I peeked in and saw the pool," she said.

"No one swims there these days?"

"Only on special occasions."

Someone was moving about inside the enclosure, and an electric light went on for a moment. Eric gave a long, low whistle. "Are those pictures on the wall?"

"They're frescoes," Molly told him. "A plaque says that the woman who painted them lived at the hotel."

"Someday I'd like to see them," he said.

"They're amazing," she told him, warming to this subject. "They show tourists at the hotel doing the things that tourists did in those days—riding bicycles through the park, swimming in the pools, drinking the water from the spring."

Eric made a face. "The tourists of yore must have been hardy souls."

Molly laughed. "Phoebe says the sulfur smell seems friendly."

"Phoebe would," he replied, and they both laughed.

Molly took care to keep a reasonable distance between them as they walked, though, if she wasn't mistaken, Eric kept trying to close it. The restaurant was only a block from the hotel, and when they entered they were seated right away. Their table was one of several occupying a wide veranda on the second floor of the old house, the former home of a lumber baron who had made a fortune by logging the pine forests that had formerly grown nearby. From where they sat, they could look out over the town, the marina, and the chain of barrier islands beyond.

After they ordered, Eric slid back his chair. "Let's walk to the end of the veranda," he said.

Her arm brushed his as he stood aside for her to pass, and she quickly pulled away. She wondered if he was aware of the sexual undercurrents passing between them, if he was trying to ignore them as she was. It was harder than she'd expected it to be.

The side of the porch that afforded the best view was narrow, and Eric positioned himself in the middle. She had a choice of standing on his left or his right, but both places left her little room. She remained slightly behind him, but he appropriated her elbow and drew her close. She felt the warmth of his body radiating through her clothes, smelled the soapy scent of his skin. She tried to concentrate on his words and to resist the urge to lean against him, to rest her head, ever so briefly, on his broad shoulder.

"I would have liked to see this town in its heyday," Eric said. "It must have been something."

His tone was matter-of-fact, normal. She took that as a sign that he couldn't tell that her heart was hammering or her palms were damp.

"It's still an amazing place," Molly said.

"My daughter's crazy about Greensea Springs," Eric said.

"Anyone would fall in love with a town like this one," she said.

"Including you?"

"I'm charmed by it," she admitted. "Greensea Springs is different from any other place I've been."

Eric nodded in agreement. "It's unique," he said, and as

they walked back to the table, she noticed him regarding her thoughtfully.

Eric seemed in a mood to talk. "This would be a good town for raising children," he said. He leaned toward her, his expression earnest. "I know your feelings on the subject of Phoebe's longing for a real home," he said. "Maybe I should explain why I haven't paid much attention to her in that regard." He paused. "Until now."

His last two words caused Molly to look up sharply from the wine list.

His gaze held hers. "I've been thinking that I'm tired of running, Molly."

"From what?"

"My own demons. When Phoebe was a baby, I left most child-care issues to Heather. I had no idea if Cocoa Krispies was a cereal or a candy bar. I had no idea how to buy a four-year-old a pair of shoes. I was overwhelmed."

He paused, seemingly lost in his own reverie, then appeared to make a conscious effort to pull himself back into the present. "After Heather died, I enrolled Phoebe in day care. I did some serious soul-searching—and you know what I thought?"

Molly shook her head.

"That no day-care provider could take care of her as well as I could, never mind that I had a lot to learn. That going to work every day was less productive than staying home with my daughter, because I couldn't concentrate on my work when I was concerned that Phoebe might be catching colds from other kids or not getting enough one-on-one attention. I quit my job, and I don't mind telling you, people thought I was out of my mind to give it up."

"Sometimes," Molly said, "it's a good idea to take a chance. Not that I've always believed this," she hastened to add. "I've only figured it out recently."

"Maybe taking chances is something we're more prepared to do once we've reached a certain level of maturity. Or perhaps we can only afford to do so after we've figured out that life has done its worst to us and that anything else coming our way would have to be better than what's gone before."

"Both of those observations are true, I think," Molly said.

"Even I wondered what I would do with myself after I quit my job. I ended up selling the house and lived on that money for a while. Phoebe and I rented a small apartment near the docks in the tiny town of Angler's Spit, and every day we walked down to the docks to watch the boaters. Soon someone needed an engine repaired right away, and the mechanic who did those things was out of town. I repaired that boat engine with Phoebe playing beside me.

"I found more work, then my apartment lease ran out, and I moved up the coast to North Carolina. It was time to enroll Phoebe in kindergarten, and she loved it. While she was there, I tore engines apart, fixed them, put them back together. When she slept at night, I studied for my captain's license. Working with my hands put me in a totally different frame of mind, helped me stop wallowing in my grief."

"Didn't you miss putting on a tie every morning?"

"Not at all. Then Phoebe and I moved onto a boat, safeguarding it for a fellow who moved away. Phoebe learned to swim like a fish, so I wasn't worried about her being around water. I started home schooling her when I began ferrying boats for yachtsmen who didn't have time to move their own boats from one place to another. By then I didn't want a house because it was just the two of us, and going back to that lifestyle would remind me of what I didn't have. I couldn't afford a mortgage. Still, I've been saving my money. Soon I'll have enough for a down payment, and then Phoebe will get her house and a real vacuum cleaner, and Cookie will come back to live with us."

"That day can't happen too soon for Phoebe," Molly said with conviction.

"I know. The way we've been living hasn't been easy on her in some ways. In other ways, she's gained a lot. How many children get to spend so much time every day with a parent? How many can name all the constellations, or so many myths from around the world, or are allowed to finish their schoolwork in the morning and play all afternoon?"

"She's a lucky little girl. I think she realizes that." Molly concentrated on her salad, spreading dressing on the greens.

"So," he said, "I took chances. Maybe I made some bad decisions, but they made sense at the time."

"You don't need to justify anything to me, Eric."

"I want to," he said slowly.

For some reason she felt embarrassed, maybe because she'd been too critical in the past. Fortunately, the main course arrived, signaling a chance to move on to other topics. As they chatted during dinner, Molly learned to her surprise that the two of them were interested in some of the same things. Eric's favorite TV news channel was Fox News, and so was hers. He didn't like to talk politics, and neither did she. He had read many of the same books, had a good basic knowledge of folk music, had been part of a student exchange program in high school that sent him to live in Switzerland for a year. He never ate brussels sprouts, claimed they gave him hives. Whether they did or not, Molly couldn't tell. She suspected he said that so he wouldn't have to eat them. When she voiced her suspicion he only laughed and said she had beautiful green eyes.

By the time dessert arrived, they had circled around to more serious topics.

"I guess what I've learned from all the things that have happened to me," Eric said, "is that life's changes are the only thing that's predictable."

At first Molly started to laugh, but suddenly understood that he wasn't joking. "You are so right," she said, and as their eyes caught and held, she recognized the depths of which Eric Norvald was capable.

She responded in kind, her finger tracing a water ring on the tablecloth. "It's odd when bad things happen to us," she said. "People always tell us, 'Don't worry, it'll turn out all right.' The fact is that it doesn't. It simply turns out. It's up to us to make the best of it."

He smiled at her. As their waiter hurried by, he signaled for the check before resuming the conversation. "That's what my life is about these days, Molly, but I wouldn't have expected that philosophy from you."

"Why not?"

"You have the manner and look of someone for whom it always turns out right."

"Hey, don't you know me better than that? Haven't I told you enough about myself to let the air out of that theory?"

"Yep, maybe you have," he said. He tucked cash into the leatherette folder for the check and stood. "We'd better get going. I don't want you to be late for your performance."

Molly had to think for a moment to figure out what he meant. Then, halfway inclined to skip the Blossom Cabaret and spend the rest of the evening with Eric, she realized that she must have been totally engaged in their discussion to have forgotten something she'd been anticipating with pleasure all week long.

He carried her harp and she remained thoughtful all the way to the Plumosa Hotel. Barriers had fallen this evening, and the thing was, she felt happy about it. Happy and scared and curious all at the same time, because she was ambivalent about where all this was going.

A couple of weeks ago, she wasn't at all interested in Eric Norvald. But as he had said, life's changes were the only thing that was predictable. And she had an idea that she was in for a big change.

Chapter Ten

Eric couldn't take his eyes off Molly as she walked sedately to the stool in the middle of the stage at the Blossom Cabaret. The spotlight sparked golden glints in her hair, glimmered on her simple earrings, made her skin seem especially soft and touchable. He found himself clenching his hands, then felt embarrassed and glanced at the people sitting on either side of him to see if they'd noticed. They hadn't. They were captivated by the sight of Molly Kate McBryde, and they were totally in her thrall when she started to sing.

She was stunning; that was the only word that could adequately describe her. Even when she was only talking her face was more animated than most, but when she sang, she managed to communicate with her eyes all the emotion that the song was meant to convey. If he hadn't been mesmerized by her face, Eric would have found himself captivated by the way her fingers evoked such melodic sounds from that harp. Or he might have concentrated on the curve of her legs, accentuated by the filmy skirt she wore. Whatever, there was no way he could look away.

She offered a sweet ballad at first, a touching song of innocence. She managed to seem innocent herself while she sang it. She followed that one with a rousing, rollicking jig that fluted up and down the scale, and for a few moments she was a vixen, a wench, a slatternly Irish maid, each in turn. This was all dramatics, reinforced again when she broke into

the familiar song of sweet Molly Malone, who wheeled her
wheelbarrow through streets wide and narrow, selling cockles
and mussels, alive alive-o. At the end of the song, which in
Eric's experience was seldom sung in its entirety, Molly Malone was dead of a fever from which none could save her. By
the time she had finished, Eric was sure there wasn't a dry
eye in the place.

The applause was thunderous, and it seemed to go on for
a long time after she took her leave. Finally Molly, his Molly,
was pushed out of the wings and walked to the center of the
stage again. There were a few whistles from the back of the
room, and more clapping. She strummed her harp once, and
everything became quiet.

"I wasn't exactly prepared," she said. "I can repeat one of
the songs from last week if you like."

If the stomping and whistling was any indication, they did
like. She began to play the Irish rebel song, and soon people
began to sway in their seats and sing along with her. Eric was
surprised that so many knew the words, but before long he
was singing, too. He knew all too well that he couldn't carry
a tune. But he wanted to join in and be part of the mood that
Molly had created in this room.

When she finished, she shook her hair back off her face,
bowed, shot him a wry glance that seemed to say "I have no
idea why they like me so much" and disappeared offstage.

He stood and pushed past the other people sitting in his
row, then loped to the back and down a side aisle with a door
leading outside. When he burst into the cool, fresh air, he
made up his mind that they would take the long way home,
even before he spotted Molly stepping out the stage door. She
cradled her harp close to her body with both hands, looking
for all the world like a little girl.

He walked up to her and cupped his hands around her
face. "That was fantastic, Molly," he told her. "You had the
crowd in the palm of your hand."

She stared up at him, her eyes wide. "Who had any idea

they'd go for Irish folk music?" she said happily. Her tone held a note of perplexity, and it was all he could do not to kiss her.

"I did," he said succinctly, letting his hands drop away. He appropriated the harp case from her, and they started down the street. After a moment, he reached over and took her hand. She didn't pull away. Instead she moved closer to him, did a funny little skip so that she'd catch up with his long stride and grinned up at him.

"Thanks for your confidence," she said.

"Last time you played for them, they liked you," he pointed out.

"I thought that was a fluke. Anyway, how do you know they liked me?" She blinked up at him, and he cut his eyes away. He'd forgotten that he'd never mentioned he'd been in the audience the first night she'd performed.

"I, um, was in the audience that night," he said uncomfortably.

"I saw someone who resembled you sneaking out at the end," she said in a faintly accusatory tone.

"I wasn't sneaking," he said in his own defense. "I had to get back to the marina."

"I'm sure you wouldn't have left Phoebe alone," she said. "How'd you manage to get away in the first place?"

"Micki came over from her boat for an hour. Phoebe was already asleep, and Micki didn't mind watching her own favorite TV program on *Fiona* while I went out."

"Why didn't you ever mention that you'd been there?" Molly asked. "You should have said something."

"I wasn't sure you'd have been happy about it." He hadn't realized he was walking faster again and Molly performed that little hitch-step again to catch up. He slowed down accordingly.

"Maybe I wouldn't. On the other hand, I might have wanted a critique."

"Do you expect one now?"

"No. I feel like Sally Field after she won her Academy Award for best actress—'You like me. You really like me.'" She laughed.

"For your information, you were fantastic both times. Your voice, your considerable onstage presence, your choice of songs, the way you looked…"

She dropped his hand, her dismay evident. "They liked me for the way I looked? Not for my music?"

"Both." He caught her sending him a sidelong glance, assessing his sincerity.

By this time they were walking parallel to the wide glass enclosure housing the indoor pool at the hotel. A door was ajar, swinging gently in the breeze, hitting with a light *thunk!* before the wind caught it and slammed it back against the wall.

"Isn't there a night watchman?" he wondered aloud.

"Selena told me that because of budget limitations, they no longer have one. Greensea Springs is the kind of place where they don't worry about vandalism."

"In that case, we'd better make sure that door is closed," he told her.

They made their way along the flagstone path, sheltered by the twisted oaks on either side, and the long streamers of Spanish moss. When they reached the door, Eric halted. "Shhh," he said. "We don't want to disturb anyone."

"We'd better make sure nobody's in there," Molly whispered.

"I'll take a peek." He handed her the harp case and stepped inside the pool house. He could hear the water lapping at the tile sides of the pool and a steady rush of the waterfall into the culvert that channeled it away. Moonlight cast dappled shadows from the Spanish moss and tree branches outside, lending the place an exotic, otherworldly ambience.

"I don't see anyone," he said, his voice reverberating against the tile walls. "If you can get past the sulfur smell, it's a neat place to be."

Molly slipped in beside him. She stood close in the tiny vestibule, her harp crowding them. "They used to have moonlight swims here in the old days," she said, still whispering, though it wasn't necessary. "See the candleholders on the pillars? I can imagine how it must have been when there were big fat candles guttering down to the end, shining on the faces and bodies of the people."

"You know," he said, assessing her mood, "I bet that would be fun. To swim here at night, I mean."

She darted a glance at his face. "You're saying we should do that? Now?"

"When will there be a better time?" he said, smiling down at her bemused expression.

She plucked at the gauzy layers of her dress. "I'm not exactly prepared," she said wryly.

"We'll go back to *Fiona*, get swimsuits and towels." He pulled her out the door by the hand, the harp case hitting against their knees. He took it from her and kept going.

"Eric, wait!" she said, lagging behind, but she was laughing. "We're not supposed to go in there."

"Sometimes it's a good idea to take a chance, don't you think?" he asked impishly, mimicking what she'd said at dinner.

"This isn't what I meant," she said.

Her voice now had a breathless quality, which he found incredibly sexy. At the dock, they made it past the marina office and the attached laundry room without attracting the attention of the lone man who sat there reading a magazine as he waited for his clothes to dry.

"Maybe we should ask permission to swim there," Molly said on the way down the dock.

"Of whom?" he asked. They reached *Fiona*, and he slung Molly's harp case over the side of the boat. He boarded first, then gave her a hand up the stairs. "You put on your swimsuit, and I'll snag a few towels. Bring a wrap to wear back to the boat—you might be cold after swimming in that warm water."

"I—"

Whatever else she might have said, he didn't hear. He wasn't in a mood to accept no for an answer, and after years of responsible fatherhood, he was ready to cut loose and enjoy being alone with a beautiful woman.

THE STREETS WERE ALMOST AS DESERTED as before, but when they crept back into the pool enclosure at the hotel like the two miscreants that they were, Molly breathed a sigh of relief. No one had seen them, she was sure of it.

Eric moved ahead of her while she dropped their towels on a nearby wicker chaise. He was a shadow against the large darker expanse of the pool.

She walked across the floor, the cold tile making her shiver. Eric reached for her as she approached, his arm going around her waist to pull her close. She didn't mind the gesture, even welcomed it.

"There's a step right in front of you, then another one. I already tried it."

Steam billowed up from the water, a swirl of mist that bound them together in this big, echoing room. It shimmered in the moonlight, caught the moonbeams and spun them into pure silver. She held her breath, stunned by the ethereal beauty of this place.

She dunked one foot into the water, was grateful for its warmth, found the next step and the next. Soon she was standing up to her chest in warm water; it eddied around her like skeins of silk. Eric stood beside her, his features beginning to come together now that her eyes had adjusted to the dim silvery light. His hair was frosted with water droplets, his eyes luminous and dark-centered. She felt buoyant, light on her feet. She sank into the water up to her neck, her hair fanning out like sea grass around her shoulders.

Eric leaned back and began a slow backstroke, even and methodical but lyrical in its grace, toward the far end of the pool. His feet disappeared in a froth of white bubbles, the hair on his chest curled and matted, his tanned arms stretched out and back, out and back, in steady rhythm. She let the water buoy her up, floating on his wake.

"Come to this end," he said. "There's a platform here with seats in the water, like a hot tub."

She swam toward him, and when she came to where he was sitting, the sight of him engendered an urging that defied logic. He pulled Molly over the edge of the raised section, his grip firm. She felt for the seat at the back of her knees and sank onto it, wishing that the steam would clear her head, make her sensible. In fact, it did just the opposite—made her thinking grow increasingly fuzzy.

"Don't sit so far away," Eric said, and his face loomed closer in the hazy light. She felt his arm glide against hers, and despite the warmth of the water, a chill shivered up her backbone with an energy that made her want him to touch her again.

"I'm not sure we should be doing this," she murmured as his arm curved around her shoulders, drawing her snug against him. Their faces were faint reflections in the dark water, rippling away into the shadows. His cheek grazed hers, and his body sent little eddies of water shimmering around them. She closed her eyes, totally relaxed by the warmth.

Eric's hand moved upward to cup her face. His eyes searched hers, delved deep inside where she never let anyone go. She didn't look away. She was totally absorbed, caught up in his presence.

"Molly," he said, and she stopped trying to keep a distance between them and floated into his embrace. He was warm and wet beneath the water, his long limbs eager to gather her in. She gave in to it.

He kissed her, but this time it wasn't with the haste of their public kiss at the beach. Now he took his time, his lips sure and knowing, the mood intense. There was nothing shy about his kisses, and he was thorough and masterful. Molly offered her lips to him without hesitation, caught up in the excitement and anticipation of the moment.

He pressed her back against the seat, and she sighed as his hands cradled her breasts. His fingers slipped inside her bra, and she felt her nipples draw into hard points against his palms. She was becoming liquid inside, melting in the warmth of the pool and the heat from his body.

His fingers coaxed the most exquisite sensations, and his breathing was soft in her ear. He moaned, or was it her name

The Mommy Wish

on his lips? She didn't know, but it didn't matter. All she cared about was being in his arms and giving in to these moments of exquisite pleasure.

"Queen Molly Kate McBryde," he said gently and teasingly, a smile in his voice. "Who ever would have thought?"

"I'm a goddess," she reminded him unsteadily. "Remember?"

"I want more, sweet Molly."

She was silent, every cell of her body attuned to his.

"We'd better go back to the boat. I didn't bring any protection."

"Eric—"

"You can still say no. You don't have to do anything you don't want to."

She knew she wouldn't, couldn't, back out now. She slipped over the side of the platform, submerged for a moment in the pool and came up with her hair sleek and streaming. A fleeting thought occurred to her: inserting distance between them might bring her to her senses, would perhaps give her a chance to think. But now it was clear to her that making love with this man was what she truly wanted. In the short time that they'd known each other she had grown to like him, to respect him and understand him. Desiring him wasn't supposed to be part of the package, but now, as he caught her to him so that the length of their bodies pressed together underwater, she admitted that she had desired him more than she would have thought possible in the early days of their acquaintance.

He kissed her with a passion that left her weak. She gazed deep into his eyes, saw affection there, and respect. Without a word she ducked underwater and began to swim toward the other side of the pool, then burst up for air in the shallow area near the steps.

She climbed up and began to dry herself, Eric close behind her. Without speaking, they gathered their belongings and crept out of the glass enclosure. Eric pulled the door securely shut behind them.

The air seemed cold, invigorating. Eric, looking conspiratorial, grabbed her hand and began to run. This was different from her early-morning jogging on the path near Lake Michigan after work, and it took her a few moments to learn to keep stride with him. Her breathing picked up, her heart beat stronger, and she felt as if they were flying with the wind as their feet pounded the shell-rock path past the playground, past the shallow pond, past the silent sentinel oaks with their beards of trailing moss. Soon they were crossing the road in front of the marina.

Eric shot her a warning look and placed a cautionary finger to his lips as they passed the laundry room, where the single male occupant now had his nose buried in a newspaper. They tiptoed past, still holding hands, still not speaking, and Molly felt like giggling as they crouched to pass Micki's catamaran. The square eye of the TV was visible through the flimsy curtains, and Micki was watching it.

No other occupants of the marina were in evidence, no dog walkers, no strollers enjoying the night air or the moonlight. She and Eric reached *Fiona* without seeing anyone and, still hand in hand, climbed aboard.

The cockpit was dark, shrouded by the lowered side curtains whose panels blurred the surrounding boats and lights into a soft panoply of colors. She was still breathing hard when Eric circled his arms around her and drew her close so that she could hear their pounding hearts beating in the same rhythm. After a few moments, when a new kind of breathing took over, he made his way down the ladder and steadied it while she followed.

The boat rocked gently on the waves, and the one lamp that they had left lit in the salon swayed overhead. Eric extinguished it, leaving the red inside running lights as the only illumination.

"Your place or mine?" he asked, his voice rumbling in her ear.

"Mine," she murmured, dropping her towel. Her swimsuit only required a couple of tugs to release, and it fell away, leaving her shivering against him.

He swung her up into his arms, his gaze catching and holding hers. "Now that I've won the goddess, I shall bear her away in triumph," he said with mock boastfulness, making her laugh as he carried her to her stateroom.

After he set her carefully on the bed, he lay down beside her, elevated himself on one elbow and smiled down at her. His even features were dappled with pale iridescent light shining through the stained-glass window over the bed. In the distance, a muted foghorn sounded.

"Eric," she breathed, and he slid over her, his belly to hers. They needed only one preliminary to make sure they were safe, and then she was gasping, aware only of her own wetness, hot and welcoming, and the ease of their joining. She braced herself against him as he drove deeply inside, establishing a frenzied rhythm that she matched stroke for stroke. His face was a dark blur, his eyes two burning coals in the dim light.

She arched beneath him, buried her fingernails in his shoulders, gasped. She may have cried out, or maybe it was Eric, but the sound was lost as she muffled her face against his wide shoulder. The taste of his skin ignited her, its heat matched hers and then, it exploded into a thousand molten sunbeams behind her eyes. It was all-consuming, this fire. She collapsed beneath him, her heart pumping wildly, her head dizzy. As reality settled in upon her, she became conscious of Eric caressing her back, whispering sweet compliments, telling her how wonderful she was.

He was heavy upon her, but she welcomed the weight. When he would have moved away, she held him, wrapped her legs around his waist to bind him more tightly to her while she basked in the waning warmth of their lovemaking. Finally, when she didn't have the strength to hold him any longer, he settled back against the bedsheets, lazily licked the nipples of her swollen breasts, kissed them one by one.

She allowed her head to be cradled on his chest, touched his cheek with still-trembling fingers. He rested his face against her damp hair for a long time before he stirred.

When she shifted in his arms so that she could look up at him inquiringly, he was smiling at her.

"Oh, Goddess Molly, someday maybe you'll explain to me why we waited so long to do this," he said, his eyes lighting with humor, but they soon drifted closed, and so did hers.

Chapter Eleven

When Eric woke up, the first thing he smelled was sulfur. Molly's head was settled comfortably on his shoulder, and after another sniff, he realized that they both reeked of it. Remembering last night and their utter disregard at the time of how it smelled, he began to chuckle.

"Hmm?" Molly said sleepily, snuggling closer.

"We smell like rotten eggs," he said.

Her eyes flew open. "Excuse me?"

"From the sulfur at the pool." He kissed her on the forehead. "How about a shower?"

Molly squinted at the bedside clock. "What time do you need to pick up Phoebe?"

"I'll call in a while and find out." He curved a hand around her breast, noticed that the nipple puckered at his touch. "That was spectacular last night."

"It was, wasn't it?" Molly said dreamily.

"You were a wild woman," he said.

"I was?"

"Absolutely. Why, after we got back to the boat, you practically ripped my clothes off."

"You carried me to bed," she said. "That was so romantic."

He lowered his lips to her breast. "I'll show you romantic," he murmured, kissing the rosy tip. "I'll teach you about ripping clothes off."

"I'm not wearing any," Molly said.

"Oh. As if I hadn't noticed."

"You're lying. And what about that shower?" she asked.

"Later," he told her.

"Later," she agreed, sighing.

A LITTLE BEFORE NOON, they borrowed Micki's kayak and paddled down the Intracoastal past huge homes sheltered by live oaks and bordered by carefully manicured green lawns. A Jet Ski plied the water near Bottlenose Island, where someone was parasailing, the big red-and-blue chute lofting in the wind.

Molly paddled in the front of the kayak, Eric in the back. She glanced over her shoulder at him as they left the marina. "It's good of the Farrells to let Phoebe visit at their house all day," she said.

"She and the other kids are playing in their pool. Dee asked if she could stay and have hamburgers with them, so I said we'd pick her up after dinner. Look," he said, pointing at porpoises surfacing nearby.

They appeared to be a pod of adults with their young. Their streamlined gray bodies arched into the air as they blew feathery spumes of water, and they didn't seem to care that they were swimming so close to humans. In fact, Molly had the distinct impression that they were racing with the kayak and were amused to be winning. About forty feet from the front of their boat, one porpoise leaped all the way out of the water. It launched itself about eight feet into the air and performed a complete flip before splashing down only a few feet from their bow.

"Wow," Eric said. "That was spectacular."

After the porpoises went on their way, Molly and Eric continued paddling through the widest part of the river, lined with the docks of private homes. Seabirds circled lazily overhead, and an anhinga swimming nearby slipped slowly underwater, to surface in the distance with a fish skewered on his beak. He tossed it into the air, swallowed it and proceeded to hop inelegantly onto a nearby piling, where he held his silvery wings akimbo to dry in the sunshine.

After consulting their borrowed chart, Molly and Eric had decided to follow the boat channel until they reached uninhabited mangrove shores immediately south of them. Micki had recommended the area and said that the trip would take several hours, so they'd packed lunch and brought plenty of water.

They entered the maze of tea-colored streams flowing through the mangroves, and the greenery soon became a dense canopy arching overhead. In some places, the stream was so narrow that they had to pull themselves along by mangrove roots. Once an eight-foot alligator heaved itself off a mud bank in front of them and submerged until only the tip of its nose and eyes were visible.

They stopped for lunch when they reached a wide canal edged by high sandy banks. It was eerily quiet here, the only sound the occasional *click-clack* of a scurrying fiddler crab. They pulled the kayak up amid a tangle of reeds, hiked a short distance inland to a clearing and began to unpack their cooler in the shade of a cluster of palmetto trees.

Today the sky was a bright blue, laced with clouds drifting toward the ocean. "I can't think of anything better than this," Molly said, gazing up at a passing airplane, which was so high in the sky that they couldn't hear its jet engines. She wondered briefly about the weather in Chicago, and in Minneapolis, too. She'd better call Emmett today; they hadn't spoken for a while.

"This place is idyllic, isn't it?" he said.

"And more. Calming, tranquil. In fact, I wish—" She caught herself up short as she realized what she had been about to say.

"You wish what, Molly?"

"I was going to say that I wish I could stay here for a time. Not go back to work. The chances of that happening, I'm afraid, are nil."

"What's stopping you? Wouldn't there be a place for you at McBryde Industries when you were ready?"

She sighed. "I suppose so, but I wouldn't like leaving Frank, my boss, in the lurch for any length of time. Then there's Grandpa Emmett. He expects a lot of me."

"Oh, Molly, you must believe that you're supposed to make up the shortfall in commitment to the family business."

"Shortfall?" She looked at him, puzzled, as he handed her a sandwich.

"Because your brother and sister didn't want any part of what Emmett built. You're worried about disappointing him, so you're determined to stick with your job, no matter how much you'd rather be doing something else."

Molly settled back against a palmetto log, twisted the cap off her water bottle, aimed a long stream of water down her throat and swallowed it. Eric's words cut too close to be comfortable. "Is loyalty a bad thing?" she asked. The question was supposed to be rhetorical.

"In some cases, maybe so. In our culture, we're taught to be loyal to our country, our team, our family, our jobs. Perhaps there are times when we should rethink what our allegiances are accomplishing for us."

"You sound like the voice of experience."

He shifted slightly against the log. "I don't mind telling you that I'm glad I didn't buy into the company line at Carolina Novelties. I'm happier out here on my own, even though I don't make as much money. Hey, sometimes I'm barely solvent." He laughed ruefully.

"That bothers you, doesn't it?"

"Only because I can't give Phoebe what she wants. On the other hand, waiting might make her appreciate a real home more when she gets one."

"Maybe. Believe it or not, Eric, I've quit and run a few times in my life," she told him. "It's not always an easy decision."

"Are you talking about your career or your personal life?" he asked curiously.

She didn't want to reveal too much. "Personal," she said, keeping her answer short in the hope that he wouldn't want her to elaborate.

His answer was to lift his eyebrows.

She only looked at him, but she couldn't help laughing. His expression was comical, and he was so clearly trying not to be nosy.

"I—well, I expect you'd like more information," she said.

"If you're willing to give it."

"Let's say that I was in a relationship recently, and it wasn't working out. I stayed, even though I was sure that I never should have gotten involved with the guy in the first place."

"How soon did you figure that?" he asked.

"Now you *are* prying," she told him, but she really didn't mind.

"Well, I'm interested," he said. "I'd like to know all the hows and whys so I'll understand better what's going on with us."

"That experience was totally different from ours. In hindsight, I'd have to say that Chuck and I gravitated toward each other because neither of us had anything better to do at the time."

"Chuck? Isn't he the man who called you on your cell phone when I answered?"

"That's the one. Do we have to talk about it?"

"No, but I've always wondered if you called him back."

"In a word, no. What Chuck and I had together—if we had anything—was over a long time ago. Besides, you remember how I said that neither of us had anything better to do? Well, Chuck found something—someone—else, and never bothered to mention it. I learned about it, and that's why I ended our relationship. Privately, I call him Chuck the Cheese. That pretty much sums up my feelings for him at present."

Eric laughed. "This sets my mind at ease. I only hope you never have to come up with a name for me."

"I won't," she said. "Besides, Phoebe already has one for you."

"Oh, right. I'm Mr. Grumpy."

Her mouth fell open. "You know about it?"

"She leaves those messages lying around sometimes before she puts them in bottles. Plus her printing is quite large and I can read it from across the room."

"Phoebe has no idea that you're onto her nickname for you. Please don't tell her that I slipped and mentioned it."

"Strictly speaking, you didn't." He made a zipping motion across his mouth. "My lips are sealed."

After they finished eating, they continued down a narrow creek that snaked through a large marshy area. They passed large mounds of shells, which Eric looked up on the map Micki had given him.

"Indian middens," he told Molly. "There was once a large native American population living around here, and they'd throw oyster shells in one place so that they piled up."

At one of the middens they got out to explore, tramping to the top of the mound and using it as a vantage point. A wide lake glimmered in the distance, and, beyond that, a major highway streamed with cars.

"We don't have time to paddle to the lake," Eric said regretfully.

"Maybe when I've come back," Molly replied, knowing as she spoke that a repeat visit here was unlikely.

When they headed back toward the marina, it was low tide, and the water level in some of the creeks was mere inches. Propelling the kayak became a heavy workout as the wind picked up on the Intracoastal, and they had to paddle hard to make progress. Considering her lack of strenuous exercise lately, Molly was sure that she'd be sore tomorrow.

After they returned the kayak to Micki and lay down to rest on the rough sun-warmed boards on a deserted corner of the dock, Eric insisted that she sit up so that he could massage her shoulders, and she did the same for him. Later, they lay down again and watched a flock of pelicans skimming the water in search of dinner. The slanting rays of the waning sun warmed Molly's face, and she felt completely and utterly relaxed.

"Happy?" Eric said, taking her hand.

"Yes," she said. She would have liked to preserve her recollections of this perfect day in a special place, a kind of memory box of the mind where she could retreat and experience all of it again when times were tough.

Thinking of tough times reminded her that she needed to phone Emmett before they went to pick up Phoebe. Reluctantly she came to a sitting position and released Eric's hand. "I'd better call my grandfather," she said.

He adjusted his hat to better shade his eyes against the sun and grinned up at her. "Tell him I said hello and that I finally understand why he was bragging about you. I thought he was exaggerating."

She smiled, liking the way his blue eyes reflected the color of the water. "And was he?"

He took her hand and raised it to his lips. "On the contrary, Goddess Molly. He didn't praise you nearly enough."

She was laughing as she headed for *Fiona* to get her cell phone. But she was also touched.

"GRANDPA?" MOLLY SAID.

The man who answered the phone didn't sound much like Emmett; his voice was gravelly.

"Depends on who this is," Emmett blustered. "Molly Kate, is that you?"

"And who else might it be?" Molly countered with a lilt in her voice. "One of your many girlfriends, maybe?"

"No, Molly, you're my one and only at the moment. Though one of the nurses here wants to take me to Fort Lauderdale when I'm through being poked and prodded."

"How's it going?" Molly asked, smiling to herself. Though he may have been feeding the nurses a steady stream of blarney since he arrived, she was sure that none of them would be accompanying Emmett to Florida. He'd fallen in love with her grandmother, Fiona, when she was nineteen years old and had adored her until the day she died. There had been no other woman for him since.

"These doctors ask impossible questions. 'When did you have measles? When did you have chicken pox?' How do I know about any of that? It was more than seventy years ago."

"Don't give them a rough time, Grandpa. They're only trying to help."

"Humph. If they really wanted to help, they'd piggyback a couple of shots of Tullamore Dew into my IV. Some good Irish whiskey would go a long way toward making this whole process less painful."

"You have an IV?" Molly asked, alarmed.

"Did I say that? I didn't mean to. Molly Kate, when will *Fiona* arrive in Fort Lauderdale?"

"I'm not sure, Grandpa. Maybe you should ask Eric. What's your doctor's name?" She reached for a pencil and paper in the chart room and sat down at the big table in the lounge.

"Which one? I have so many. Don't get any ideas about talking to them behind my back. They won't tell you any more than they tell me."

"Grandpa," she said, her patience wearing thin, "I want the name of your head doctor."

"Head doctor? You think I need a psychiatrist?" His tone was mock indignant.

"Very funny. What's his name?"

"It's Talwani. Or Shupta. Or something like that."

"What do you mean, 'something like that'? Can't you give me a straight answer?"

"Only if you tell me what's going on between you and Eric," her grandfather said slyly.

Molly's mouth dropped open, and she quickly shut it again. "How do you know anything is going on? If it is, I mean."

This brought forth a hearty cackle. "Like you said, I talk to Eric once in a while," he retorted. "He keeps me posted with bulletins about *Fiona*."

Eric couldn't have told Emmett anything personal. There was nothing to tell. Until last night, of course, but she was sure that Eric hadn't spoken to Emmett since then.

"I can figure things out for myself," Emmett said, then began to cough.

"Grandpa? Are you all right?"

"Sure, I am that. Say, Molly Kate, what do you hear from your brother and sister?"

"Patrick intends to stay in County Sligo until he's finished researching leprechauns, and Brianne is on her way back to the U.S. They're concerned about you, Grandpa. We all are."

Emmett ignored this. "Leprechauns! That boy needs to hurry home from Ireland and get down to earth. As for your sister, don't get me started. I told her she ought to practice photographing gears and switches. How she can find kangaroos and koalas more fascinating than plastic parts for industrial components is beyond me. Patrick and Brianne should be working at McBryde Industries. Like you, Molly Kate."

"I'm not sure Patrick and Brianne don't have the right idea," she said.

"Bite your tongue! For shame," and he began to cough again.

"Grandpa, maybe you'd better call a nurse," Molly said uneasily when the coughing stopped.

"And here comes a cute little colleen to check on me right this minute, wouldn't you guess."

Molly heard voices, and Emmett quickly covered the phone.

"She says I've got to hang up. Says there are things she wants to do to me. They wouldn't be anything indecent, now would they, darlin'?"

"Maybe you should let me talk to her," Molly said firmly.

"Goodbye, Molly dear. You're in good hands if you're with Eric. No, I mean *Fiona*'s in good hands. Oh, I don't know what I mean," he said, sounding vague and distracted.

"I'll call your doctor tomorrow," Molly said, but she didn't think Emmett heard her before the connection was broken.

WHEN ERIC AND MOLLY ARRIVED at the Farrells' house, Phoebe ran up and hugged them both. She had a backpack slung over her shoulder.

"Oh, Dad, we've been having so much fun! Corduroy gave me his old backpack. Isn't it wonderful? That's a picture of a dinosaur on it. Lexie and I played Barbies—and can I have a Barbie? And a Ken? And Corduroy showed me this hut he made in the woods out of scrap boards and palmetto fronds. It's soooo cool! And guess what? Jada said 'Mama.' I heard her. She's never said it before, Lexie says. Can we invite Lexie and Corduroy to the boat? Can we? Huh?"

For an answer, Eric swung Phoebe up in his arms, and she was giggling when he set her down. Dee emerged from the house, Craig close behind her.

"Come on in," Dee said. "We ate supper early, and I'm taking advantage of Jada's early bedtime to accomplish some sewing."

"How about if you show Molly what you're doing?" Craig said. "I have a couple of questions to ask Eric about that boat motor in the garage."

After Eric followed Craig around the corner of the house, Dee led the way inside. She settled the children on the porch with foil packets of juice and brought out her sewing.

"These are costumes for the puppets at the puppet theater," Dee told Molly. "Selena said you'd stopped by, and I thought you might like to see them."

The little costumes were elaborate, complete with delicate tucks and lacings. Dee had fashioned riding habits and ball gowns, tuxedos and swimwear. As she spread them out on the kitchen counter, Molly exclaimed over them.

"These are wonderful!" she said, fingering the delicate lace on a baby's cap. "Where did you find the patterns?"

"I made them myself," Dee said with modesty. "As Selena told you, the puppet theater has budget problems. I convinced a drapery company to donate fabric, and I sew these in my spare time. Ralph Whister's brother is making the puppets, and by changing their costumes for each production, we won't need to have so many. If there's any way to keep the costs minimal, we will."

"Selena said the lighting system cost more than anyone expected," Molly said, recalling their conversation.

"Everything was more expensive than we ever thought, but

counting our pennies has caused us to be all the more creative."
She interrupted herself to instruct Corduroy to look in the
snack drawer for granola bars, then began to fold the costumes
into squares of tissue paper. Molly helped, and by the time they
had finished, Eric and Craig were stomping in from the garage.

"Eric says I should deep-six that engine and forget about
using it again," Craig said cheerfully.

"Good," Dee replied. "It's old anyway, and you're never
going to need it now that you've bought a new one."

This set off lively banter between husband and wife while
Craig poured everyone a glass of iced tea. They sat on the
porch around the pool to drink.

When the evening began to grow dark, Eric called to
Phoebe. "Let's go, Peanut. Time to head back to *Fiona*."

They said their goodbyes and began sauntering along the
wide streets toward the marina. Phoebe jabbered nonstop
with Eric, which Molly thought was all to the good. She was
suddenly self-conscious, sure that Phoebe would detect the
change in their relationship. Now that she and Phoebe's father were intimate, Molly was unsure how to act. Should she
let her hand reach for Eric's as they waited for the light to
change at the intersection of Water Street and Vendue Lane?
Should she avoid his eyes on the chance that Phoebe would
notice the warm light in his when he looked at her? She'd
never been in a situation like this before.

Yet Eric slid his arm casually across her shoulders as they
walked, seeming not to care if Phoebe noticed this affectionate gesture, and he took her elbow as they crossed the street
in front of the marina. Molly wished that they'd had the fore-
sight to discuss what their behavior should be in front of
Phoebe. She'd be sure to tackle that tonight after Phoebe had
gone to bed.

By the time they reached *Fiona*, Phoebe had convinced
Eric to buy the Blaine doll as well as the Barbie.

"Blaine is Barbie's new surfer boyfriend—she broke up
with Ken. Molly, can you sew?"

"Not much," Molly said as she helped Eric slap together

a quick meal of spaghetti and garlic bread. Her experience was limited to a sewing course she'd taken as a teenager.

"Lexie has the best-dressed Barbies in the world. Her mother sewed their clothes out of scraps."

"We have a small sewing machine on *Fiona*," Eric said. "Your grandfather keeps it around for mending sails."

Molly, who was eager to change the subject before she was wheedled into doing something she didn't really know how to do, said, "I talked with Grandpa today."

"How is he?" Eric stirred the spaghetti sauce, and Phoebe sat down to work on her latest drawing, the one of the Robo-Kleen. Eric kept an eye on its progress, clearly wishing that Phoebe were drawing something else.

"He seemed tired and cranky. And—" Molly stopped talking before adding that there was something else about her grandfather that worried her, his reticence about his condition and the name of his doctor. "He wanted to know when we're going to get *Fiona* to Fort Lauderdale."

Eric snorted. "So do I. The fuel injection pump is due any day now."

"I'm going to try to call my grandfather's doctor tomorrow. Grandpa seems to have trouble remembering the person's name, or else he was obfuscating."

"What does that mean?" Phoebe asked, looking up from her drawing.

"Trying to confuse me. Probably so that I won't find out whatever Grandpa doesn't want me to know."

"Obfuscating," Phoebe repeated. "That's a good word."

"Don't get any ideas about doing it," Eric warned sternly. "I'm confused enough as it is."

Phoebe smiled and bent over her drawing again.

"You sound worried about Emmett," Eric said in a low tone.

"I can't help it. He's a seventy-nine-year-old man with heart trouble. He's never been forthcoming with information about his health, either. Fortunately, my sister returns from her stint in Australia this week, and she'll be catching a flight from O'Hare to Minneapolis right away. I expect her to check in with my brother and me when she gets there."

"Let's hope you're worrying for nothing," Eric said comfortingly.

"We have other things to fret about," she said pointedly. It had not escaped her notice that Phoebe was covertly watching them, a small secret smile on her face when she thought no one was glancing her way.

"Oh. You mean—?" Eric spared a quick and almost imperceptible twitch of his head in Phoebe's direction.

"The same," Molly said.

"Little pitchers do have big ears," Eric said. "One might wish to be careful about one's choice of topics."

"I'll let you set the tone," Molly murmured. "This isn't easy for me."

"What are the two of you talking about?" Phoebe demanded. "Could you please speak up?"

"We're discussing who's going to put the garlic bread in the oven," Eric said.

"Yeah, right," Phoebe said, clearly not fooled.

"I'm in charge of the bread," Eric said, "and then I'm going to set the table. Phoebe, away with you and your drawings, my child. Do you want me to put a plate out for you?"

"Nope, I'm not hungry. I ate two hamburgers at the Farrells'," Phoebe said as she gathered her pencil, papers and crayons.

"Okay," Eric answered, but as soon as Phoebe's back was turned, he swooped the hair off Molly's neck and planted a light kiss at the nape.

"Eric!" she warned, her voice an outraged whisper.

He only afforded her a maddening grin. "Molly, me goddess," he said in a fake Irish brogue. When he reached for her again she had to make tracks for her own stateroom. With her neck still tingling where Eric had kissed her, she sank onto her bed, wondering how they were going to keep their relationship within bounds while living in such proximity with a child. Molly didn't mind a few stolen kisses. She didn't mind being caressed. But she most certainly would mind if Phoebe got her hopes up. All those sand wishes had made Molly all too aware of what Phoebe wanted from her.

LATER, WHEN PHOEBE was asleep in her narrow bunk in the middle of the boat, Eric led Molly to his stateroom. Here in the bow, they could hear every slap of every wave, and outside a freshening wind blew in from the north. There was no moon, and the chilly damp air curled down through the open hatch and around them so that Eric wasted no time in pulling Molly close.

"I don't think I'm handling our new situation very well," Molly confessed, resting her forehead against Eric's shoulder.

The two portholes admitted soft illumination from the lights of the boat in the next slip. The yellow glow played across Eric's features, and Molly lifted her head to admire for the umpteenth time that day the straightness of his nose, the fullness of his lips.

"Handling what?" Eric said. He reached under her shirt, unhooked her bra.

"Don't act like you don't know. *Phoebe*," she said as he eased her shirt over her head. "She suspects what's going on. I'm sure she does."

Eric tossed both garments to one side. "Realizes that we're having a great time? I certainly hope so."

The ends of his mouth curved into a smile as he shrugged out of his shirt. The hair on his chest glimmered in the half darkness, begged to be touched. She ran her hands up his taut torso, across his well-developed pectoral muscles.

"She may know that we've slept together," Molly said, swallowing hard. She couldn't believe how rapidly she became aroused from only touching him.

"How is that possible?" He kicked off his shoes and helped her shimmy out of her jeans.

"She sees things. She hears things," Molly said. Her nipples were tight nubs, and she guided his hands to them.

"She's sound asleep. Don't worry."

"Easy for you to say. Phoebe's likely to walk up to me tomorrow and ask, 'Are you and Dad having sexual intercourse?' What am I supposed to tell her, Eric?"

"She doesn't understand anything about sex. She's only seven years old. I guess you could tell her you're satisfying me like no other woman in a long time. Tell her—"

Molly removed his hands from her breasts. "Excuse me? 'Like no other woman in a *long time*'?"

Eric looked abashed. "There hasn't been anyone since Heather. Well, no one important. There were only quick couplings in the dark, and I don't even remember the women's names. And they happened a long time ago. I thought…" His voice trailed off, and his reflective tone caused Molly to touch her fingertips gently to his cheek. He twisted his head and kissed them. "I thought I could overcome my grief by having sex with people I didn't care about. I was wrong."

"Eric, you don't have to tell me this," Molly said as he pulled her down on the bed beside him. She lay back on rumpled sheets; he'd never bothered to make the bed that morning. Not that she cared, because there was something even more intimate about sheets where you'd made love before.

"I want you to know everything about me." His fingers found her breast and began to trace easy circles.

Eric's caresses made it difficult to concentrate on anything but his soothing ministrations. His hand moved lower, and she closed her eyes. To give in to the sensations, to reach for him and anticipate the sensuous pleasure of skin against skin, was so easy.

"We should talk about the Phoebe situation," she managed to say as he began kissing her open mouth, ran his hands up into her hair and down her back to press her closer. She reached down and touched him, wrapping her fingers around him.

"Later," he said. "First let's turn Mr. Grumpy into Mr. Happy."

She smiled, and he nuzzled her neck. "Hey, I'm the one who should be smiling," he said.

She continued her ministrations, and he rolled over so that

she was on top. By this time, she was ready for him and realized the pointlessness of further conversation. She guided him inside her, gasping as he found his mark. Then she gave herself over to him, wishing only to possess and be possessed. Her consciousness was limited to their lovemaking, to the utter passion of the experience.

Eric. He was everything in those moments, everything and more. What that "more" might entail was not at all clear, and she didn't care. She clung to him, cried out at her climax and held him fiercely close when he had his. Afterward, they lay pressed together in silent communion with their legs and feet tangled in the V of the berth, hardly able to tell where one ended and the other began.

Eric slept before she did. Finally, after lying awake for a long time, she disentangled herself from him and slipped out of his bed. She found her clothes and clutched them to her chest as she made her way naked through the quiet cabin, steadying herself against the to-and-fro motion of the boat. A peek into Phoebe's stateroom revealed a child who was sleeping soundly and looking particularly angelic.

Molly continued on to her own room and shut the door before falling into bed. As much as she would have liked to spend the whole night with Eric, she didn't want Phoebe to discover them together in the morning. Maybe, as Eric said, the kid didn't know anything about sex. But Molly certainly hoped she wouldn't find out from them.

Chapter Twelve

"Don't forget your picture," Molly cautioned Phoebe as they prepared to go to Art in the Park the following Sunday. Phoebe was wearing one of her new shorts outfits and had blown her hair dry herself. She looked adorable.

"Oh, I've already put it in my backpack. It's the Robo-Kleen I've worked on so hard. Dad, hurry! I want Mr. Whister to hang my drawing up on the kids' display so everyone will see it."

Eric emerged from the cabin into the cockpit and kissed Molly on the cheek while Phoebe's back was turned.

"Let's go," he said, and Phoebe began to clamber over the side of the boat. To Molly he said in a low tone, "She's displaying a vacuum cleaner picture? Why can't she take the one she drew in art class of the Farrells' house?"

"I don't know, Eric." Molly pulled a hat down over her curls and grabbed the sunscreen from its usual place near the ship's wheel.

"Hurry up, you two," Phoebe called up to them.

They joined her on the dock and started to walk past the nearby boats. On one, Mrs. Peeler was hanging clean laundry on a line strung between the two masts of her husband's small sloop. On another, a sleek white cat sat grooming his whiskers while his owner, Lainie Kallbeck, read the newspaper on a deck chair nearby. Phoebe waved to Lainie, and she waved back.

"Hi, Phoebe," she called.

"Hello, Mrs. Kallbeck. Come see my picture at Art in the Park."

"I will, honey." The woman spared a cordial nod for Molly and Eric before picking up another section of the paper.

"Who's that?" Eric asked.

"Phoebe and I met her in the laundry room the other day," Molly explained.

"She's on her way to Miami. She spends the winter there," Phoebe added.

"Well, Phoebe, you sure do get around," Eric teased.

"Oh, I've talked with most everyone at this marina. Mrs. Kallbeck's cat's name is Jody. He lives on the boat with her. The boat at the end of our dock, *Argonaut*, has a dachshund on it. He lives with Mr. and Mrs. Vrooman. And then—"

Eric chuckled. "Okay, Peanut, we get the picture." He paused and said to Molly, "She does this everywhere we go. The kid's never met a stranger."

Phoebe grinned. "I've met lots of strangers, Dad, but I turn them into friends." She ran ahead when she saw Micki standing at the open door of the marina office.

Micki greeted Phoebe enthusiastically, and Eric and Molly stopped to talk.

"Going somewhere?" Micki asked.

"To Art in the Park," Molly told her.

"I'm planning to walk over there after I close the office around noon," Micki said. "Eric, we've got a boat coming in and they say they need a quick fix on their engine. You available?"

"Sure. I'll check with you when I get back."

"Phoebe, we could keep your dad busy full-time repairing engines," Micki said with a wink. "He's good at it."

"I wish you would," Phoebe replied. "Then maybe we wouldn't have to leave Greensea Springs, ever."

Micki grinned. "I'd like to stay here, too, but when my husband returns from the Middle East, I'll be going to Norfolk. That's where he'll be stationed."

"Will he be back soon?" Eric asked.

"In a month or two. I've told the marina owners that I'll be out of here then."

"You'll be hard to replace," Molly said, remembering all the times she'd been in the office and seen Micki at work. The woman could field three phone calls, hand out quarters for the laundry machines and sort mail, all at the same time.

"I'm not sure I'll hire someone else. There's talk that they plan to sell the marina."

"Why? It's a going concern, and someone told me the new dock section was added only a year ago," Eric said.

Micki shrugged. "I suspect the owners are ready to retire and go fishing. Can't say that I blame them." She laughed and handed a key to the showers to a marina guest who had just ducked into the office.

"Dad, we need to go," Phoebe said, tugging at his arm.

"See you later," they told Micki.

After they crossed the street, Phoebe ran ahead of them, her dinosaur backpack bobbing behind her. "You know what she carries in that backpack? Her new Barbie and Blaine and all her vacuum cleaner drawings," Eric said.

"In other words, the things that are most important to her," Molly suggested.

Eric sighed. "Yeah. Except for you."

"I'm not—"

"Oh, but you are. She thinks the world of you, Molly."

Before Molly could reply, Dee waved at her from across the street and hurried over to join them. She carried Jada in a blue canvas sling across her front, and Jada smiled and gave an eager wriggle when she recognized Molly.

Molly, charmed, held out a forefinger and let the baby grasp it. Jada immediately tried to gum Molly's finger, and Molly, laughing, pulled it away.

"She's teething," Dee explained. "She tries to shove everything in her mouth."

"It's cute," Molly said, watching Jada as she blinked in the bright sunlight, then laid her head against Dee's chest. The baby was wearing a pink sunbonnet and a seersucker sunsuit with strawberries on it. The bonnet emphasized the perfection of her tiny head and the sweet vulnerability of her neck. Jada smiled shyly and batted her silky eyelashes. Molly wondered if all babies were so irresistible.

"Craig brought our two eldest over earlier," Dee said, shading her eyes with her hand. "Lexie and Corduroy were gung-ho to compete in the sand castle contest."

"Oh, what's that?" Phoebe asked, hopping from one foot to the other.

"The organizers trucked in a big mound of sand and let kids build castles with it. Prizes are awarded for the best ones."

"First I have to find Mr. Whister." Phoebe pulled off her backpack and removed her drawing. "Dad, can you help me find him?"

Eric and Phoebe set off through the crowd, and Molly and Dee continued toward the sand castle competition.

"I'm glad that Phoebe is enjoying Corduroy's old backpack," Dee observed. "She insisted that she wanted it when I mentioned we were going to give it to Goodwill. I hope you don't mind."

"Of course not. By the way, I found Grandpa's sewing machine on *Fiona*. I just might be able to make clothes for Phoebe's Barbie doll." She had her misgivings about this, but the dress that Barbie was wearing when she came home from the store at the beginning of the week was showing signs of wear. Phoebe kept putting it on the doll and taking it off again.

"Molly, I am certain you can do it. Tonight when we come to the boat for dinner, I'll bring fabric remnants and some spools of thread. Patterns, too."

"Don't expect too much," Molly warned. "I'm not an experienced seamstress."

Dee only laughed. "Trust me, Molly, Barbie won't care."

They had reached the huge pile of sand, where children were working at top speed to build some of the most fantastic sand castles Molly had ever seen. Phoebe, when she arrived with Eric, jumped right in beside Lexie and Corduroy, who were erecting an extravagant structure that so far outclassed all the competitors.

Eric sauntered over and casually draped an arm across Molly's shoulders. "Hey there," he said to Jada after greeting Dee. The baby smiled and hid her face in her mother's shoulder.

"Don't worry, she likes you," Dee said. "She's bashful, that's all."

"So was Phoebe at that age," Eric said.

"You'd never know it now," Dee observed as they watched Phoebe running to get more sand, then laughing at the way Corduroy dumped it on the mound that Lexie was molding into a tower for their castle.

Dee moved closer to call encouraging words to the children, and Eric squeezed Molly's shoulder. "So you like babies, huh?" he asked.

"I didn't realize I did until I got to know Jada better," she admitted.

"Haven't you ever dreamed of children of your own?"

Molly shook her head. "I'm afraid not. After dealing with Brianne in her tempestuous teenage years, I hoped to stay as far away from that kind of trouble as possible."

He drew her into the shade of a towering magnolia tree. "You get along with your sister all right now, don't you?"

"Yes, I suppose so." She remembered something and glanced at her watch. "Brianne's plane should be touching down at O'Hare Airport right about now, and she's going straight to visit with Grandpa in Minneapolis. I'm eager to hear her report."

"Do you need to go see him, Molly?"

She shook her head. "I'm very concerned, but I managed to talk to Dr. Talwani the other day, and he told me that my grandfather is most anxious for *Fiona* to be in Fort Lauderdale so that she'll be there when he arrives. The doctor suggested that I do whatever I can to expedite things here. Speaking of which, what's new on the engine part?"

"Oh, I forgot to mention that I talked with the representative at the German company yesterday afternoon, and he said that the fuel injector pump has finally been shipped. It should arrive in Jacksonville tomorrow."

"That means I'll have something worthwhile to report to Grandpa when I next speak with him. The news will cheer him."

Eric pulled her close and nuzzled her cheek. "You know what would make *me* a lot happier? If you'd stop being so uptight in public."

"Eric, I'm not uptight. I like being affectionate, but I worry about Phoebe and what she might suspect."

"Phoebe," he said as he pulled her closer, "is busy digging a moat right now."

Molly wrested herself away. "I'd like to see Phoebe's picture hung with the others," she said, taking Eric's hand. She called to Dee, "We're going to look at the paintings. Would you mind keeping an eye on Phoebe for a few minutes?"

"We'll join you as soon as they've judged the castles. Lexie has a coat-hanger sculpture on display."

Fingers linked, Molly and Eric strolled over to the kids' art section. Phoebe's picture was posted right in the middle of the bulletin board. An elderly couple were admiring it.

"Will you notice that detail, Gloria! Whoever drew that picture really put a lot of effort into it, I'd say."

The woman leaned closer, peering through her trifocals. "It was drawn by a seven-year-old girl, can you believe that?"

The couple moved away, but Eric's pride was evident in his expression. "I can't wait to tell Phoebe what those people said about her work."

"She's talented. No doubt about it," Molly said.

"Should I stop bugging her about her vacuum cleaners? I don't want to suppress a great artist in the making."

"I'll leave that up to you, Eric, but I caught her drawing Barbie yesterday."

"You did? Really?"

"Yes, really."

"Maybe she's not weird after all. You think?"

Molly only grinned. "I never thought she was weird in the first place, merely different. And there's nothing wrong with that."

"Hmm. Maybe you're right," Eric said, and he seemed more thoughtful than usual.

PHOEBE AND HER FRIENDS ran up, their sneakers kicking up white puffs of dust from the shell-rock path. "Dad! Dad! Our castle won first place!" She, Lexie and Corduroy waved shiny, gilt-embossed blue ribbons in the air.

"Congratulations, Peanut," Eric said, swinging Phoebe up in his arms. She immediately clamored to get down. Lately she was refusing to be treated like a little kid, and this made him sad. He wasn't all that eager for Phoebe to grow up.

"Did you see my picture?" Phoebe asked.

"People have been admiring it," he told her, and then Molly related the compliments they'd overheard.

"I can't wait to go to my next art class," Phoebe said. "My teacher is going to bring pastel crayons for us to use. They're like colored chalk, he says. I'm already thinking what I might draw."

As Phoebe ran off to join Lexie and Corduroy at the kids' display, Eric and Molly exchanged looks. If *Fiona*'s engine part arrived tomorrow as scheduled, they would be on their way to Fort Lauderdale soon and Phoebe might well miss her next art class. Eric didn't relish breaking this news to his daughter. He'd have a fight on his hands if she dug her heels in and said she didn't want to leave Greensea Springs.

"Don't worry," Molly told him as they walked past a display of kinetic sculptures made of copper tubing. "Phoebe will understand."

"Will she?" he mused, not at all sure of this.

"I'll try to prepare her. I'll tell her about Grandpa, and how happy he'll be that the engine will soon be repaired, and how much she'll enjoy seeing him again in Fort Lauderdale."

Eric retreated into silence. He and Phoebe would be leaving *Fiona* when they reached Fort Lauderdale, and Molly was certainly aware of that. Did she really expect that they could continue their relationship when they reached their destination?

He tried to recall if he'd ever mentioned what his plans were after delivering *Fiona*, and he didn't think he had. So far, he really hadn't figured out what he and Phoebe would do. Staying in Fort Lauderdale, where rents were high during this, the winter season, was not an option. Buying a house there was also out of the question, since when he settled, he wanted to live in a smaller city rather than a larger one.

A place like Greensea Springs.

"HAVE ANOTHER KEBAB," Eric urged Craig. The four of them were gathered around a table in *Fiona*'s cockpit, chowing down after drinks on deck. Dee's parents were baby-sitting the Farrells' children, and Phoebe was below, playing with her dolls in her bunk.

"Thanks," Craig said, holding out his plate as Eric served the skewer of shrimp and vegetables. Micki had sent over a bucket of shrimp, payment from a local shrimper who owed the marina money for diesel fuel. Earlier Eric had dug Emmett's old barbecue out of one of the storage lockers and affixed it to the bow railing. Molly had learned how to marinate the kebabs from the label on a salad-dressing bottle, and she had also contributed rice and a tossed salad.

"If you need any other material for those doll clothes, Molly, you let me know," Dee told her. "I've accumulated bags and bags of scraps over the years."

Molly got up to get more ice cubes. "Thanks, Dee. I'm going to be busy, aren't I."

When she stepped off the ladder below, she heard Phoebe playing with her dolls in her bunk. Molly didn't pay much attention as she removed the bag of ice cubes from the freezer, but as she prepared to start back up the ladder, she couldn't help overhearing.

Phoebe was visible through the partly closed door of her

room. Barbie and Blaine were arrayed on a folded-over towel that served as a couch, and Phoebe, talking in a high, sweet voice, was pretending to be Barbie.

"But, Blaine, I don't want to play my harp. I don't want to go back to my job. I only want to stay with you."

Now Blaine replied, this time in a deep stern voice. "Barbie, if you stay with me, we will have no place to live. We will have to live under a bridge or someplace like that. Or on the beach in a hut and go surfing all the time."

Barbie again: "I don't care where we live, Blaine, my one true love. I only want to be with you. And your wonderful dog, Phoebe."

Molly stifled a bout of giggles over that, but there was more.

"Now, Blaine, let's kiss and forget all about having no house to live in. Mmmm-*smooch*. Oooh, Blaine, that was a wonderful kiss."

"I know. Now, come to sleep in my bed. Don't tell Phoebe, though. She thinks you sleep in your own bed."

"Ha-ha, that's very funny, Blaine. I have an idea! Let's let Phoebe sleep in my bed. She will enjoy it so-o-o-o much." It must have been the dog's turn to say something, because the real Phoebe said, "Arf! Arf!" She was using a fuzzy chihuahua on a key chain as a play dog.

Molly had heard enough. She climbed the ladder and joined the others on deck, chastened by these revelations. Clearly she'd better have a serious talk with Eric—and soon.

DEE AND CRAIG WENT HOME EARLY, and by the time Eric and Molly started to carry dishes down from the cockpit, Phoebe was sleeping, her head pillowed on Barbie and Blaine's towel "couch," the key-chain chihuahua clutched in her fist. Since her head was at the foot of the bed, Eric covered her with an extra blanket and gently removed Blaine and Barbie to the shelf above the bunk.

Molly scraped soggy leftover salad into the garbage can. "Eric, we have to talk," she said.

He moved behind her and wrapped his arms around her shoulders. "I'd rather do something more fun. Like this," he said, curving a hand around her breast.

She brushed him away. "I'm worried about the effect we're having on Phoebe. I mentioned how I've been concerned about what she thinks is going on between us, and now I've got reason to believe we're not fooling her at all."

Eric's hands dropped away and he leaned back against the counter. "Okay, you must be on to something."

Quickly she related what she'd heard when she'd returned to the cabin for ice. "She knows we sleep together," she said in conclusion. "That's probably not so good."

Eric raised his eyebrows. "Oh, it's very good," he began, but Molly interrupted.

"For us, yes. For a seven-year-old girl to comprehend, maybe not."

"I'd better have a talk with her."

"What will you say?"

He sighed. "Hey, how about if you tackle the subject?"

Molly blinked. "I must not be hearing this correctly. Do you honestly believe that's a good idea?"

"We could both be there. We could tell her that when two people like each other, sometimes they want to be really close."

Molly abandoned the cleaning-up process and sank onto the lounge. "The thing that troubles me is that Phoebe—" She stopped, at a loss for a cogent way to express herself. She was about to say that Phoebe was heavily into happily-ever-after, and that the child would likely extrapolate any mention of liking each other into love. Neither Molly nor Eric had mentioned the treacherous *L* word, and to bring up the topic now would suggest that she, Molly, was angling for more of a commitment than she was ready to accept.

But Eric was regarding her with an empathy and understanding that she hadn't expected. He reached for her hand. "Molly, don't worry so much. Phoebe is my responsibility. I'll deal with this."

Molly, her thoughts in a jumble, bit her lip. "Can you?" she murmured, searching his expression.

He smiled and squeezed her hand. "As a responsible parent, I have to say yes," he said.

"But *can* you?"

He stood, ran a hand up the back of his neck. "We'll find out," he said. He pulled her up beside him and kissed her in a way that left no doubt that an evening of lovemaking would follow, and Molly found a great deal of pleasure in the idea.

As he reluctantly released her lips, she leaned her forehead against his. "You're the first guy I've ever dated with a child who lives with him full-time. This is all new to me, Eric."

"Well, relax. We'll muddle through it, you know."

"I wish I were so confident," she admitted.

"I doubt that it's only the Phoebe problem that rattles you. In case you're wondering, I don't mean to trifle with your feelings. I care about you deeply, Molly. As for what will happen in the future, I know from experience that we never can predict anything. I've learned that the best thing to do is to enjoy what you have at the moment and forget about tomorrow."

Molly considered this. It was a new thought, but she didn't feel capable of living only in the moment where Eric was involved.

"How about if we use this particular time to its best advantage?" Eric said, trailing a string of kisses down the side of her neck.

She wrapped her arms around his waist, rocked by the realization of how important he had become to her.

"I think it's time to adjourn to the bedroom," he murmured close to her ear, but at that moment, her cell phone rang.

She pulled away, wishing she could let her message service pick up, but with her grandfather sick and her sister due to check in soon, that wasn't a possibility.

"Right after I answer my phone," she said, hurrying to her stateroom to dig it out of her purse.

"Molly," said her sister, Brianne, "I'm here at the clinic with Grandpa."

She'd have a chance later to ask Brianne about her trip and catch up on other news. "How is he?"

Brianne hesitated. "He's so pale and gaunt. I haven't seen him in several months, but I was shocked."

Molly lowered herself to the edge of the bed. "When I talked with Dr. Talwani, he didn't linger on health reports. He seemed more concerned over Grandpa's sense of urgency about our getting *Fiona* to Fort Lauderdale."

"Maybe the doctor didn't want to alarm you. Today when I first walked in, Grandpa didn't seem to know who I was. I don't look any different, I don't sound any different, but he seemed confused. The nurse said she thought he'd had a mini-stroke recently."

Molly's heart sank as she took in this information. "I'd better come to Minneapolis," she said heavily.

"No, Molls, don't do that. You're in charge of getting the boat to Fort Lauderdale, and I understand there's some delay. You've got enough to do."

"I could be with you in a few hours if necessary," Molly reminded her. "I'm only about an hour from the Jacksonville airport."

"I'll tell you if you need to come. Gosh, Molly, I thought he was getting better. I—" Brianne choked. "I was going to say that it's terrible to see someone that I always considered strong and invincible now weak and sick," she said when she recovered. "I thought he'd go on for a long time. Now I'm not so sure."

"I'm sorry, Brianne. I would have prepared you if I'd known how bad things were."

"Well, I've got a good handle on the situation now, and I have an appointment with Dr. Talwani first thing in the morning. My list of questions is a yard long, and I'll update you when I can."

"Thanks, and I'll be eager to hear from you."

They hung up, and Molly sat pensively for a moment, wishing she could be with Brianne. Thinking that she'd better touch base with her brother, she dialed his number in Ireland, but hung up before it rang. She'd almost forgotten the time difference; it was two o'clock in the morning there. She'd have to call Patrick later.

WHILE MOLLY WAS TALKING on the phone, Eric went on deck to give her privacy. Only thin partitions divided *Fiona* into rooms, and it was easy to overhear things said in normal tones. From the little Eric had heard of Molly's present conversation, he surmised that she was talking with her sister. Or perhaps Chuck, even though she'd told him that she'd never called the guy back and didn't intend to do so.

He pictured Chuck in his mind. He was probably one of those corporate types, a solid type-A kind of guy and upwardly mobile, as they used to say in business school. Compared with Chuck, he was sure that he, Eric, didn't have much to offer.

He leaned over the railing, staring down into what seemed like a vast quilt of stars. The water was calm tonight, scarcely a ripple, and the sky was clear. He found that he was gazing at the reflection of Vega, Heather's star, and he wished he hadn't thought of her. Usually he welcomed memories of his wife, or at least that was the way it was before he and Molly got involved.

Involved. That was such an impersonal word for her effect on his emotions, on his life. In a short period of time, Molly had become so important to him that he didn't like to think of that inevitable day when she would go back to Chicago.

Was it inevitable? Probably.

Melancholy settled over him as he realized that he and Molly were ill-matched in various important ways. From everything that she and Emmett had said, he'd gathered that Molly had been a child of privilege. Emmett had made it clear that his three grandchildren would inherit everything he owned, which was considerable. One day Molly would be rich. And Eric was barely making ends meet.

He didn't hear Molly as she stepped out on deck. When she came to stand beside him at the railing, he glanced up, saw that she was visibly upset.

She related the conversation with her sister, and before she had finished, he put an arm around her shoulders. He had never seen her so distressed. "I'm sorry," he said. "I wish the news was better."

"Grandpa has been such an important influence in our lives," Molly said in a low tone. "I don't know how we will get along without him when he goes."

"Let's hope he'll pull through this, Molly. I wouldn't count Emmett McBryde out yet."

She leaned her head on his shoulder. "I'm not."

They stood like that for a long time. Finally a large cabin cruiser motored past, creating a wake that rocked *Fiona* until they both had to grasp the railing to keep from losing their footing on the deck. Vega's reflection fractured, along with that of all the other stars, and this only increased Eric's descent into the doldrums. Soon, like the reflection of the star that was hers, his memories of Heather would disappear. He didn't know if he could bear it when he could no longer recall the exact way her mouth curved up at the edges just before she laughed, or the scent of her hair, or the smoothness of her skin when he reached over to touch her at night.

Molly sighed, and he was about to echo it when she spoke. "If you don't mind, I think I'd like to be alone. I'm not very good company right now."

He did mind, he discovered, and fiercely. Hard on the heels of his yearning for Heather came a new and disturbing emotion, one even more unsettling than memories of his loss. He might not remember those things about Heather, but he was most aware of the sweet upturning of Molly's mouth when she smiled, and the way her hair smelled when freshly washed with whatever shampoo she used, and how sometimes at night she rolled toward him with the motion of the boat and settled gratefully into his arms. Which is where he wanted her right now.

She treated him to a brief, brisk kiss on the cheek and turned. As she pushed past him, he reached for her, but she was already too far away and didn't even notice.

"Good night, Eric," she called over her shoulder. "I'll see you in the morning."

Not in the morning. Come with me to bed, he wanted to say, but he respected her wish for privacy and understood that at the moment, it took precedence over his own needs. He watched her mutely until she had disappeared down the companionway.

When he turned back toward the railing, the water had regained its previous calmness, and the stars had again become a softly rippling quilt. But Vega, if he wasn't mistaken, was not nearly as bright as it had been before.

Chapter Thirteen

Molly spent a restless night, alternately waking and sleeping. Once when she woke, she heard Eric moving around the cabin. It sounded as if he was getting a drink from the fridge. Toward morning, she moved toward him, wanting the comfort of his warm body, but he wasn't there. Later, she heard the pump switch on and knew he was taking a shower. When she woke for good, she lay gazing up at the watery reflections on the ceiling and wondering what would happen when she returned to Chicago. How long would it take before she stopped expecting Eric to be there in the night? Would she immediately get back into the groove of eating alone, sleeping alone, going places alone?

Finally, around six-thirty, she rose and wrapped her robe around her before going up on deck. She'd thought that it was too early for Eric, but he was there before her. He didn't look as if he'd slept any better than she had; his beard was bristly, and deep purplish circles rimmed his lower eyelids.

He smiled and handed her a cup. "I thought you'd be up early. I couldn't sleep last night, either."

She accepted the coffee and sat beside him, drawing her feet up under her. During the night, a dank fog had settled over the marina, and a pale scrim of mist swirled around the boats. Molly shivered even in her thick velour robe. "I guess I didn't want to be alone as much as I thought," she admitted. The warm steam rising from the cup carried with it the full, fragrant smell of coffee, making her feel better already.

"We can fix that tonight," he said. He placed his arm across the back of the seat and caressed her shoulder. His hand was warm, gentle.

She took heart from his smile. "What's our plan for today?"

"Since you asked, can you look after Phoebe? I have to drive to Jacksonville to get the engine part. Micki said I can take the van as long as I deliver some anchor chain to a customer along the way, and I figure that's faster than waiting for the part to arrive here in Greensea Springs."

"Phoebe and I can work on the Barbie clothes after she finishes her school assignments. Then, while you're repairing the engine this afternoon, we could visit the Farrells."

"That's cool." He drained his coffee. "I'm going to cook breakfast for all of us. Bacon or sausage with your eggs?"

"Bacon. I like the way you do it." Instead of frying, Eric broiled bacon, which made it crispier and less greasy.

"Three breakfasts, coming up," he said. They heard Phoebe opening the door of her small stateroom, and Eric cadged a stealthy kiss before his daughter could climb up the ladder. Molly grinned at him as he disappeared below.

Yes, how would she ever accustom herself to life without Eric? Somehow she couldn't imagine such a thing.

MOLLY CALLED HER GRANDFATHER from the laundry room, where she was overseeing the washing of Phoebe's clothes while Phoebe, sitting in the nearby bougainvillea arbor with her head bent over a textbook, worked on her reading lesson.

"Hi, Grandpa," Molly said with forced cheeriness when Emmett picked up the phone.

"M-Molly Kate, is that you?"

"Yes, and I'm phoning early in the day because I'm concerned about you."

Emmett cleared his throat. His voice wasn't hearty by any means. In fact, he sounded more frail than she'd ever heard him.

"No need to worry, Molly. I'll be out of this looney bin in a few days, and when I am, we're all going sailing on *Fiona* again. You, me, Patrick and Brianne, like old times."

"That's right. Eric is going to get the engine part today—did he mention that? The pump arrived in Jacksonville this morning."

"No, but that's good news. How long before you arrive in Fort Lauderdale?"

"Less than a week, probably."

"Good, Molly." He hesitated as if gathering his thoughts. "Molly, dear, how did you get back to Florida? You were here last night. Did you catch a plane in the middle of the night?"

Molly digested his words as she watched the clothes spin around and around in the dryer. "Why, no, Grandpa. I've been right here in Greensea Springs all along. Brianne arrived in Minneapolis last night. She caught a flight from Chicago after her plane from Australia landed at O'Hare." Had he confused his only granddaughters? Except for red hair, she and Brianne looked nothing alike. Her sister was short, only five-two. Brianne had freckles and her eyes were brown.

"Your sister was here?" Her grandfather stumbled over the words and began to cough.

"She's meeting with your doctor this morning. Maybe that's why you haven't seen her today."

"She'll be back? She won't be returning to the Outback?"

"Brianne is home for the foreseeable future, Grandpa. You behave yourself and don't give her a hard time."

"She should find a guy and settle down. You, too, Molly Kate. Marriage between two like souls is the greatest gift you'll ever know. My Fiona and I were married for fifty years, and I wouldn't be the man I am today if not for her gentle guidance and support. Through thick and thin—as she used to say, through sick and sin. Though there was no sin on either part, mind you. I want to see you happily settled with someone you love. Sharing experiences with a spouse is the only way to find real happiness."

It was on the tip of Molly's tongue to inform him that she'd never found a person with whom such a relationship would be remotely possible, but she realized with a jolt that this was no longer true now that Eric was a part of her life.

"Does your silence mean that you agree with an old man's ramblings, Molly Kate?"

"Perhaps," she managed to say.

Emmett's voice was kind as he responded. "I've had a wonderful life with a lot of love in it," he said. "I wish the same for you."

"Thank you, Grandpa," she replied, a lump in her throat. "Would you mind if I called you later today? I miss you so much."

"Why not. There's nothing else to do around here." He sounded as if he had rallied.

"You'll have Brianne nearby. That should make it more interesting," she said, blinking tears from her eyes. She'd always been the closest of any of them to their grandfather, and it pained her that she couldn't be with him when he was so sick.

"Let's hope so. Goodbye, Molly Kate. I love you."

"I love you, too. Get well soon, and we'll be sailing together before long."

After she hung up, she sat in the webbed lawn chair provided by the management and stared at the washing machine, which was clicking off after the final rinse. She was concerned about Emmett and his mistaking Brianne for her. His confusion about everyday events seemed to grow every time she talked with him.

Well, Brianne would have phoned if she was through talking with Dr. Talwani. Molly could do nothing but wait.

"Phoebe, how is your lesson coming along?" she called.

"I'm almost finished. Give me a few more minutes and I'll be ready for lunch. What can we have?"

"Peanut butter and jelly?" Molly had learned through experience: when in doubt, peanut butter and jelly was the way to go.

"That's good. I have a sand wish I need to make today," Phoebe replied before bending over her book again.

Molly herself had some she wanted to make. It might not help to wish for her grandfather's improved health on a peanut butter sandwich, but it probably wouldn't hurt, either.

ERIC IDLED THROUGH the drive-in window at a burger place just off I-95 after picking up the fuel injection pump for *Fiona*. He ordered a burger, engaged in the usual crackling exchange of words with the girl at the register, neither of them understanding what the other was saying, and as a result ended up with no fries, even though he'd ordered the large size. For a few seconds he considered driving through again, but decided it wasn't worth the hassle. While waiting for traffic at the stoplight, he unwrapped the burger and ate it on the way back to Greensea Springs.

This time away from Molly was a good chance to think things over, and the main thing on his mind was that after he'd installed the part, they'd head for Fort Lauderdale. Assuming good weather, the trip might take five days, six at the most. Then Molly would catch a flight out. She was eager to be with Emmett and wouldn't delay her departure. In his mind's eye he visualized Phoebe crying as Molly said goodbye. He would be stoic, calm.

No. He'd be in agony over losing the only other woman in the world aside from Heather who had ever meant anything to him.

For a few minutes, he allowed himself to indulge in daydreams about how it might be if Molly didn't have a sick grandfather and a job that needed tending. He could get work on a boat in the Virgin Islands; tourists intent on island-hopping often required a captain. Lots of times, couples worked on yachts where the man sailed the boat and the woman cooked. Scratch that one—Molly, though trying valiantly and improving daily, didn't cook with enough skill for them to pull that one off. Besides, they would have Phoebe in tow, and delightful though his daughter was, he'd be the first to admit that people wealthy enough to own their own yachts usually didn't enjoy sharing their limited space with kids.

Perhaps the three of them could take up residence on some remote Caribbean island where they'd farm pineapples and plantains, live in a palm-thatched hut and play all day on the beach. He'd have plenty of time to spend with Phoebe, which meant that they could speed ahead with her home schooling. However, his daughter needed other children; he understood this now that he'd seen her in action with the Farrell kids. And Molly wouldn't take to living in the middle of nowhere with little intellectual stimulation. He wouldn't be able to watch *Jeopardy!*, either.

So maybe he and Molly could buy their own boat. A catamaran, perhaps, that didn't draw much water, which meant that they'd be able to sail right up to those beautiful white beaches in the Bahamas. The ocean would provide most of their sustenance; they'd eat fish and lobster. And where would they get enough money to buy such a boat? His paltry savings didn't amount to much. As for borrowing, his credit rating probably wasn't even on the books anymore. Molly had more money than he did, but he was too proud by far to let her buy the boat or own a bigger share of it than he did.

Speaking of which, what made him think Molly Kate McBryde would stick by him for the long haul, anyhow? Again he asked himself, what did he have to offer her? He had no job, no real money, no good prospects. All he had was his love for her and a seven-and-a-half-year-old child.

He loved Molly. He could picture the two of them together for the rest of their lives. But ask her to marry him? No way. He wouldn't be a bit surprised if she laughed in his face.

And he wouldn't blame her if she did. He wasn't up to her speed, and he knew it. Had known it from the beginning. So maybe the best thing to do was to let this thing play itself out to its natural end and say "so long." That was a depressing thought, and he felt glum all the way back to the marina.

Once there, he busied himself with *Fiona*'s engine. Now that he had the engine part, repair would be a snap. They'd soon be on their way. This should have cheered him, but it didn't.

"DOES THAT MEAN you'll be leaving?" Dee asked Molly in resignation. Eric was back on *Fiona* installing the new part, and Molly and Phoebe were visiting the Farrells.

Somberly, Molly nodded. "It'll be a couple of days, most likely." She tried to concentrate on hemming the tiny troll costume that Dee was making for the puppets, but it was difficult when out of the corner of her eye she could see Phoebe playing so happily with Corduroy and Lexie in the backyard. They had built a fort out of an old cardboard refrigerator box, and Lexie, wearing a gilt-paper crown on her head, was cheering on Corduroy and Phoebe, who were jousting. They were riding old brooms, which served as their horses, and their lances were foam noodles, the kind kids play with in the swimming pool.

"I wish we didn't have to go," Molly said unhappily. "It will break Phoebe's heart."

Dee, after lifting the baby out of her high chair, came to the window to watch the kids. "Lexie and Corduroy will miss her. You'll have to bring Phoebe back to visit." She colored quickly and attempted to cover up her gaffe. "I mean," she said, "it would be fun if you could."

"Perhaps Eric can," Molly said, her spirits taking a dive. Merely thinking about being separated from Phoebe and Eric made her sad.

Dee sat beside her on the window seat and smoothed Jada's dress. "I keep forgetting that you're not Phoebe's mother. I'm sorry if I embarrassed you."

Molly tossed aside the costume and got up to get a glass of water from the refrigerator. "You didn't. I realize it must seem strange to people that we're not really a family. I mean, people see us together all the time. It's—it's hard to believe that we only met a few weeks ago when—when—" It was no use. She couldn't hide her anguish from Dee, her best friend here. She set the half-full glass carefully on the counter and buried her face in her hands. The tears wouldn't stop; they stung her eyes, dribbled through her fingers, splashed on the tile floor.

Dee settled Jada in the playpen and rushed to give Molly

a hug. "Molly, I'm sorry," she said soothingly. "I shouldn't have brought it up."

"It's—it's that I love him. And I love Phoebe. I can't imagine going back to Chicago and resuming a life that seems cold and lonely by comparison. I thought I was happy, Dee, but maybe I wasn't."

"Sometimes," Dee said softly, "we get a wake-up call. Maybe getting stranded in Greensea Springs was yours."

Molly dried her eyes. "Wake-up call? This is more like a fire alarm. What am I going to do?"

Dee picked up her glass and filled it. "You're going to have a glass of water, and you're going to talk it out. You'll feel better afterward, I promise." She led Molly back to the window seat and planted the glass in her hands. Then she handed Jada a teething biscuit and sat down. "I'm all ears," she said. "Suppose you tell me why you can't stay with Eric and Phoebe."

"It's complicated," Molly said distractedly. In the backyard, Corduroy had evidently bested Phoebe at jousting, and Lexie was rewarding him with a garland made of oak leaves. Phoebe was writhing on the ground, groaning realistically but stopping occasionally to offer advice about how Corduroy could keep his new headgear from falling over one eye.

"Never mind that it's complicated," Dee advised. "I'm here to listen."

Molly summoned her thoughts and attempted to bring some order to them so she could relate them coherently.

"In the first place," she told Dee, "he doesn't know I love him."

"Fine. So tell him. Next?"

"You think it's that simple?" Molly asked incredulously.

"Nothing is ever simple, but you've got to start somewhere."

She hadn't wanted Eric to make such a declaration to her because once he stated that he loved her, she'd be required to act on the information. She'd have to say that she loved him, too, or that she didn't. Either answer would kick over a whole can of worms in their relationship. She'd never once thought about saying the words first.

She sprang up from the window seat. "Dee, you're brilliant," she said.

"But—"

"No, I mean it. I'll talk to him about it tonight."

"Talk to him? Why don't you create a setting—candles, moonlight, Phoebe in bed asleep—before you spring this on him?"

"Like I said, you're brilliant. I'll stop and buy candles on the way home."

Dee went to a nearby drawer. "I'll give you some. You can have flowers from the camellia bush in the backyard. Let me know how it goes."

"I will," Molly said. She was already planning to stop and buy something special for dinner.

BACK ON *FIONA*, Eric was finishing up for the day, wiping his greasy hands on a rag, when Micki called to him from the dock.

"Eric! It's important."

He hurried up the ladder. The concerned expression on Micki's round face was punctuated by a frown. "You have a phone call in the office. She says it's an emergency."

He tossed the rag aside. "Who is it?" he asked. Myriad possibilities flitted through his mind—his brother's wife's pregnancy, his friend Steve washing overboard on his trawler? Worse yet, something to do with Phoebe?

Micki immediately set his mind at ease on that count. "She said her name's Brianne. She sounded as if she had been crying."

Eric trotted up the dock slightly ahead of Micki, who was forced to double-time to keep pace. "That's Molly's sister's name. I've never met her." A sense of dread washed over him.

Eric burst through the office door and grabbed the phone up from the counter.

"Eric here," he said brusquely.

"Eric, this is Brianne McBryde, Molly's sister."

"Yes," he said. Emotion blocked his airway, made it difficult to breathe.

"I have bad news, and I didn't want to call Molly on her cell phone, since I don't know where she is at the moment or what she's doing," Brianne began.

"It's Emmett, isn't it?" He tried to temper his alarm, soften his tone.

"Yes. He—he died around four o'clock—" Brianne's voice broke, and he heard a rustle, as if she were brushing a tear from her cheek.

Eric didn't speak for a moment. He hadn't expected this. He didn't think Molly had either, at least not so soon after she last spoke with her grandfather.

"I'm sorry. Is there anything I can do?"

"Please, Eric, could you tell Molly for me? I have to phone our brother in Ireland, and I could call her afterward, but this is very difficult for me, as I'm sure you know."

"Brianne, I'll tell her. She'll be devastated."

"They were close. Grandpa was special to all of us, but he and Molly seemed to be on the same wavelength. She—and my brother and I—will miss him."

"I will, too. I got to know him when he came to stay on the boat while I did some repairs. He was a great guy, a true gentleman, an accomplished raconteur."

"Yes, he certainly was. Thank you for your kind words, and thanks in advance for breaking the news to Molly. I'll talk to her later about arrangements. Right now I'm trying to pull myself together enough to inform the people he'd want me to tell. Close friends, his lawyer, the McBryde Industries board of directors."

"Don't worry, Brianne. Again, I'm sorry for your loss. I'm sure we'll talk again soon."

They hung up, and Micki stopped shuffling papers long enough to send him an inquiring look. "Molly's grandfather?"

"Yes, it's Emmett. This is going to be a big blow to her."

"If there's anything I can do," Micki began, but he silenced her by aiming a significant nod toward the window. They could see Molly swinging up the other side of the street, carrying a couple of plastic bags from the grocery store. Phoebe, clutching a bouquet of pink flowers, was scampering along beside her, chattering at top speed. The two of them looked happy, as if they'd had a lovely afternoon.

"All I can think of right now, Micki, is to find something for Phoebe to do so I can talk with Molly privately."

"I'll close up the office. It's time, anyway. And Phoebe and I will go visit Lainie Kallbeck and Jody while you're with Molly. Will that work?"

"Thanks, Micki," Eric said. He'd enjoyed Emmett's company in their short time together, and he'd looked forward to seeing him again in Fort Lauderdale. They had discussed sailing together sometime, maybe to the Turks and Caicos islands, perhaps to Bermuda. He'd never dreamed that Emmett was so sick, and he would miss him.

MOLLY SHIFTED HER PARCELS from one hand to the other and waved at Eric as he approached. He was wearing faded denim cutoffs and flip-flop sandals, and a baseball hat sat low over his brow. He wasn't the kind of guy she would have given more than a casual nod a couple of months ago, and yet now, as he walked toward her, her heart brimmed with happiness and anticipation.

"Dad! We bought more Chunky Monkey ice cream, your favorite! And Corduroy lost a tooth, and Lexie got new tap shoes. Can I take tap dancing lessons, Dad? Can I?"

Eric relieved Molly of the grocery bags and wrapped an arm around her waist. "We'll talk about it later, Peanut. Say, Micki is locking up the office and she wants you to go with her to visit Jody on Mrs. Kallbeck's boat. Why don't you run ahead, and Molly and I will be along soon."

"Sure!" Phoebe pressed the bouquet of camellias into Molly's hands and was off like a shot.

As soon as she had rounded the corner of the marina office, Molly leaned over and kissed his cheek.

"Hi, guy," she said. "How's work on the engine coming along?"

"Almost done. I'm going to replace a filter later, check a few other things." He started to guide her toward the bougainvillea arbor, but she hung back.

"I bought food for dinner, and I should get started on it right away. Dee gave me one of her favorite recipes, and I'm going to make asparagus casserole for dinner tonight. I thought we'd eat late, just the two of us. Phoebe says she'll be happy if we let her heat up a can of ravioli, and—"

"Molly," he said, and she identified a new quality in his voice that made her swing her head around sharply. "I need to talk with you."

His eyes were dark with gravity and something else, as yet unidentifiable. A flicker of apprehension penetrated her mood and, unobjecting, she let him lead her to the arbor.

"Sit down," he said gently, and she lowered herself to the bench. Nearby, boats bobbed in their slips. Somewhere a motor chugged into action, the sound receding as the boat headed toward the inlet.

"What's wrong?" she asked as a sudden premonition emptied her lungs, made it difficult to breathe.

"I'm sorry, Molly, but I have bad news." His gaze held hers, and for the first time she saw the compassion clouding his eyes. Another emotion simmered beneath their depths: sorrow.

"It's—it's my grandfather, isn't it." The bouquet fell unheeded to her lap.

He took both her hands in his. "Yes, Molly." He paused, seemed to gauge her reaction before plunging ahead. "He's gone."

Eric's face swam before her, and a buzzing began in her ears. "You mean—?"

"Brianne called and asked me to break the news to you. He died this afternoon. I'm so sorry."

"Oh, no," she heard herself say. She'd known he was very ill, but she couldn't believe that he was really gone. She couldn't imagine getting along without Emmett. If only she'd visited him despite his insistence that she stay with *Fiona!* If only— But it was too late now.

And then the tears came, a flood of grief that she made no attempt to hold back. Eric wrapped her in his arms and let her cry, rocking her gently and saying, "It's okay, Molly, just let it go."

Which was all she could do for the moment.

Chapter Fourteen

She didn't know how long she cried. It could have been ten minutes—it could have been twenty—but when her sobs tapered off, Eric handed her his handkerchief.

"It's just such a shock," she said before blowing her nose. "What else did Brianne say?"

"Only that she was going to notify your brother and the people at McBryde Industries as well as his lawyer. She said she'd talk with you soon."

Molly nodded even as tears welled again.

"Don't worry, Micki's looking after Phoebe. We can stay here as long as you like."

"I was—" She gestured at the bags, sending a flurry of camellia petals floating to the ground. "I was planning something special."

"We'll get takeout tonight."

She sighed, thinking of the romantic dinner she'd had in mind. "I'm not hungry at all, Eric. You and Phoebe can go get a pizza. She'd like that."

"Not tonight, and don't worry about us." He smiled at her, took the handkerchief from her hands and blotted at a lone tear rolling down her neck. Then he kissed her softly on the lips.

"Thank you, Eric. If I had to hear bad news, I'm glad you were the one to tell me." He was so tender, so kind. No wonder she loved him.

"It's never easy to hear something like that," he said. "Even when you expect it."

Molly was reminded of his grief, and he seemed lost in his thoughts for a few moments. Whatever her pain at this unwelcome news, his must have been even worse. Losing a young wife to a terrible disease would be much harder than saying goodbye to a grandfather who had lived to the fullest.

She reached for his hand, knowing for the first time how deeply Heather's death must have affected him. "I think I want to go back to *Fiona*," she said.

His answering smile and nod were reassuring, though they didn't diminish her heartache. Eric kept his arm around her shoulders as he walked beside her down the dock, carrying the bags of groceries. When they passed the boat where Phoebe was visiting with Micki, Lainie Kallbeck and her white cat, Phoebe called from the deck, "Dad, may I stay and eat hamburgers with Mrs. Kallbeck and Micki? Oh, and Jody, of course." The cat peered out from under a tall potted palm on the deck.

"Sure. I'll come over to get you in about an hour."

"Goody! Mrs. Kallbeck said I could brush Jody." She disappeared below.

"Make it more like two hours," Micki suggested, hurrying aft from the bow as they were turning to leave. "We're still thawing the meat. Molly, I'm sorry about your grandfather."

Though bleary-eyed, Molly managed a smile. "Thanks. He was wonderful, and I'll miss him."

"Don't worry about Phoebe. I'll bring her over when we're through eating," Micki told Eric. "Incidentally, she asked me why the two of you were spending such a long time in the arbor. I hope you don't mind, but I thought it best to tell her."

"What did she say?" Eric asked.

"That Emmett was in heaven with her mother. And then she started playing with Jody and asked if she could brush him. She took it well, I think."

"Thanks, Micki," Molly told her. "I would have found it difficult to break the news." Although Phoebe hadn't known

The Mommy Wish

Emmett well, they'd liked each other. She'd mentioned to Molly that he had always brought her a bag of M&Ms when he went out and insisted on her sharing with him, though he would only eat the green ones because they were the color of shamrocks. That was so like Emmett, and thinking about it now eased her grief.

After they boarded *Fiona*, Eric started to put away the food, and Molly went into her bathroom, where she splashed her cheeks with cool water. She stared at her face in the mirror; it was pinched and white, her eyes red-rimmed from crying.

"I want to call Brianne. I'd like to know what happened. I didn't expect him to go so fast," she said to Eric when she came out.

"I'll fix you a sandwich, if you'd like."

"I don't think I'll be able to eat," she said. In fact, it was the last thing she wanted to do.

"You should try."

"Maybe in a few minutes," Molly said, reaching for her cell phone and retreating into her stateroom.

She called Brianne, who told her that their grandfather had simply slipped quietly away while napping, that he hadn't suffered and that she had been sitting beside his bed at the end. Brianne had notified everyone who needed telling, and his lawyer would be in touch with all of them soon.

"Should I come to Minneapolis?" Molly asked her.

"No, Molly, it's not necessary. Grandpa wanted to be cremated and his ashes scattered in the Gulf Stream. I think you should continue on with *Fiona* to Fort Lauderdale as planned, and perhaps you and I could take care of the ashes later."

"Of course," Molly said, wiping away the tears that wouldn't stop. She recalled that Emmett had hated funerals and always said he didn't want one because they were a waste of money.

"Patrick wanted to come back from County Sligo, but I told him not to bother. He can join us for the scattering of the ashes if he likes."

"Agreed. I'll mention that to him when we talk. How are you holding up?"

"Fine. I'll be visiting Frank and his family in Lake Forest. They've invited me to stay with them. I'm on my way to the Minneapolis–St. Paul airport now."

"In Chicago, you can stay at my apartment. The guest room is always ready for company."

Brianne sighed. "Thanks, Molls, but I want to be with people. Frank and Elise and their brood are like family."

"I know. We're lucky in that respect."

"Are you okay, Molly?"

"I'm doing as well as could be expected. Eric has been wonderful."

"I liked the way he sounded when I called. He was eager to be helpful, and I knew somehow that he was the right one to break the news."

"Yes," Molly said softly, recalling the concern in Eric's eyes. She could see through the doorway to where Eric stood in the galley, cutting a sandwich in half, his brow furrowed as he focused on the task. He had been fond of Emmett, she knew. Shifting light penetrated the glass of the nearby porthole to cast shimmering reflections on Eric's face, and she felt the bond of their shared sadness tighten in her chest.

Brianne sighed. "I'd better hang up. We're getting close to the airport now."

"Bye, Brianne. I love you."

"Love you too, big sis. I'll be in touch."

After they hung up, Molly kicked off her shoes and lay back on the bed, tears pooling in her eyes and trickling freely down her cheeks. Memories flashed through her head; the years fell away, and she recalled Emmett dressed as Santa Claus, hauling bag after bag of presents into their house on Christmas Eve, knowing full well that three sets of eyes followed his progress from behind the stair railing and putting on a show to make it worth their while. She remembered how he had built each of them kites out of newspaper one windy March weekend and spent hours patiently teaching her, Patrick and Brianne how to fly them. And she'd never forget how her courtly grandfather had treated her to a gourmet dinner at a restaurant, followed by dancing afterward at a grown-up nightclub, when she and her boyfriend broke up right before the senior prom.

When Eric entered into her stateroom, he stood silhouetted against the light in the salon. "I brought you this," he said, holding out a tray bearing a sandwich and a mug. "Try to eat, won't you?"

Molly wiped away the tears and pushed herself up against the pillows. As he settled the tray across her knees, she said, "Thanks, Eric. Maybe I can manage a few bites."

He sat on the edge of the bed, and she bit into the sandwich. The mug contained hot herbal tea, and she forced down a few small swallows.

She shifted the tray to the bedside table. "I'm sorry, Eric. I don't have any appetite."

"Would you like me to rub your back? It might help you to relax."

Obediently she turned over on her stomach, and Eric began to massage her shoulder muscles. After a while, his hands moved to either side of her spine, then to her waist. When he slid his fingertips under her blouse, she didn't object.

He unhooked her bra, caressed her skin. It wasn't about sex—she knew that. This was comfort.

After a while, he pulled her blouse down again and caressed her hair. "I'll go now. It's almost time for Phoebe to show up. I hope you can go to sleep."

She reached up and put her finger lightly to his lips. "I doubt it. I can't stop thinking that I'll never see him again."

"Wait. I have something that might help." He went away for a few minutes and returned with an over-the-counter sleeping aid. "These are left over from when Heather died. One might get you through this first night."

She accepted the pill gratefully and washed it down with the rest of the tea. After Eric left, she took off her clothes and slipped a comfy oversized T-shirt over her head, then climbed beneath the covers. The last thing she heard as she drifted off into welcome sleep was Eric whispering with Phoebe as they boarded the boat. The sound of them talking nearby soothed her, and she felt comforted that two people so dear to her were close by during this difficult time.

ERIC SLEPT UNEASILY, and during his waking periods, his mind kept drifting back to Molly in the stateroom at the other end of the boat. He wanted to go to her, but he didn't want to upset her. The thought of her sleeping alone in that big bed dismayed him, yet he couldn't go where he wasn't invited. Finally he slept, but not well.

He woke up later than usual to the beep of the coffeemaker signaling that coffee was ready. He slid out of bed, pulled on his shorts and stepped into the salon to find Molly, already showered and dressed, holding a mug out to him.

"I didn't expect you to be up so early," he said.

She lifted a shoulder and let it fall. "The sleeping aid worked. I feel okay this morning, but it's hard to accept the finality of Grandpa's death. I halfway expect him to step down that ladder, booming out plans for the day's sailing."

"I know you'll miss him. What did your sister have to say?"

Molly filled him in on yesterday's conversation with Brianne. "After Patrick arrives home from Ireland, the three of us will grant Grandpa's final wish. We'll scatter his ashes at sea, and if I can talk them into it, maybe we'll sail to the Bahamas for a week or so. It would be a fitting tribute to our grandfather to enjoy his boat one last time."

"Last time?" Eric repeated. "You mean you'll sell her?"

"I suppose so. None of us has the kind of life that allows time to appreciate a sailing yacht like *Fiona*." She sounded regretful, even sad.

"You still want to take her to Fort Lauderdale?"

"Of course."

"I see." He drank all his coffee in one long gulp. "I'm going up on deck. I noticed some spots that need caulking before we leave."

He thought her gaze followed him as he climbed the ladder, but he didn't speak again and neither did she.

ERIC WAS SETTING OUT caulking materials when Molly appeared on the foredeck.

"What's going on?" he asked.

She knelt beside him. "I talked to my brother. He's devastated, as you can imagine. He says he's not coming home until spring."

"That's what you expected, right?"

"Pretty much. I miss him, that's all." She heaved a sigh and picked up a tube of caulk. "Do you need some help."

He kept his head down, taping the teak so the caulking material wouldn't stick to it. "Why don't you take it easy today?"

"I should call Frank at the office, ask if Grandpa's passing has changed anything around there. I'm putting it off. Talking with Patrick made me feel even worse."

He looked at her then, really looked at her. Her swollen eyes and pale cheeks cut to his heart. "Hey," he said softly. "Are you okay?"

"I'm holding myself together. Phoebe offered me comfort food. She poured me a bowl of her Cocoa Krispies and said they'd make me feel better. She's been very solicitous, and it's sweet."

"How'd you like the cereal?"

"Not bad. I'll probably eat more tomorrow morning."

He chuckled, and she smiled. "Should I go below and check on Phoebe?" he asked.

Molly shook her head. "She's watching a TV program about volcanoes. She hinted, by the way, that she wouldn't mind seeing a real one."

"If I got a job in the South Pacific, she would. Whether it would be erupting is another thing." He accepted the tube of caulk from her before squeezing out a long line of the black paste between two rows of teak.

"Would you really do that? Take Phoebe so far away from home, I mean?"

"We have no home. You've reminded me of that a few times."

"Eric—"

Sensing that he had really upset her with his remark, he glanced at her. She'd scrunched her hair carelessly on top of her head with a small terry-cloth band—he wasn't sure of the correct name for it. It was the same color as her shirt, which was bright blue. A bit of cleavage showed above the scooped neckline, and his hands grew damp as he contemplated the pleasures that would accompany peeling it away from her body to expose her beautiful breasts. He swallowed, made himself look away.

"I haven't decided yet what Phoebe and I will do next," he said gruffly.

She was quiet for a time, and then she stood. "If you don't need any help here, I'm going to wash Phoebe's breakfast dishes, and then I'll call Frank."

"I can manage. You should relax, not plan on doing any work today."

She shook her head so that a few loose strands of golden hair fell across her forehead. "I learned when my mom died that the best way to get through something like this is to keep busy. I'll spend time with Phoebe, maybe clean out the refrigerator." She stood and picked her way carefully across the lines that secured the dinghy, then disappeared into the cockpit.

Eric leaned back and wiped his brow. He knew he had to give Molly her space right now, let her mourn in her own fashion. This was not the time for heavy discussions about their future or daydreams about how they might stay together. Neither of them had spoken about forever. That had never been an option, and he'd realized it from the start.

Eric lowered his head again, squeezing out more caulk and spreading it between the boards. If he knew what was good for him, he'd learn to regard this interlude on *Fiona* with Goddess Molly as a mere blip on the radar screen of his life.

Molly would go back to Chicago soon, and she'd forget him and Phoebe. Saying goodbye was going to be hard for him, and he could only imagine how difficult it would be for his daughter.

He had reached the point of grasping at straws. Perhaps he and Phoebe could follow Molly to Chicago. A college classmate of his lived there, had something to do with the board of trade. Don would have contacts in important places, would put in a good word for Eric, would help him get a job.

But Eric couldn't imagine himself living in Chicago. City life wasn't what he wanted for Phoebe, either.

Boats plied the Intracoastal, lazily stirring the water into foamy white wakes. Down the dock, someone was cleaning fish, and a bevy of gulls circled overhead waiting for handouts. Life around a marina was endlessly fascinating and had always had a calming effect on him. Some of Eric's happiest times had been spent around boats. This was what he liked to do, what made him happy. He couldn't imagine giving it up.

But he would have to, eventually, for Phoebe. The sensation of impending loss enveloped him. Somewhere, he admitted ruefully to himself, was a regular nine-to-five job that he would soon fill, a tedious means of making a living and nothing more. It would provide a pension plan and health insurance, and he'd have a manager who might or might not like his work, who would have to be flattered, mollified and pleased, not necessarily in equal amounts. As he contemplated the loss of Molly and of the work he loved, it seemed too much to bear.

He bent to his task, taking heart from the knowledge that he and Phoebe would have a few more days with Molly, at least. They would leave for Fort Lauderdale shortly after dawn tomorrow.

"YOU DIDN'T GET A CHANCE to tell him?" Dee's voice on the phone was incredulous.

Molly, sitting on a bench one dock away from *Fiona*, propped her feet on a nearby boat box and kept her eye on

Phoebe, who was tossing bread crusts to ducks swimming in the water. "I wasn't in the mood after I found out about Grandpa. The romantic dinner didn't happen."

"Oh, Molly, what are you going to do?"

"I'll wait until we reach Fort Lauderdale. By that time, I'll be ready to get back to normal. Whatever that is," she said with a rueful laugh. She was glad that Phoebe was too far away to hear and that the dock was otherwise unoccupied, because this was a private conversation.

"We'll miss you in Greensea Springs," Dee said. "Are you going to come over before you leave?"

"I don't know, Dee," Molly said, troubled. "It might make it even harder on Phoebe."

"I could bring the kids over to the marina in the morning. We could wave you off."

"That would work. Say, stop by for breakfast. It might be cereal for the kids and frozen bagels for the adults, but at least we'd have a chance to say goodbye."

"Invitation accepted," Dee said. She sighed. "I hate to see you leave, Molly. I was hoping to recruit you to help me sew puppet costumes. Selena even mentioned that you'd be a good addition to the puppet theater's board of directors."

"I'll miss you and your family and Selena and the Blossom Cabaret crowd and—well, all of it," Molly said. "But listen to this, Dee. I have an idea of how to help the puppet theater in a very important way. Do you have a minute?"

"I have an hour, if you need it. Tell, tell."

Molly, knowing that she had come up with a fitting memorial for Emmett, began to outline her plan.

ERIC WAS TAKING A BREAK from the hot midday sun when Phoebe showed up on *Fiona*.

"Hi, Dad," she shouted as she jumped down off the deck into the cockpit. She started down the ladder.

Eric looked up from the navigational charts that he'd spread across the table in the chart room and watched his daughter as she appeared, feet first, red plaid shorts and matching shirt next, then the rest of her.

"Hi there, cutie. I thought you and Molly were going to be doing something this morning," he said.

Phoebe heaved a sigh. "We fed the ducks all the old bread, or at least I did. Mommy—I mean Molly—is talking on the phone with Mrs. Farrell."

When Eric glanced out the chart room porthole and saw Molly sitting on a bench the next dock over, looking engrossed in her conversation. That Phoebe had slipped and called her "Mommy" hadn't escaped his notice.

"Phoebe," he began patiently, then noticed that his daughter was pouting. The strain of having to leave Greensea Springs was written on her face.

"Would you like me to make lunch?" she asked, which diverted him from the lecture he needed to give her.

"I didn't know you could," he said.

"Molly taught me how," she said, brightening. "I only know how to do peanut butter sandwiches, but they're my favorite."

They definitely weren't Eric's, but that was okay. "I'd like that," he said.

Phoebe went into the galley and started to assemble peanut butter, jelly and bread. He studied her silently as she worked, marveling at how efficiently she went about the job. Even though the counter was too high for her, she managed to spread the peanut butter and jelly on the bread without making much of a mess.

"I'm going to leave the sandwiches whole because Molly doesn't like me to cut them. She says the knives we have are all too sharp."

"I'll see if I can find one you can use when we get to Fort Lauderdale," he said.

Carefully Phoebe transferred the sandwiches from the cutting board to small plates, and carried one to him where he was working. "Here," she said. "I know you're busy figuring out the boat channels and stuff." Phoebe, veteran of many voyages, understood the drill.

"Got a kiss for your dear old dad?" he asked, pulling her close.

She pecked him on the cheek. "Can I turn on the TV?"

"Sure, it won't bother me."

She brought him a bottle of juice and he twisted off the cap for her. She dug around in a drawer until she found a drinking straw, and then she climbed on the lounge and began to eat her lunch.

He munched on his sandwich, thinking that it tasted pretty good. In the salon, the TV switched on, and he heard some inane advertisement for hair products.

Over the noise of the commercial, he also heard Phoebe making a wish. She kept her voice low, but when he figured out what she was saying, he put down his sandwich and listened.

"This is my last sand wish here in Greensea Springs," she said. "Please, please, *please,* like I've asked so many times before, could Molly be my new mommy? There's not much time left. We'll be in Fort Lauderdale soon, and you know what *that* means. So *please* could I have my wish?" The urgency in her tone was heart-wrenching, even desperate.

Shaken to the core, Eric half stood and started to go to her, then changed his mind and fell back onto the seat. Is *that* what Phoebe had been wishing for? For Molly to be her mother?

He was familiar with Phoebe's sand wishes for a new house and a real vacuum cleaner and to have Cookie back. He had heard her make those requests innumerable times and had pegged them as harmless. The sand wish thing was a little unusual, perhaps. The things she asked for were, well, touching. But this mommy wish of hers was something he hadn't heard before.

Suddenly things added up, made sense. He realized that Phoebe had been subtly and not so subtly paving the way for him to fall in love with Molly from the moment she'd arrived on *Fiona.* Since Phoebe was his daughter, and only seven years old besides, he hadn't credited her with being so manipulative.

Of course he'd played right into her fantasy. He'd done exactly what Phoebe had wanted—he'd fallen in love. The difference between him and Phoebe was that he had always known the risks. He'd made a big mistake in letting his daughter think that there was any possibility that Molly Kate McBryde could remain part of their lives.

He pushed the plate with the sandwich aside and massaged his eyes wearily. In the salon, Phoebe clicked the channel to a kids' cartoon network. She would be eating her sandwich, drinking her juice.

As for him, he wasn't hungry anymore. In his heart, he'd realized all along how this relationship would end, though he'd been reluctant to admit it. As Molly had said once, things didn't always turn out all right, they simply turned out, and it was up to them to make the best of it. He'd deal with losing her somehow. He was an adult and would get over her, eventually.

For Phoebe, however, who had been forced through no fault of her own to say goodbye to so many people and places she loved, it would be a lot harder than it was for him. He should have taken drastic measures to make sure that Phoebe hadn't grown to care about Molly as much as he did. He lowered his head to his hands.

MOLLY CAME BACK from saying goodbye to Micki that afternoon and found Eric in the cockpit, making a list of last-minute supplies to buy for the boat. Phoebe was sitting quietly beside him, writing.

"We need sugar and coffee, maybe some canned goods," Eric told her as he tucked the list in his pocket. He looked tired and out of sorts, probably due to his working on deck in the hot sun.

"I didn't think about stocking up," Molly told him. "I could have shopped earlier, while you were still working here."

He smiled thinly, and she thought he was more pale than usual under his tan. He also seemed more distracted, but that was to be expected. Sailing *Fiona* to Fort Lauderdale was a big responsibility.

"I don't expect you to worry about things like that," he said. "You're still mourning."

"I'm feeling better now that I'm focusing on positive things," she said. "I want to memorialize Grandpa in a special way, one that will take into account his enthusiasms and bring pleasure to others. Would you like to know what I have in mind?"

His eyes took on a bit of their old sparkle, and he sat down on the cockpit bench opposite her. "I certainly would," he said.

"I'm going to donate a large amount of money to the art center's puppet theater in Grandpa's memory," she announced.

Phoebe, who sat quietly beside her composing another message for a bottle, looked up with wide eyes.

"What a great idea," Eric said.

"He'd love it. I'll set the money aside in a trust, and it will pay for supplies and training and anything else they need. Selena and Dee will be co-chairs of the board governing how the money is spent, and I'll visit every once in a while to take in a puppet show or two."

"Molly, that's impressive. Emmett would be so proud of you."

"I hope so. My grandfather wouldn't have liked to see me crying, and I'm going to make sure something good will come out of my grief."

He stood, and for a moment she thought he might say something else. Then his eyes flicked in the direction of Phoebe, and he drew himself up, seemed to have made a decision about something.

Molly gazed at him inquiringly, but all he said was "I'd better be on my way. How are we fixed for dinner?"

"I'm cooking," Molly said. "It'll be something special to commemorate our last night in Greensea Springs."

"I'll bet it's that asparagus casserole," Phoebe chimed in. "Corduroy says he hates it."

"You can have the ravioli," Molly told her. "Remember how you said that's what you'd like?"

"Asparagus sounds good to me," Eric replied.

Phoebe stopped writing. "Do you think I'll ever see Corduroy and Lexie again, Dad?"

"I hope so, Peanut. You never know."

Phoebe's eyebrows knotted in a scowl. "That's what he always says when the answer is no," she told Molly. When she began to write her bottle message again, she bore down so hard on the pencil that the lead broke. She stared at it in dismay. "I hate when that happens," she said. "Now I've got to sharpen it."

"Don't make a mistake and stick your little finger in the pencil sharpener," Eric said, but this time Phoebe didn't smile, only shot him a murderous look and disappeared down the companionway.

For a moment, Eric fidgeted as if he were at loose ends. "I guess she isn't too happy," he said finally.

Molly touched his hand briefly in a rush of sympathy, but he seemed aloof and cool, his mind on other things.

"I'd better go," he said, starting to walk up the dock.

Molly noticed then that the sun had slipped below the western horizon and the sky was darkening. "Let's take the cushions on deck and watch the stars pop out after you finish writing your message," she called down to Phoebe.

"Let's do it now," Phoebe called back. "I can finish my message later."

Molly dragged the cushions onto the deck, and Phoebe joined her. This time she snuggled right up to Molly, and Molly wrapped her arms around her, inhaling the sweet little-girl smell of no-tears shampoo and bubble gum.

"I'm going to miss Greensea Springs an awful lot," Phoebe said with a slight catch in her voice.

"I know, Phoebe. I will, too."

"Are Lexie and Corduroy and Jada and Mr. and Mrs. Farrell all really coming to say goodbye tomorrow?"

"They're going to eat breakfast with us," Molly assured her.

"We're leaving so early. Are you sure they'll get here in time?"

"Positive," Molly said.

Phoebe didn't reply. She only sighed deeply.

After a while, she spoke. "You want to hear what my dad said one other time when we moved? That even though I have to leave the people I love, my mommy's star goes with me everywhere. He's right. There's Mommy's star right there," Phoebe said, pointing toward Vega. "Does your mom have a star, too?"

Molly blinked back her own tears. "I suppose so," she said.

"Was she pretty, Molly? As pretty as you?"

"Prettier," Molly said. Her memories of her mother involved brown eyes flashing with merriment at the pranks of her three children and the light, citrus-scented cologne she always wore. To this day, when Molly got a whiff of that scent on an elevator or in a restaurant, she was instantly transported back to her childhood.

"I bet that's her star, right over there above *Miss Take*," Phoebe said.

"Maybe it is," Molly agreed. She hugged Phoebe closer.

"And your grandfather must have a star, right? Which one is it, do you think?"

By now, all the stars had appeared, gleaming against the velvety background of the sky in an incandescent display. Molly selected a bright one hovering over the tall gables of the Plumosa Hotel. "That would be Grandpa Emmett," she said. "He's shining down on the puppet theater that will bear his name."

"Oooh, Molly, you're going to name it after him?"

"The board of directors will probably vote to call it the Emmett McBryde Puppet Theater."

"Mr. Emmett would like that," said Phoebe. "He was a nice man."

"Yes, he was," Molly said. She'd look up the name of that star later, and when Patrick and Brianne joined her in Fort Lauderdale, she'd share this story with them.

"You know what I think, Molly? That babies who aren't born yet have their own star up there, maybe a little tiny one."

"What makes you say that?"

"It's because I'm sure there's a brother or sister for me somewhere," Phoebe said contemplatively, settling more securely into the curve of Molly's embrace. "That's where I think they'd want to be."

Through a blur of tears, Molly gazed up into the heavens, wondering if any of the smaller stars were her unborn children: her son, Nicholas; or her daughter, Emma. Of course, she'd never wanted any kids before, but that was before this sojourn on *Fiona*.

If she were ever lucky enough to have children, Molly would want them to be just like Phoebe.

Chapter Fifteen

Eric drove the marina van to the mall and bought Phoebe a box of pastel crayons and a bathrobe she had admired on their shopping trip. The presents wouldn't compensate for their leaving Greensea Springs, but he wanted to do something to make things easier for her. Then he called his friend Steve in Thunderbolt, Georgia.

"Eric," Steve boomed in his hearty voice. "We haven't heard from you for a while. Joyce and I have been wondering when we can expect a visit from you and that sweet little girl of yours."

"You've still got that camper trailer where you said we could live for a while? And the job on your fishing boat is available?"

"Correct on both counts. When can you get here?"

"I can probably be there sooner than you think," Eric said. Then he proceeded to explain what he had in mind.

IT WAS ALMOST NINE O'CLOCK before Eric returned to *Fiona*. Phoebe was asleep in her bunk, breathing softly. He dropped the packages with the pastel crayons and bathrobe at the foot of the bed and went back to the galley, where Molly was removing a pan containing twice-baked potatoes from the oven.

"I didn't know you were waiting dinner for me," he told her. "I thought you and Phoebe would have eaten by this time."

"You took a little longer than we expected," Molly said. "Phoebe went to sleep about half an hour ago after she polished off a can of ravioli." She started toward him as if she might kiss him on the cheek, but he sidestepped her and pretended to inspect the salads, which she had arrayed artistically on two individual plates.

"You must be hungry," Molly said. She seemed upbeat, cheerful, and he was swept with guilt for what he was about to do.

"We need to talk," he said heavily.

Her smile faltered, and a succession of conflicting emotions flitted across her face. "Sure," she said, easing down on the lounge beside the table.

She sat staring up at him, and the tensing of her shoulders indicated that she sensed the importance of what was about to be said.

"I've been thinking, Molly," he said, keeping his voice low so that he wouldn't wake Phoebe. "This isn't working between us." He sat beside her, focusing his eyes on her lovely face. He didn't like being the bearer of more bad news; she'd had enough for any one person in the past couple of days. But he couldn't wait to tell her this because, in his view, more harm would be done by putting it off than by making a clean break.

She paled, but her gaze didn't waver. "I thought it was working quite well," she said levelly.

He shook his head. "You need to find another captain to get *Fiona* to Fort Lauderdale. I'm off the job as of tomorrow morning. I can give you the name and phone number of someone who can take you the rest of the way. It's someone I met at the Farrells' party. He's well qualified."

Molly's face flushed and she stared at him incredulously. "What's wrong, Eric?"

"I shouldn't have stayed this long," he said doggedly. "I should have left as soon as we got to Greensea Springs, found someone else to install the fuel injection pump."

"I don't understand why you're saying this," Molly said in

disbelief. "I don't want another captain, and the past few weeks have been the best time of my life."

Her bewilderment seemed to be turning into anger, but then, that shouldn't be a surprise. How could he expect her to take this news without putting up a fight?

"Maybe we should go up on deck to finish this discussion," Eric said, glancing toward the closed door of Phoebe's state-room, where he had heard a rustle of the bedcovers.

"Fine," Molly said through gritted teeth. She climbed up the ladder and charged through the cockpit, then made her way to the aft deck. He followed, realizing that though they hadn't had much privacy below, there was even less here. A party boat trolled past in the distance, its occupants talking loud enough to be heard over raucous music. A dog walker strolled two docks over, his poodle prancing along in front of him.

"I can't believe you'd do this, Eric," Molly said. "I thought we had a relationship. I—"

"Molly," he said placatingly. "This is for your own good. Of course we've had a relationship. You're a wonderful per-son, and you've done so much for Phoebe. I'm grateful, and I always will be."

Her chin shot up. "Abandoning ship right now isn't the way to show how you appreciate me," she pointed out. "I care about you and Phoebe. I doubt if you understand how much."

"Maybe I do," he said softly. "Maybe I don't think it's a good idea."

"'Good idea'? What does that mean, Eric?"

"I'm crazy about you, Molly Kate McBryde, but I have nothing to offer you. You called me a boat bum in one of your angrier moments, and I deserved that. I have no job, no home, nothing but myself and a seven-year-old girl who unfortu-nately got her hopes up much too high."

Molly tossed her windblown hair back off her face, "Please don't run yourself down. You're intelligent, and good at what you do, and Phoebe is a big plus to our relationship. When I called you a boat bum, I didn't mean that you're not a fine person. I wanted to bring you to your senses about Phoebe's needs. Let's cut to the real topic here. Have I done something to anger you?"

He was nonplussed. "Of course not," he said.

"You're breaking off with me because you think you're not good enough?"

"I don't deserve you, Molly. You're beautiful, talented, fun and smart. You could find someone who has as much money as you do, who can buy you the kind of house where you'd feel comfortable."

"This is about *money?*" Her tone had taken on a tone of disbelief.

"You've inherited a bundle. Emmett spoke to me of his bequests to you and your brother and sister. I'm not a rich man, Molly. Sometimes I don't know where I'm going to get my next dime. I have a little nest egg for Phoebe, but that's all. We're not in the same league, and I've realized it from the start."

Molly sank onto one of the chairs where they sometimes sat under the stars at night. When she spoke, she invested her words with heavy irony. "I was going to tell you tonight that I'm in love with you. If, in this age of disposable relationships, that makes any difference."

Words left him, and he felt as if she'd socked him in the stomach. Out of the corner of his eye he became aware of a blur of movement. *Phoebe,* he thought. She had probably already heard more than he would have liked. She was edging along the railing toward the bow, intent on her task, and while he caught his breath, tried to figure out what to say, he heard a soft splash. She was tossing one of her messages in a bottle overboard; he waited until she went back down below to speak.

"I'm sorry, Molly. I shouldn't have let it go this far," he said.

"'This far'?"

"Phoebe has been making sand wishes that you'd be her new mom. I should have realized, should have put a stop to such nonsense."

"So your daughter's wishes are as meaningless as our relationship?" Her eyes had gone stony and dark.

He cleared his throat, wishing he were anywhere but here and doing anything but this. He couldn't lie to her, tell her he didn't love her. He knew now that he had loved Molly Kate McBryde almost from the first moment he set eyes on her, when she had ordered him about and looked down her nose at him. She had changed his perspective, brought him out of his grief, made him hopeful about his future.

"Leave Phoebe out of this for the moment, okay? I care about you deeply, Molly. I want only the best for you." *And that's not me,* he would have liked to add, but he didn't. In that moment he wished with all his heart that it didn't have to be like this. "Actually," he said, his voice sounding to him as if it came from a great distance away, "I've already made plans. Phoebe and I will be leaving tomorrow for Thunderbolt, Georgia."

"Georgia? Why?"

"A friend has offered me a job on his shrimp trawler."

"Oh."

"Believe me, it's better this way." Though, as he spoke the words and drank in her beauty, he doubted that this way was better after all.

She treated him to a long, hard, blistering stare. "Better than for the two of us to be together? Oh, I don't think so. Better than for Phoebe to have her mommy wish? Again, I don't think so."

Tears shimmered in her eyes, and he felt like a jerk for doing this to her. Against his better judgment, he reached for her, but she pushed past him.

"I'll save you the trouble of leaving, Eric. I'll catch a plane back to Chicago tonight. Patrick and Brianne and I can meet here and sail *Fiona* to Fort Lauderdale ourselves."

Then she was down the ladder and all he could do was stare after her. He didn't know what he had expected, but it was not this. He'd never considered that Molly might leave *Fiona.* He scrambled down the ladder after her, knocking his shin against one of the supporting columns in the salon. She had marched straight into her stateroom and slammed the door behind her, and he heard her opening and closing drawers, dragging her duffel out of the closet.

"Molly!" he said, limping across the salon and pounding on her door. "Molly? You don't need to go anywhere tonight. How will you get to the Jacksonville airport? What makes you think you can get on the next flight? Stay, Molly. You don't want to sit up all night in an airport waiting room."

"Go away," she shouted. "I don't want to talk to you ever again."

"Molly?"

A weight slammed against the door, and he winced. She'd thrown something. He listened for the sound of Phoebe waking up in her own room, but all was quiet. Nevertheless, he lowered his voice.

"Molly!"

She didn't reply, and he stood there breathing heavily until the door flew open. Her hair was a red-gold aureole. She'd pulled on a jacket and was lugging her harp case.

"Get out of my way," she said.

Without speaking, he stood to one side. She barged past him and up the ladder, tossing her harp into the cockpit. When she came back, she glared as she brushed past him and grabbed her duffel.

"Can't you be reasonable?" he asked with exasperation. "Can't you at least stay overnight?"

"No," she said. Her face softened as she drew even with the door to Phoebe's stateroom. "If—if I may, I'd like to look in on Phoebe. I won't wake her."

"Go ahead," Eric said, his heart aching. How he would explain Molly's sudden leavetaking to his daughter was unclear, and he knew he wouldn't do a good job of it.

Molly opened the door quietly, and he expected the light from the overhead lamps to fall upon Phoebe sound asleep, her face pillowed on her hands, her Barbie and Blaine dolls settled beside her on the pillow.

Phoebe's bunk was empty. Her dolls weren't anywhere in sight, and her backpack was missing. The pastel crayons and the bathrobe he had bought her were still at the foot of the bunk, but she was gone.

WHEN MOLLY DISCOVERED that Phoebe was missing, all thoughts of fleeing evaporated.

"We'll search the boat," Eric said immediately, and even though she was furious with him, she warmed to the way he took charge.

"I'm sure she's not in my stateroom, but I'll check the shower and closet," she said, moving swiftly. While she did that, Eric disappeared into his room and emerged almost immediately.

"She's not there," he said.

"Could she have fallen overboard?" she asked.

"We'd better have a look," Eric said, anguish visible on his face. "I saw her throwing her bottle message off the bow during the first few minutes of our discussion up there, but I know for certain that she went back below. I didn't see her leave again."

"I didn't, either," Molly said. The words between them had flown furiously at some points, and she'd assumed that Phoebe was asleep in her bunk.

On deck, they shone lights down upon the dark water surrounding the boat, but they saw no sign of Phoebe. A damp mist was rolling in from the ocean, and Molly went below to get her windbreaker. When she returned to the deck, she spotted a bit of fabric fluttering in the breeze halfway down the dock and jumped off the boat to check it out. It turned out to be one of Phoebe's headbands, and she held it up so Eric could see.

"Phoebe had this on when she went to bed," she said, returning to the boat.

A quick inventory of Phoebe's belongings told them that she must be wearing the same red shirt and plaid shorts that she'd had on all day.

"I believe she left *Fiona*, Eric."

"But why?"

"Maybe she heard us arguing," Molly said. Anxiety twisted in her stomach, burned behind her eyes.

"Where would she go?"

"To say goodbye to the Farrell family?" Molly suggested hesitantly. "I don't think she was convinced that they would be here early enough in the morning."

"I'll call them right away," Eric said.

Molly silently handed him her cell phone and he punched in the number.

Dee and Craig were getting ready for bed, and they expressed surprise and then concern that Phoebe was missing. "She hasn't turned up here," Craig said before insisting on joining the search.

Adrenaline kicked in, mobilizing them into action. While Eric checked the marina's laundry room and the small lounge housing the book exchange, Molly hurried to Micki's boat to see if Phoebe was there. She wasn't, and Micki suggested that they both go see if the child was visiting with Lainie Kallbeck and Jody. As they were rousing Lainie from bed, they managed to waken several other occupants of the marina, and soon an uneasy search party had assembled on the dock beside *Fiona*.

"We'll fan out through the whole marina," Micki said quickly. "Check all the little nooks and crannies. If she's here, we'll find her."

"What if she fell in the water?" asked Lainie, looking alarmed.

"Phoebe is an excellent swimmer. We've spent so much time around water that I made sure she learned. Besides, Molly and I would have heard a splash. No, she walked off the boat," Eric said.

"She was upset about leaving Greensea Springs," Molly told the assembled group. "I'm sure her disappearance has something to do with that." She tried not to focus on all the dangers that could befall a seven-year-old child.

They spread out over the marina, stopping at each slip to ask if anyone had seen Phoebe. One man who had been on the deck of his cabin cruiser unjamming a reluctant hatch mentioned that he'd spotted a child wearing a backpack walking with determination toward the marina office shortly after nine o'clock; he'd considered it strange, but since the laundry facility was open until midnight, he thought that she was going there to meet her mom or dad.

When Phoebe didn't turn up, Eric grimly decided that it was time to call in the police. Sergeant Raul Blanco, his hair bristling around his head in an overgrown brush cut, showed up at the marina office. Molly and Eric, both struggling to quell their fears on Phoebe's behalf, talked with him under the cold fluorescent lights in the marina office while he took copious notes. He said he'd notify all the local officers as well as the state clearinghouse for missing children. All this sounded ominous to Molly, and Eric looked beside himself.

As they talked, the sergeant received a phone call from a police officer who had been strolling his beat on Water Street. He had stopped to help a motorist with a flat tire on his SUV, and the man said that he'd noticed a small girl traversing the playground behind the Plumosa Hotel Arts Center while he was pulling his spare tire out of the back of his vehicle. He'd thought about calling someone to report it, but when he turned around again, she was gone.

Eric became even more agitated at this news, and he began to question Sergeant Blanco extensively. "Can you be sure that this man's not involved in Phoebe's disappearance?" he demanded. "Did you check him for any violations?"

The sergeant shook his head emphatically. "I know him personally. He lives on my street. In fact, his wife and baby were with him in the car, and they were driving home from a church function. No, I'm positive he couldn't have anything to do with Phoebe's disappearance. I think she's wandered off."

Eric walked outside abruptly and went to the dock railing. Moonlight touched his hair with silver and cast his profile in stark relief. Molly's first instinct was to go to him, but Sergeant Blanco had more questions for her.

"Now, Ms. McBryde, suppose you tell me what Phoebe was wearing when she disappeared."

Molly, feeling increasingly bereft, haltingly described the red T-shirt and plaid shorts that were missing from Phoebe's room. In her hands she held the headband that Phoebe had dropped on the dock.

"Thanks, Ms. McBryde," Blanco said, snapping his notebook closed. "Don't worry, we'll do our best to find her. Greensea Springs is a safe place. We have a low crime rate. I have a feeling that Phoebe will turn up soon."

"I hope so," Molly said fervently. A glance out the window told her that Eric was no longer standing at the railing, and she excused herself to find out what he was doing.

The wind had picked up, and Micki, Craig Farrell and some of the others who had aided in their earlier search of the marina huddled in a knot outside the laundry room. "Any luck?" Micki asked.

Molly shook her head and wrapped her windbreaker more closely around her. "Did any of you see where Eric went?"

"He jumped off the dock, started walking along the beach," Craig told her.

In the bright moonlight, Molly spied Eric making his way along the narrow apron of sand exposed by low tide. He scuffed at debris, his head down and his shoulders slumped. He seemed walled inside his own pain, beaten down by worry.

As she watched, he bent and scooped something up from the ground. He stared at it, held it up to the light. Though the wind was not cold, a chill swept through her and clamped icy fingers around her heart.

"Eric," she called. "What are you doing?"

"Come here," he said. He sounded shaken.

It was only a short jump over the edge of the dock to the earth below. Wind-driven sand stung her face as she made her way toward Eric. She prayed that whatever he had found would lead them to Phoebe.

When she drew closer, she saw that Eric was twisting the cap off a plastic soda bottle. He shook out a piece of paper rolled into a tight cylinder and unfurled it. "One of Phoebe's messages," he said.

As he held the sheet of lined notebook paper out to her, she saw that it bore that day's date.

Phoebe had drawn a picture of a house with three people standing in front of it; one of them was Eric, identifiable because he was taller than all the rest, with a gray baseball cap on his head. It was easy to figure out that the woman with the red hair was Molly, and Phoebe was most certainly the child in the picture, because she wore a red headband and her favorite red plaid shorts. There was even a black-and-white spotted dog, whose leash the girl held in her fist. Cookie, thought Molly. And the house, drawn in some detail with a red door and a chimney, was undoubtedly the home that Phoebe wanted so much.

"Read it," Eric said unsteadily, his voice raw with emotion.

DEAR PERSON,
HERE IS A PICTUR OF THE HOUSE I WANT. THAT'S DAD AND MOLLY AND ME IN FRONT. I GOT MY DOG COOKIE BACK. MY LIFE WILL BE WUNDER-FULL AT LAST.

Then there was a long space, and a watery splotch that had almost obliterated the next words, though Molly could still read them.

THEY ARE ~~FITTING~~ FITING. OH IT IS AAWFUL. IN-STEAD OF SAYING THEY LUV EACH OTHER THEY ARE BRAKING UP. ALL MY SAND WISHES DID NOT WORK. I HATE THEM. I NEVER WANT TO SEE THEM AGAIN. I AM GOING AWAY. AT THE CONTEST I WILL FIND SOME ONE ELSE AND LIVE WITH THEM.
I DON'T NO WHEN I WILL SEND MY NEXT MES-SAGE. MAYBE NEVER.
YORE FRIEND
PHOEBE ANNE NORVALD

"What contest?" Eric asked, looking dumbfounded.

Molly remembered Phoebe's avid interest in the vacuum cleaner competition and related as much about it as she could recall. "It's in Jacksonville this weekend," she told him.

"A vacuum cleaner competition?" he said as if he couldn't believe it. "She's never mentioned it."

"She's well aware that you don't approve of her interest in vacuum cleaners," Molly reminded him.

"Where would she go if she were trying to get to Jacksonville? The bus station? The highway out of town?"

Molly considered this as she gazed out across the marina. The wind had whipped the surface of the water into a light chop. The boats rocked restlessly, tugging at their lines. She turned back to Eric. "I think she'd ask Ralph Whister for a ride. He said he was going, and he was looking forward to it. He said—"

"Never mind what he said. Where does he live?"

"I have no idea. I'm sure Phoebe doesn't, either. She'd know that he'd be opening up his shop in the morning, and it's near the playground."

"Let's go," Eric said urgently, grabbing her hand. He jumped up on the seawall, pulled her after him. The next moment, they were racing down Water Street, past parked cars, past the moss-hung trees, past the quaint wrought-iron benches lining the sidewalks.

Eric's hand in hers felt warm, and Molly was heartened that they were united in this task of finding Phoebe. After the harsh words they'd exchanged earlier, it seemed strange and yet so right to be working as a team. She should have been out of here by now, out of his life and Phoebe's, too. But as long as Eric's daughter was in jeopardy, Molly knew with great certainty that her place was beside him.

The sign outside A Perfect Vacuum swung gently in the breeze. "We should call Ralph Whister, ask him to come open his shop," Molly said as they halted in front of the big plate-glass windows. She pulled her phone out of her pocket and prepared to dial the emergency number posted on the front door.

Eric stared through the window. It was illuminated by the streetlights so that the sparkle finish on the shiny Orvasweep vacuum glinted invitingly; in the window on the other side of the door, the Robo-Kleen robotic vacuum went about its endless cleaning duties.

"Look," he said, pointing at what appeared to be a bundle of clothes next to the case of Orvasweep attachments.

Molly stepped closer and saw that Phoebe was curled up beside the vacuum cleaner, her head pillowed on her backpack, her Barbie and Blaine dolls propped nearby. Her chest rose and fell gently with each breath, and though her face was tearstained, she seemed peaceful and so innocent. Best of all, she was safe.

Relief washed over Molly, and she gripped Eric's arm. He tapped on the window, and Phoebe opened her eyes. Dazed confusion was followed by relieved recognition when she found herself staring back at her father and Molly. She raised her tousled head.

"Dad," she said in a tone of wonder. "Molly. You came for me."

Even though the words were muted by the window between them, they tugged at Molly's heart. If she had left before they discovered that Phoebe was missing, she never would have seen her again, and right now that seemed unbearable. Somewhere between the hairstyling lessons and manicures, the bedtime stories and peanut butter sandwiches, Molly had grown to love Phoebe as if she were her own.

Slowly Eric raised his outspread fingers and pressed his hand against the glass, and Molly, following his lead, did the same. Phoebe knelt on the other side of the window, her gaze never wavering from them, and held her two smaller hands up to theirs. The three of them were connected like that when Ralph Whister arrived with the keys.

Chapter Sixteen

Eric lay flat on *Fiona*'s foredeck, lost in the twinkling benevolence of the star that he had long ago designated as Heather's. Tonight it shone with a special radiance, like a diamond affixed to the fabric of the sky.

He had carried Phoebe home from the vacuum cleaner shop where she'd sought refuge, her sleepy head nodding against his shoulder. Now Molly was below, putting her to bed.

He sighed and adjusted his position; the deck was hard beneath his back. He hadn't bothered with the cushions, thinking that he wouldn't stay up here long. But he would do nothing to interrupt Phoebe's time with Molly, since it seemed so important to her. And to Molly, too, of course. She had shed tears of joy when they'd found Phoebe, and she'd held his daughter's hand tightly on the short walk back to the boat.

Phoebe had apparently crawled into Ralph Whister's shop through a pet door at the service entrance in the back. It had been left unsecured for some reason, even though the dog that once used it no longer accompanied his master to work. Since the vacuum cleaner competition in Jacksonville was coming up over the weekend, Phoebe had intended to talk her friend into taking her along. She'd headed for her favorite vacuum cleaner, the Robo-Kleen in the window, and sat watching it at work until she felt sleepy. Then she'd climbed in the neighboring window and curled up beside the Orvasweep to go to sleep. Phoebe had never been in any danger, Eric was convinced of that.

He heard a quiet footstep on deck and turned his head to see Molly walking carefully toward him, holding on to the railing. She eased down beside him and clasped her hands around her knees.

"Phoebe's asleep," she said. "She's exhausted."

Molly's hair, teased by the wind, fell over one shoulder, a tumbling cascade of color. He reached for her hand, prepared for her to pull it away, but she didn't.

"You were wonderful with her," he said. "You comforted her when she started to get upset that you might leave before she woke up tomorrow, and you settled her down with a glass of milk before she had a chance to bring up our argument."

"I didn't do much. I feel so guilty that she ran away because of the things I said."

"That *we* said," Eric corrected her. "We never intended her to hear us."

Molly didn't speak, only stared resolutely toward Bottlenose Island.

"Molly?"

"You've got Phoebe back. I'm going to bed."

"Wait," he said, turning on his side so that he could see her expression. She looked beautiful and determined and sad.

She skewered him with a glance. Her eyebrows lifted slightly as if she were asking a question, and he recalled a time when that expression had seemed imperious, demanding.

"I'm numb, Eric. I don't have the emotional reserves to handle any more tonight."

He was all too aware of the many ups and downs of the past week. Her grief over Emmett, her dashed hopes about their relationship and Phoebe's disappearance had all contributed to emotional overload. "Please stay here awhile," he said. He reached up and slid his hand under her hair, brought her lips in line with his. He kissed her, an exploratory kiss, and when she didn't pull away, he deepened it.

She was the one to end the kiss, but not immediately. The scent of her skin filled his nostrils, a heady perfume. Her hair was soft against his cheek.

"We shouldn't be doing this, Eric," she said, her voice a mere whisper.

"Who says?" he whispered back. He kissed her again, more intensely this time.

"Maybe it's not only Phoebe I want back. Maybe I want you, too," he told her when they broke away.

"You can't get back something that wasn't yours to begin with," she said with unexpected spirit.

"Oh, but you were always mine. I knew it in my heart from the moment I saw you."

"Eric, don't say things you don't mean."

"I never do," he said. "In fact, I'm going to say something momentous in a few seconds." He sat up and took her into his arms. He was surprised to find that she was trembling.

"Dearest Molly, I love you. I never want us to be apart. I've been wrong about us, just as I've been wrong about a few other things in my life. Luckily for me, I've had an epiphany of sorts, and it was brought about by my daughter's disappearance. I panicked when I thought I might lose her, and it made me realize how important both of you are to me. I couldn't live without Phoebe, and I can't live without you, either." He paused to catch his breath, noticed Heather's star.

"See that star up there? Heather's star? I've been lying here on deck, trying to figure out what to do, and while I was staring at it, it seemed to twinkle a bit brighter. Some people might believe that's because of conditions in the earth's atmosphere or because the moon isn't as bright as on some nights, but I believe it's Heather telling me that I've found the right woman for me."

"I don't think—"

He gently placed a finger to her lips. "Stop, Molly. Just say yes. Will you marry me? Be my wife forever and ever? Be Phoebe's new mommy?"

She studied him as if he'd lost his mind. When she finally

found her voice, she stammered, "D-didn't we have a big discussion about this very topic? Where you told me that you couldn't offer me anything? Where you ran yourself down and I got angry because I can't stand for you to undervalue yourself when you're one of the finest, most intelligent, loving men I've ever known?"

He managed a sheepish grin. "Well, I guess we did have quite an argument, but I've reconsidered. Without you, the freedom to wander becomes a prison. I still don't have many material possessions to offer you, Molly, but I can give you the most important thing of all. Love, Molly. I love you more than you'll ever know, and it will last a lifetime."

He had a few moments' concern when she looked up at the heavens, at the water rolling by, at the flag billowing on the cabin cruiser across the way.

"Eric," she said with great deliberation, "I do love you. I told you that earlier tonight, and you broke my heart when you said you wanted to end it between us. There were so many things I wanted to say to you, but you never gave me a chance. I accept you as you are, Eric—as a kind, loving man who chose an unconventional way of dealing with the problem that fate dished out to him. I don't fault you for that. If you and Phoebe hadn't been on *Fiona*, I wouldn't have met you, and my life is so much richer and more meaningful with the two of you in it. I love you and I love Phoebe, and in answer to your marriage proposal, my answer is…yes. Yes, yes, *yes!*" She shouted the last word so loudly that everyone in the marina could have heard.

Eric began to laugh, starting with a long chuckle. He leaped to his feet and pulled Molly along with him. "I'll find some way to earn a decent living, Molly, I won't disappoint you," he said. Their joy burst into an impromptu waltz along the length of the foredeck. They danced to music only they could hear, sidestepping cleats and piles of rope and the open hatches that provided ventilation below.

One of the hatches creaked open even more, and a small head popped out. "Dad?" said Phoebe in a voice fuzzy with sleep. "Are you and Molly fighting again?"

Holding Molly's hand, Eric knelt beside his daughter. "Absolutely not, Peanut. This is what people in love sound like when they're making up. I've just asked her to marry me."

Phoebe's eyes grew wide. She blinked at Molly. "Did you say yes?" All the awe and concern she must have felt were contained in those short words.

"I certainly did," Molly told her.

"Wow. Oh, *wow,*" Phoebe said. She looked from one to the other, a wide smile spreading across her face. "I can't believe it."

"Come up here with us, Phoebe. We're going to have a family celebration." Eric reached down and eased her up through the open hatch, then settled back on the deck with her in his lap.

"What do you do for a celebration like this one?" Phoebe asked, wide-awake now.

"I'm not exactly sure," Eric said, smoothing her nightgown. He winked over the top of her head at Molly. "Before we find out, I have a story I want to tell."

Phoebe perked up at that. "A story? What kind?"

"It's something like the Greek myths and the Egyptian ones. In fact, you might call the story a Norvald myth, except that it's true," he said, improvising as he went along.

"Tell it, Dad."

"Well, once upon a time, there was a true goddess, and her name was Molly Kate McBryde. She had long and beautiful hair in a color that looked as if gold and copper had been melted together."

Phoebe wriggled delightedly. "Eric," Molly began, laughter in her voice, but he silenced her with a wink.

"The beautiful goddess Molly Kate lived in a cold, hard land called Chicago. Sometimes she was lonely and gazed up at the stars from her window, thinking about how much fun it would be to ride away on the flying horse Pegasus to play her harp. Unfortunately, she had other duties, and this was never possible. One day, she escaped from Chicago due to the kindness of a sage old man named Emmett. She got on a big silver bird and traveled to a faraway place where she boarded a magic boat. There she met an angel named Phoebe and a man called Mr. Grumpy."

Phoebe darted a surprised look up at him. "You know about that name?" she asked with trepidation.

"Yes, but it's okay," he said. When Phoebe relaxed, he went on spinning his tale, enjoying the telling of it. "Mr. Grumpy was lonely, but he loved the angel Phoebe, who was his daughter. Together they went on many travels. Sometimes Mr. Grumpy felt as though he carried the whole world on his shoulders, and—"

"That wasn't Mr. Grumpy's job," Phoebe interjected. "Nut, the enormous naked blue giant woman, was supposed to do that, like in the Egyptian myth."

"Sometimes Mr. Grumpy forgot that the world wasn't his responsibility. Lots of times, the world became too heavy for Mr. Grumpy, so he was tired and crabby and hurt the angel Phoebe's feelings. When Goddess Molly Kate appeared on the boat, Mr. Grumpy wasn't too happy about it. Worse yet, Molly Kate didn't like him at first. Then she played her harp, creating music so beautiful that it enchanted Mr. Grumpy. After that, he was much more agreeable and pleasant. The angel Phoebe was so grateful for the change in her father that she became Molly Kate's good friend."

"Let me tell it," said Phoebe, sitting up straight.

"Okay," Eric said.

Phoebe's eyes sparkled as she continued the story. "The angel Phoebe loved Molly Kate very much and hoped that she would become her new mommy. Phoebe tried to cast a spell on Mr. Grumpy and Molly Kate, but sometimes it didn't seem like it was working. The angel Phoebe sent messages, many messages, to the gods and goddesses of the ocean, asking them to help her. She made sand wishes, hoping that something, anything would help Goddess Molly and her father fall in love. Then, just when the angel Phoebe thought that the two of them really loved each other, Mr. Grumpy and Molly Kate had a big fight—it sounded like maybe they were throwing thunderbolts at each other across the deck of the magic boat.

So the angel Phoebe ran away. She wanted to find another kingdom where everyone was happy."

"Now it's my turn," Molly said.

Phoebe clapped her hands and regarded Molly raptly.

"When Mr. Grumpy and Molly Kate realized that the angel Phoebe had flown away, they were very frightened. They didn't want anything to happen to the dear, sweet angel that they both loved so much. So they searched everywhere, knowing that they would never stop looking until they found her. When they did, they were so happy, and after they took Phoebe back to the magic boat, they realized that the three of them should never be apart again."

"Never," said Phoebe.

"Never," echoed Eric. All was silent for a moment as *Fiona* rocked between the water and the sky, the stars twinkling above and below.

"And that, my girl," Eric said after a time, "is our story."

Pheobe regarded him solemnly. "We'll never be apart again? Honest?"

"Honest," chorused Molly and Eric.

"I think this calls for a celebratory dish of Chunky Monkey," Eric suggested.

"I'll go get it," Molly said. "You two wait here."

She hurried below, and Phoebe treated Eric to an expansive grin. "Our story didn't say anything about getting our dog back. Or buying a house."

"Cookie will be here as soon as I can arrange it. I was thinking that we might want to find a place right here in Greensea Springs."

"What about Molly's job?" Phoebe asked, as Molly reappeared carrying a tray with three dishes of ice cream.

"I'm going to find work I like better. I'm pretty sure it's going to have something to do with music and puppet shows," Molly said. "My boss will manage very well with the marvelous Mrs. Brinkle to take over my job. She's fully capable, and Frank will feel relieved that he won't have to promote her to the Legal Department."

As Molly handed around the dishes of ice cream, Phoebe frowned. "Okay, so you don't have to go back to your old job. But music and puppet shows all at the same time?"

"I'll make music at the Blossom Cabaret, and maybe there's still a seat available on the board of directors of the new Emmett McBryde Puppet Theater."

Eric listened to them chatter excitedly about the future, and he smiled to himself. Finally he, too, had something to anticipate, that would make his life happier. The three of them had many details to discuss, but he had no doubt that it would all work out. His eyes sought Molly's, and as they exchanged smiles over Phoebe's head, he thought he must be the luckiest guy in the world.

He reached for Molly's hand, the one that wasn't holding the ice-cream spoon, and squeezed it. She squeezed back.

She loved him. He had come close to losing her, and that made what they had—and what they would have in the future—all the more precious. Sitting out here on deck, making plans, telling stories and discussing dreams, the three of them were a family, and had been, in fact, since he and Molly had learned to work as a team. The thought warmed him, and out of curiosity, he glanced up at Heather's star again, occupying its own special place in the universe. As did he. As did all of them.

The star still shone brightly, but it imparted no special message. Then again, he hadn't expected that. He already knew that he had made the right choice.

"MAIL CALL!" Micki said. "Eric, you have an overnight letter."

Molly opened her eyes, sat up and stretched. Eric pulled aside the curtain at the porthole in Molly's stateroom to reveal Micki's stocky figure firmly planted on the dock beside *Fiona*.

"You stay in bed," Eric said after dropping a swift kiss on her forehead. "Anyway, if we hope to preserve the fiction that we're not sleeping together, Phoebe shouldn't find me here."

"We're getting married soon," she said, though she still

couldn't believe her good fortune. "Maybe it's okay to sleep together if we're engaged?"

"I'll leave figuring that out to you. For now, I'm outta here." He yanked on his shorts and went into the salon.

She heard him climbing the ladder and, afterward, exchanging short pleasantries with Micki.

She jumped into the shower and was out again in a matter of minutes. After throwing on a pair of shorts and a shirt, she checked on Phoebe, who was sprawled across her bunk and snoring slightly, then hurried up to the cockpit. Eric was seated on one of the long benches and staring at a letter in his hand.

"You won't believe this," he said. His voice was hoarse, his tone unbelieving.

She sat beside him, leaned forward to read the letterhead.

"'Graham, Segars, St. Bernard and Pyne'? Those are Grandpa's attorneys."

"I know," he said. "Read it." He passed the letter to her, and she leaned back to study it.

"This is about my grandfather's will?" she asked, darting a glance in Eric's direction. He still looked stunned.

"Keep reading," he said.

"'Dear Mr. Norvald,

"'This is to inform you that according to the stipulation of the last will and testament of our client, Emmett C. McBryde, you are entitled to $1,000,000, payable in a—"

She stopped reading, unable to comprehend for a moment. She knew that Emmett had left the bulk of his fortune to her and her brother and sister, and she had been informed long ago that he would make bequests to friends and others that he considered worthy, but she had never suspected that Eric was one of those.

"Eric?" she said, her voice no more than a croak. She cleared her throat. "Were you aware of this?"

He shook his head. "Of course not. It's a complete surprise. Keep reading."

"'…the sum of $1,000,000, payable in a lump sum. Enclosed is a letter that Mr. McBryde asked to be forwarded to you in the event of his death.'"

There was more, mostly legal jargon, and Molly skipped it.

"Here's the letter," Eric said, passing her the envelope. "I haven't opened it yet."

"Go ahead," Molly said. "If you want to read it in private, that's okay."

"You're part of everything I do from now on, Molly. We'll read this together."

He opened the envelope, removed the paper within and draped an arm around Molly's shoulders:

Dear Eric,

I'm glad we became friends, and if you are reading this, you know I am gone. I had a wonderful life, a caring family and good times, some of which were with you as we sat on the deck of *Fiona* and talked. I admire you, Eric, for following your own path and for being such a terrific father. Phoebe is a lucky little girl to have you for a dad.

When I first decided to leave you a million dollars in my will, I wanted to put restrictions on it. In other words, you would inherit it only if you and my granddaughter, Molly Kate McBryde, pursued a relationship ending in marriage. From talking with you, I had an idea that the two of you would be well suited. Then I decided that to do such a thing would be unfair. Molly Kate has a mind of her own. Furthermore, you deserve to inherit this money because my bequeathing of it isn't based on whether she likes you or you like her. I am giving it to you so that you can pursue your dreams. If they happen to include my granddaughter, that's even better.

Wherever the voyage takes you, whoever your companion on the journey, Godspeed.

With all best wishes,
Emmett.

"Oh, Eric," Molly said, resting her head on his shoulder. "I had no idea he was doing this."

"Nor did I," Eric said. "I still don't believe it."

Molly dried her eyes. "Does this windfall make you feel any better? Does it put us on a more equal footing?"

"It provides an opportunity, Molly. Instead of a job, I can have my own business. What would you say if I bought this marina? As Micki said, it's for sale. Greensea Springs is growing, and as more people discover that this is a great place to live, the marina will expand. I'll be working around boats, and the marina will provide a steady and ever-expanding income." He looked excited, happy, energized.

"I like it!" Molly said.

Phoebe emerged from the companionway and rubbed the sleep from her eyes. "What are you two talking about? *What* do you like, Molly?"

Molly drew her close and hugged her. "Your father and I were talking about living in Greensea Springs."

Eric picked up his baseball cap and twirled it on one finger before jamming it down on his head. "You'd better get dressed, Peanut. We're going shopping for a house as soon as we've finished eating breakfast."

"Can it have a red door and an azalea bush? And—"

Eric laughed. "Whoa, kiddo! Let's not get ahead of ourselves. Hurry and get dressed, we've got a lot of things to do."

"A red door and an azalea bush sound great to me," Molly interjected.

"Our new house should have lots of bedrooms, so I can have brothers and sisters. And we need a doghouse." Phoebe clambered down the ladder, and they could hear her clattering around below.

Eric took Molly into his arms. "Is that okay with you, Goddess Molly? Lots of brothers and sisters for Phoebe?"

"First a girl, then a boy. What do you think?"

"Names?"

"Phoebe likes the name Thoth for a boy," she warned him. He made a face. "And how about you?"

"Nicholas for a son, Emma Kate for a daughter."

"Hey, I think it's a plan," he said, and then he tried to kiss her. The bill of his cap got in the way, and she laughingly turned it around so that the back of the hat was in the front.

He did kiss her then, and it was a kiss full of hope and happiness and the promise of even better things to come. A promise of life lived to the fullest with the one person in the world who could make it all beautiful. And fun. And worthwhile.

"Dad? I'm ready. Can we go shopping for our house right now?" Phoebe climbed up the ladder and presented herself on deck.

"We sure can," Eric assured his daughter, and Molly's heart expanded with joy when she saw the delight that sprang into the little girl's eyes.

"My mommy wish worked," Phoebe said. "It really worked!"

"I guess it did," Eric said, gazing at Molly as though he never wanted to stop.

Molly was so happy that she couldn't speak. All she could do was look from Eric's dear face to Phoebe's. This pristine moment would become part of their collective history, as much as Emmett's bequest to Eric, or the story of Nut the giant blue goddess, or finding Phoebe curled up sleeping beside a vacuum cleaner. This was their family circle. They were meant to be together, through thick and thin, through sick and sin.

"I love you both so much," she said unsteadily. Then they were all hugging, and laughing, and crying, and she knew that now that they had found one another, they would never let go.

Epilogue

One Year Later

MESSAGE IN A BOTTLE

DEAR WHOEVER,

THIS WILL BE MY LAST MESSAGE TO YOU. I THINK.
I AM VERY BUSY EVERY DAY PLAYING WITH MY
NEW SISTER EMMA KATE. SHE IS ~~TINNY~~ TINY AND
SHE HAS RED HAIR! I GO TO SCHOOL WITH COR-
DUROY AND LEXIE AND I AM TAKING TAP LES-
SONS! ART LESSONS TOO. SO YOU SEE THERE IS
NOT MUCH TIME LEFT FOR MESSAGES.

I AM SENDING A PICTURE I DREW OF OUR NEW
HOUSE. IT HAS A RED DOOR AND A BUNCH OF
AZALIA BUSHES. AND A BACK YARD WITH A SWIM-
MING POOL! I SWIM ALMOST EVERY DAY! THAT IS
DAD AND MOMMY HOLDING HANDS. EMMA KATE
IS IN THE STROLLER. I AM HUGGING COOKIE THE
DOG, SHE IS HAPPY TO BE BACK WITH US.

WELL THATS ALL. GUESS WHAT, THE SAND
WISHES WORKED. I HAVE THE BEST MOMMY IN

THE WHOLE WORLD. SOMETIMES I FORGET AND
CALL HER MOLLY BUT SHE SAYS THATS O.K.

LUV FROM YOUR FRIEND,
PHOEBE ANNE NORVALD
P.S. I GOT RID OF MY PRETEND VACUUM CLEANER.
WE HAVE A REAL ONE NOW.

Welcome to the world of American Romance!
Turn the page for excerpts from
our July 2005 titles.

A SOLDIER'S RETURN
by Judy Christenberry

TEMPORARY DAD
by Laura Marie Altom

THE BABY SCHEME
by Jacqueline Diamond

A TEXAS STATE OF MIND
by Ann DeFee

We hope you enjoy every one of these books!

Bestselling author and reader favorite Judy Christenberry delivers another emotion-filled family drama from her Children of Texas miniseries, with A SOLDIER'S RETURN. Witness a touching reunion when the Barlow sisters meet their long-lost older brother, and find out how the heart of this brooding warrior is healed by an irrepressible beauty—an extended member of his rediscovered family.

Carrie Abrams was working on her computer when she heard the door of the detective agency open.

She turned her body to greet the entrant, but her head was still glued to the computer screen. When she reluctantly brought her gaze to focus on the tall man with straight posture standing by the door wearing a dress uniform, she gasped.

"Jim! I mean, uh, sorry, I mistook you for someone I—um, may I help you?" She abandoned her clumsy beginning and became as stiff as he was.

"I need to speak with Will Greenfield."

"And your name?" She almost held her breath.

"Captain James Barlow."

"Thank you, Captain Barlow. Just one moment, please."

She got up from her desk, wishing she'd worn a business suit instead of jeans. *You're being silly. Jim Barlow wouldn't care what she was wearing.* He didn't even know her.

She rapped on Will's door, opened it and stepped inside.

"He's here!" She whispered so the man in the outer office wouldn't hear her.

"Who—" Will started to ask, but Carrie didn't wait.

"Jim! He's here. He's wearing his uniform. He wants to speak to you."

Will's face broke into a smile. "Well, show him in!"

Carrie opened the door. "Captain Barlow, please come in."

She wanted to stay in Will's office, but she knew he wouldn't extend the invitation. And she wouldn't ask. It wouldn't be professional.

As she leaned against the door, reluctant to break contact with the two men inside, her gaze roamed her desk.

"Oh, no!" she gasped, and rushed forward. Jim's picture. Had he seen it? She hoped not. How could she explain her fascination with Vanessa's oldest brother? She'd been enthralled by his square-jawed image, just as Vanessa had been. He was the picture of protective, strong…safe. The big brother every little girl dreamed of.

Her best friend, Vanessa Shaw, had probably dreamed those dreams while being raised as an only child. Then, after her father's death, her mother had told her she had five siblings. That revelation had set in motion a lot of changes in their lives.

Carrie drew a deep breath. It was so tempting to call Vanessa and break the news. But she couldn't do that. That was Will's privilege.

All she could do was sit here and pretend indifference that Jim Barlow had returned to the bosom of his family after twenty-three years.

TEMPORARY DAD is the kind of story American Romance readers love—with moments that will make you laugh (and a moment now and then that'll bring you to tears). Jed Hale is an all-American hero: a fireman, a rescuer, a family man. And Annie Harris is just the woman for him. Join these two on their road trip from Oklahoma to Colorado, with three babies in tow (his triplet niece and nephews, temporarily in his care). Enjoy their various roadside stops—like the Beer Can Cow and the Giant Corncob. And smile as they fall in love….

Waaaaaaaaaaaaaaa! Waa huh waaaaaaaaaAAAHH!

From a cozy rattan chair on the patio of her new condo, Annie Harris looked up from the August issue of *Budget Decorating* and frowned.

Waaaaaaaaaaa!

Granted, she wasn't yet a mother herself, but she had been a preschool teacher for the past seven years, so that did lend her a certain credibility where children were concerned.

WAAAAA HA waaaaaaa!

Annie sighed.

She thought whoever was in charge of that poor, pitiful wailer in the condo across the breezeway from hers ought to try something to calm the infant. Never had she heard so much commotion. Was the poor thing sick?

WAAAAAAAAA WAAAAAAA WAAAAAAA!
WAAAAAAA Huh WAAAAA!
WAAAAAAAAAAA!

Annie slapped the magazine back to her knees.

Something about the sound of that baby wasn't right.

Was there more than one?

Definitely two.

Maybe even three.

But she'd moved in a couple weeks earlier and hadn't heard a peep or seen signs of any infant in the complex—let alone three—which was partially why she'd chosen this unit over the one beside the river that had had much better views of the town of Pecan, Oklahoma.

WAAAAAA Huh WAAAAAAAAA!

Again Annie frowned.

No good parent would just leave an infant to cry like this. Could something else be going on? Could the baby's mom or dad be hurt?

Annie popped the latch on her patio gate, creeping across grass not quite green or brown, but a weary shade somewhere in between.

WAAAAAAAAAA!

She crept farther across the shared lawn, stepping onto the weathered brick breezeway she shared with the as-yet-unseen owner of the unit across from hers.

The clubhouse manager—Veronica, a bubbly redhead with a penchant for eighties rock and yogurt—said a bachelor fireman lived there.

Judging by the dead azalea bushes on either side of his front door, Annie hoped the guy was better at watering burning buildings than poor, thirsty plants!

Waaaaaa Huhhhh WAAAA!

She looked at the fireman's door, then her own.

Whatever was going on inside his home probably wasn't any of her business.

WaaaaaAAAAA!

Call her a busybody, but enough was enough.

She just couldn't bear standing around listening to a help-less baby—maybe even more than one helpless baby—cry.

Her first knock on the bachelor fireman's door was gen-tle. Ladylike. That of a concerned neighbor.

When that didn't work, she gave the door a few good, hard thuds.

She was just about to investigate the French doors on the patio that matched her own when the forest-green front door flew open—"Patti? Where the?— Oh, sorry. Thought you were my sister."

Annie gaped.

What else could she do faced with the handsomest man she'd ever seen hugging not one baby, not two babies, but three?

Like Alli Gardner, the heroine of THE BABY SCHEME, Jacqueline Diamond knows about newspapers. She worked as an Associated Press reporter for many years. You'll love this story of a woman who puts her investigative talents to the test—together with a very attractive private investigator—as the two try to unravel a blackmail scheme targeting parents who've adopted babies from a Central American orphanage.

"I'm here about the story in this morning's paper," Alli said to her managing editor. "The one concerning Mayor LeMott."

"Ned tells me you were working on something similar." J.J. eased into his seat. "He says Payne warned him you might have a complaint."

"It wasn't similar. This is my story," Alli told him. "Word for word."

"But you hadn't filed it yet."

"I'd written it but I was holding off so I could double-check a couple of points," she explained. "And there's a sidebar I didn't have time to complete. Mr. Morosco, Payne's planted spyware in my laptop. He stole every bit of that from me."

The editor's forehead wrinkled. He'd been working such long hours he'd begun to lose his tan and had put on a few pounds, she noted. "The two of you have never gotten along, have you? He'd only been here a month when you accused him of stealing your notebook."

"It disappeared from my desk right after he passed by, and the next day he turned in a story based on my research!"

"A guard found your notebook outside that afternoon, right next to where you usually park," the M.E. said.

"I didn't drop it. I'm not that careless." Alli hated being put on the defensive. "Look, you can talk to any of the people I quoted in today's story and they'll confirm who did the reporting."

"Except that most of your sources spoke anonymously," he pointed out.

"I was going to identify them to Ned when I handed it in!" That was standard procedure. "Besides, since when does this paper assign two people to the same story?"

She'd heard of a few big papers that ran their operations in such a cutthroat manner, but the *Outlook* couldn't afford such a waste of staff time. Besides, that kind of competition did horrible things to morale.

"He says Payne asked if he could pursue the same subject. He decided to let the kid show what he could do, and he beat you to the punch."

How could she win when the assistant managing editor was stabbing her in the back? If she were in J.J.'s seat, she probably wouldn't believe her, either.

"Give Payne his own assignment, something he can't steal from anyone else," she said. "He'll blow it."

"As it happens, he's going to have plenty of chances." J.J. fiddled with some papers. "I'm sure you're aware that I've streamlined two other sections. In the meantime, the publisher and Ned and I have been tossing around ideas for the news operation. I'm about to put those proposals into effect."

Why was he telling her this? Allie wondered uneasily. And why was he avoiding her gaze?

"The publisher believes we've got too much duplication and dead wood," he went on. "Some of the older staff members will be asked to take early retirement, but I'm going to have to cut deeper. After careful consideration, I'm afraid we have to let you go."

American Romance is delighted to introduce a brand-new author. You'll love Ann DeFee's sassy humor, her high-energy writing and her really entertaining characters. She'll make you laugh—and occasionally gasp. And she'll take you to a Texas town you'll never want to leave. (Fortunately you can visit Port Serenity again next June!)

Oooh, boy! Lolly raised her Pepsi in a tribute to Meg Ryan. Could that girl fake the big O! Lord knows Lolly had perfected the very same skill before Wendell, her ex, hightailed it out to Las Vegas to find fame and fortune as a drummer. Good old Wendell—more frog than prince. But to give credit where credit was due, he had managed to sire two of the most fantastic kids in the world.

Nowadays she didn't have to worry about Wendell's flagging ego or, for that matter, any of his other wilting body parts. Celibacy had some rewards—not many, but a few.

Meg had just segued from the throes of parodied passion to a big smile when Lolly's cell phone rang.

"Great, just great," Lolly muttered. She thumped her Pepsi on the coffee table.

"Chief, I hate to call you right at supper time, but I figured you'd want to handle this one. I just got a call from Bud out at the Peaceful Cove Inn, and he's got hisself something of a problem." An after-hours call from the Port Serenity Police

Department's gravel-voiced night dispatcher signaled the end to her evening of popcorn and chick flicks.

Chief of police Lavinia "Lolly" Lee Hamilton LaTullipe sighed. Her hectic life as a single mom and head of a small police force left her with very little free time, and when she had a few moments, she wanted to spend them at home with Amanda and Bren, not out corralling scumbags.

"Cletus is on duty tonight, and that man can handle anything short of a full-scale riot," Lolly argued, even though she knew her objections were futile.

Lordy. She'd rather eat Aunt Sissy's fruitcake than abandon the comfort of her living room, especially when Meg was about to find Mr. Right. Lolly hadn't even been able to find Mr. Sorta-Right, though she'd given it the good old college try. Wendell looked pretty good on the outside, but inside he was like an overripe watermelon—mushy and tasteless. Too bad she hadn't noticed that shortcoming when they started dating in high school. Back then his antics were cute; at thirty-seven they weren't quite so appealing.

"I'd really rather not go out tonight."

"Yes, ma'am. I understand. But this one involves Precious." The dispatcher chuckled when Lolly groaned.

Precious was anything but precious. She was the seventeen-year-old demon daughter of Mayor Lance Barton, Lolly's boss and a total klutz in the single-dad department. She and Lance had been buddies since kindergarten, so without a doubt she'd be making an unwanted trip to the Peaceful Cove Inn.

"Oh, man. What did I do to deserve that brat in my life?" Lolly rubbed her forehead in a vain attempt to ward off the headache she knew was coming. "Okay, what's she done now?"

"Seems she's out there with some guys Bud don't know, and she's got a snoot full. He figured we'd want to get her home before someone saw her."

Lolly sighed. "All right, I'll run out and see what I can do. Call her daddy and tell him what's happening."

She muttered an expletive as she marched to the rolltop desk in the kitchen to retrieve her bag, almost tripping over Harvey, the family's gigantic mutt. She strapped on an ankle holster and then checked her taser and handcuffs. In this business, a girl had to be prepared.

Amanda, her ten-year-old daughter, was immersed in homework, and as usual, her fourteen-year-old son had his head poked inside the refrigerator.

"Bren, get Amanda to help you with the kitchen." Lolly stopped him as he tried to sneak out of the room and nodded at the open dishwasher and pile of dishes in the sink. "I've got to go out for a few minutes. If you need anything call Mee Maw."

Her firstborn rolled his eyes. "Aw, Mom."

Lolly suppressed the urge to laugh, and instead employed the dreaded raised eyebrow. The kid was in dire need of a positive male role model. Someone stable, upright, respectable and…safe. Yeah, safe. It was time to find a nice, reliable prince—an orthodontist might be good, considering Amanda's overbite.

"I'm leaving. You guys be good," Lolly called out as she opened the screen door.

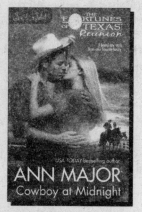

If you enjoyed what you just read,
then we've got an offer you can't resist!

Take 2 bestselling
love stories FREE!
Plus get a FREE surprise gift!

Clip this page and mail it to Harlequin Reader Service®

IN U.S.A.
3010 Walden Ave.
P.O. Box 1867
Buffalo, N.Y. 14240-1867

IN CANADA
P.O. Box 609
Fort Erie, Ontario
L2A 5X3

YES! Please send me 2 free Harlequin American Romance® novels and my free surprise gift. After receiving them, if I don't wish to receive anymore, I can return the shipping statement marked cancel. If I don't cancel, I will receive 4 brand-new novels every month, before they're available in stores! In the U.S.A., bill me at the bargain price of $4.24 plus 25¢ shipping & handling per book and applicable sales tax, if any*. In Canada, bill me at the bargain price of $4.99 plus 25¢ shipping & handling per book and applicable taxes**. That's the complete price and a savings of at least 10% off the cover prices—what a great deal! I understand that accepting the 2 free books and gift places me under no obligation ever to buy any books. I can always return a shipment and cancel at any time. Even if I never buy another book from Harlequin, the 2 free books and gift are mine to keep forever.

154 HDN DZ7S
354 HDN DZ7T

Name _____ (PLEASE PRINT)

Address _____ Apt.# _____

City _____ State/Prov. _____ Zip/Postal Code _____

Not valid to current Harlequin American Romance® subscribers.

Want to try two free books from another series?
Call 1-800-873-8635 or visit www.morefreebooks.com.

* Terms and prices subject to change without notice. Sales tax applicable in N.Y.
** Canadian residents will be charged applicable provincial taxes and GST.
   All orders subject to approval. Offer limited to one per household.
   ® are registered trademarks owned and used by the trademark owner and or its licensee.

AMER04R   ©2004 Harlequin Enterprises Limited

BLACKBERRY HILL MEMORIAL

Almost A Family
by **Roxanne Rustand**
Harlequin Superromance #1284

From Roxanne Rustand,
author of *Operation: Second Chance*
and *Christmas at Shadow Creek*,
a new heartwarming miniseries,
set in a small-town hospital,
where people come first.

As long as the infamous Dr. Connor Reynolds stays
out of her way, Erin has more pressing issues to
worry about. Like how to make her adopted children
feel safe and loved after her husband walked out on
them, and why patients keep dying for no apparent
reason. If only she didn't need Connor's help. And if
only he wasn't so good to her and the kids.

Available July 2005 wherever Harlequin books are sold.

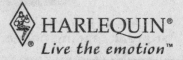

HARLEQUIN®

AMERICAN *Romance*®

is thrilled to bring you
a heartwarming miniseries
by bestselling author

Judy Christenberry

Children of TEXAS

Separated during childhood, three beautiful
sisters from the Lone Star state are destined
to rediscover one another, find true love and
build a Texas-sized family legacy they can
call their own....

You won't want to miss the third installment
of this beloved family saga!

A SOLDIER'S RETURN
(HAR #1073)

On sale July 2005.

HARLEQUIN®

AMERICAN *Romance*®

COMING NEXT MONTH

#1073 A SOLDIER'S RETURN by Judy Christenberry
Children of Texas

Ever since he was a kid and his orphaned family split, sending him into foster care, Captain James Barlow knew he was a jinx to anyone he loved. He'd hidden out safely in the marines…until a detective found him and most of his siblings. The captain had seen battle, but no enemy made him uneasy like his newfound family—and the beautiful Carrie Rand.

#1074 TEMPORARY DAD by Laura Marie Altom
Fatherhood

After her last "romantic" experience, Annie Harnesberry has sworn off men— especially single fathers. Now she just wants to start her new job and redecorate her condo. But when her neighbor—of the gorgeous male variety—needs help with his five-month-old triplet niece and nephews, it's Annie who can't seem to help *herself*….

#1075 THE BABY SCHEME by Jacqueline Diamond

Alli Gardner may be out of her reporter's job thanks to an underhanded competitor on her newspaper, but she's not out of story ideas—or an investigative partner. She and hard-nosed private detective Kevin Vickers are about to have their hands full looking into a blackmail scheme involving babies from a Central American orphanage. Soon Alli and Kevin will also have their hands full with each other….

#1076 A TEXAS STATE OF MIND by Ann DeFee

Lavinia "Lolly" LaTullipe, a single mother of two, is busy enough as police chief of the little Texas town of Port Serenity, but her job becomes even more complicated when the bodies of drug dealers start floating into the town's cove. Enter Christian Delacroix, undercover DEA cop sent to help solve the murders. When he and Lolly meet the sparks fly—literally!

www.eHarlequin.com

CNMHAR0605